A disturbing revelation

Spit's bony knees were drawn up to his ribs and his mouth hung open: a dark void surrounded by broken teeth.

Hylas stopped binding his knees and stared at the gaping mouth. A terrifying thought had occurred to him.

He woke Zan and dragged him to the mouth of the den.

"What's this about?" growled Zan, rubbing his eyes.

"If a snatcher gets you," breathed Hylas, "it can reach down your throat—yes?"

"That's what they say. So?"

"So that means it can get *inside* you."

"They're spirits, they can do anything. Why?"

"What's he saying?" Beetle stood behind them with his arms at his sides.

Hylas motioned them closer. "The first night I came, I asked what was wrong with Spit, and Zan said a snatcher'd nearly got him." He swallowed. "I think you were wrong, Zan. I think a snatcher already has."

Beetle's face went still. Zan's scowl deepened. *"What?"*

Hylas pointed at the sleeping boy and whispered, "He's possessed. *It's inside him.*"

Hylas pictured the evil spirit coiled in the pulsing red darkness under Spit's heart. Who knew what it would make him do next?

Other Books You May Enjoy

GODS AND WARRIORS

THE BURNING SHADOW

GODS AND WARRIORS

THE BURNING SHADOW

MICHELLE PAVER

BOOK

2

PUFFIN BOOKS
An Imprint of Penguin Group (USA)

PUFFIN BOOKS
Published by the Penguin Group
Penguin Group (USA) LLC
375 Hudson Street
New York, New York 10014

USA * Canada * UK * Ireland * Australia
New Zealand * India * South Africa * China

penguin.com
A Penguin Random House Company

First published in the United States of America by Dial Books for Young Readers,
an imprint of Penguin Group(USA), 2014
Published in Great Britain by Penguin Books Ltd, 2013
Published by Puffin Books, an imprint of Penguin Young Readers Group, 2015

Text copyright © 2013 by Michelle Paver
Maps by Fred van Deelen copyright © 2013 by Puffin Books
Logo design by James Fraser copyright © 2012 by Puffin Books

THE LIBRARY OF CONGRESS HAS CATALOGED THE DIAL BOOKS FOR YOUNG READERS EDITION AS FOLLOWS:
Paver, Michelle.
The burning shadow / by Michelle Paver.
pages cm. – (Gods and warriors)
Summary: "In his search for his sister, Issi, Hylas is kidnapped and sold into slavery and must
escape the Crows with the help of his friend Pirra and a lion cub"—Provided by publisher.
ISBN: 978-0-8037-3880-5 (hardcover)
[1. Kidnapping—Fiction. 2. Brothers and sisters—Fiction.
3. Voyages and travels—Fiction. 4. Prehistoric peoples—Fiction. 5. Human-animal
communication—Fiction. 6. Gods—Fiction. 7. Bronze age—Fiction.
8. Mediterranean Region—History—To 476—Fiction.] I. Title.
PZ7.P2853Bur 2014 [Fic]—dc23 2013017791

Puffin Books ISBN 978-0-14-242285-4

Printed in the United States of America

1 3 5 7 9 10 8 6 4 2

GODS AND WARRIORS

THE
BURNING
SHADOW

THE WORLD OF GODS AND WARRIORS

THALAKREA

THE MOUNTAIN

Blasted Ridge

Crater

Obsidian Trail

Village

Black Plain

Pools

Mines

Guards Camp

Broom Thicket

Forested Ridge

Wild Pear Tree

The Neck

Crossroad

Furnace Ridge

Kreon's Stronghold

Obsidian Ridge

Smithy

White Ravine

Cave of Green Mudpool

N

W   E

S

1

"Go *away!*" shouted Hylas.

The boar threw him an irritable look and went on wallowing in the mud. She and her piglets were having a lovely time at the spring, and she wasn't going to make room for some scrawny boy who needed a drink.

A chill east wind tore across the hillside, rattling the thistles and probing the holes in Hylas' tunic. He was tired, footsore, and his waterskin had been empty since last night. He had to reach that spring.

Loading a pebble in his slingshot, he landed the boar a smack on the rump—which she ignored. He blew out a long breath. Now what?

Suddenly the boar scrambled to her feet, jerked up her tail, and fled, with her piglets racing after her.

Hylas dropped to a crouch behind a thornbush. What had she sensed?

At that moment, the wind dropped to nothing. The hairs on the back of his neck rose. The silence felt thick and strange.

The lion came out of nowhere.

Bounding down the slope above him, it halted two paces from where he hid.

He didn't dare breathe. The lion was so close that he could smell the musky heat of its fur, and hear the dust settling around its enormous paws. He saw how its tawny mane stirred in the windless air. Silently, he begged it to spare his life.

The lion turned its great head and looked at him. Its golden eyes were stronger than the Sun—and it *knew* him. It saw his spirit, like a pebble at the bottom of a deep, clear pool. There was something it wanted him to do. He didn't know what, but he felt its command.

Again the lion lifted its head and tasted the air. Then it bounded down the hill. Hylas watched it leap a clump of boulders and land without a sound—then vanish into a thicket. Now all that was left was its musky scent and the prints of huge paws.

The wind returned, hissing dust in Hylas' eyes. Shakily, he rose to his feet.

Near the spring, the lion's tracks were filling with water. Hylas knelt by a paw print as big as his head. Water from the paw print of a lion gives you strength. He stooped and drank.

Something heavy smacked into him and knocked him off his feet.

"That might've made you stronger," said a voice, "but it didn't make you lucky."

"Where are they taking us?" moaned the boy next to Hylas.

No one answered. No one knew.

The ship was packed: ten slaves tied to the oars on either side, twenty huddled on deck, and eight fat overseers with copper-tipped whips.

Hylas sat crammed against the side of the creaking, pitching vessel. His wrists throbbed, the rawhide collar was chafing his neck, and his scalp hurt. Two days before, one of the slavers had hacked his fair hair short.

"Where you from?" the slaver had barked, stripping him of his gear and tying him up with brutal efficiency.

"He's on the run," his companion had muttered, peeling back Hylas' lips to check his teeth. "You can always tell."

"That true, boy? Why're you missing a bit of your ear? They do that to thieves where you're from, eh?"

Hylas had stayed grimly silent. He'd paid a herdsman the last of Pirra's gold to cut off the bottom of his earlobe, because the notch in it would have marked him as an Outsider.

"He understood that," said the smaller one, "so he must be Akean. Which part, boy? Arkadia? Messenia? Lykonia?"

"Doesn't matter," the other growled. "He looks strong enough, he'll do for a spider."

What's that? Hylas thought numbly

And who *were* they? They wore rough wool tunics and greasy sheepskin cloaks, more like peasants than Crow warriors; but they might be working for the Crows. They mustn't find out who he was.

A wave splashed him in the face, wrenching him back to the present. The boy beside him groaned and threw up in Hylas' lap.

"Thanks," muttered Hylas.

The boy gave a feeble snarl.

Trying to ignore the smell of vomit, Hylas turned back to the Sea. The ship sat low in the water, and he'd been watching for dolphins. So far, nothing. He thought of Spirit, whom he'd befriended last summer. At least the dolphin was happy and free with his pod. Hylas clung to that.

And maybe far away on Keftiu, Pirra had managed to escape. She was the daughter of the High Priestess, and unimaginably rich, but she'd told him once that she would do anything to be free. At the time, he'd thought she was mad. Now he knew better.

A fin sliced the water, alarmingly close to where he sat. The shark fixed him with its lightless black eye and sank out of sight.

That's why no dolphins, thought Hylas. Too many sharks.

"That's the seventh since we set out," said the man on the other side of the seasick boy. He had a broken nose that had set crooked, and there was a weariness in his brown eyes, as if he'd seen too many bad things.

"Why are they following us?" mumbled the seasick boy.

The man shrugged. "Dead slaves get chucked overboard. Easy meat."

A whip cracked out and struck his cheek. "No talk!" yelled a fat-bellied overseer.

Blood trickled into the man's beard. His expression didn't change, but something in his stare told Hylas that he was picturing burying a knife in the overseer's hairy paunch.

Judging by the Sun, Hylas guessed that they'd been heading southeast since dawn—which meant a long way from Akea. He was furious with himself. All his efforts wiped out by a moment's carelessness.

Sorry, Issi, he told her in his head.

The familiar guilt gnawed at his guts. His one memory of his mother was of her telling him to look after his little sister—and he'd failed. The night the Crows had attacked their camp, he'd decoyed them away, but afterward he hadn't been able to find Issi. Did she know that he'd done it for her? Or did she think he'd abandoned her to save his own skin?

That had been a year ago. Since then, all he'd found out was that Issi *might* be in Messenia, the westernmost chieftaincy of Akea. Last summer he'd bought passage on a ship, but it had wandered from island to island before putting in at Makedonia—hopelessly far north.

For eight moons he'd struggled through an unknown land of hostile peasants and savage dogs: always in hiding, always on his own. The image of his fiery, talkative little sister had gradually faded, till he could scarcely remember her face. That frightened him more than anything.

He must have slipped into a doze, because he was woken by a ripple of apprehension among the slaves. They were approaching land.

In the red glare of sunset, Hylas saw a vast, black, cloud-wreathed mountain rising from the Sea. Its peak was weirdly flat, as if some god had lopped it off in a fit of rage.

Below it, he made out a bay of charcoal sand between twin headlands that curved inward, like jaws agape. As the ship slid between them, he heard the screams of seabirds and a din of hammers. He caught a strange smell, like rotting eggs.

Craning his neck at the western headland, he glimpsed smoky fires high on a ridge. On the opposite headland, a steep rocky hill was crowned by a massive stone wall spiked with torches, like all-seeing eyes. That had to be the stronghold of a chieftain. From there you'd have an eagle's view of the whole island. You'd see everything.

"What *is* this place?" whimpered the seasick boy.

The man with the broken nose had gone pale beneath his windburn. "It's Thalakrea. They're sending us down the mines."

"What's a mine?" said Hylas.

The man threw him a sharp look, but just then an overseer grabbed Hylas' collar and hauled him to his feet. "It's where you're going to spend the rest of your life."

2

"What *is* a mine?" muttered Hylas to the man with the broken nose.

After an evil trudge, they'd reached a crossroads. Tracks led off to both headlands, another inland—and the fourth ended here, at the mines: a great red hill heaving with half-naked slaves. Men pounded livid green rock, women and girls washed it in troughs, small boys picked it over; all under the watchful stares of overseers. Higher up, more slaves swarmed in and out of holes in the hillside, like flies at a wound.

"A mine," said the man with the broken nose, "is what men do to get bronze. You dig till you hit the greenstone. Hack it loose, crush it, burn it till the copper bleeds out. Then mate it with tin." He nodded at the smoky ridge. "Furnaces. That's the smith's domain."

Hylas swallowed. In Lykonia, where he'd grown up, peasants said sorry to the earth before they plowed their barley patches—even though plowing didn't really hurt Her and the scars soon faded. This tortured hill had been cut too deep to heal.

At last their bonds were untied, and an overseer passed down the line, appraising each slave. "Hammerman," he grunted, and the man with the broken nose was led away. "Hauler. Crusher." He glanced at Hylas. "Pit spider."

A bigger boy jerked his head at Hylas to follow, and they scrambled over piles of red rubble dotted with shards of glossy black rock. Hylas recognized it as obsidian. Crow warriors used it to make their arrowheads: Last summer, he'd dug one out of his arm. Pretending to stumble, he grabbed a shard and hid it in his fist.

They reached a hollow cut into the lower slope, and the boy told Hylas to wait for the other pit spiders, then left.

The hollow seemed to be some kind of den: Hylas saw four small piles of rags in four patches of trodden earth. He slumped down, too exhausted to care where he sat. He couldn't remember when he'd last eaten or drunk, and the din of hammers was making his head pound. His new tattoo stung. After they'd splashed ashore, a man had grabbed his forearm and pricked it over and over with a bone needle, rubbing in a paste that smelled like soot. The result was a grimy zigzag, like a mountain with twin peaks: his owner's mark.

The Sun set and the hollow filled with shadow. The hammers fell silent—except for one, which rang out from the furnace ridge.

Four boys appeared at the mouth of the den and glared at Hylas as if he was something they'd forgotten to chuck on the dung heap. They were covered in red dust and their scrawny limbs were pocked with odd greenish scars. They wore nothing except sweat-soaked rags tied around their heads, hips, and knees.

The tallest looked a couple of years older than Hylas, with a hook nose and heavy black brows that met in the middle. On a thong on his chest he wore a shriveled strip of dried meat the size of a finger. He was clearly the leader; he shot Hylas a challenging stare.

The youngest was about seven, with bandy legs and weak eyes. He squinted up at the older boy for reassurance.

The third had black hair and haughty features. He reminded Hylas of an Egyptian he'd seen last summer.

The fourth was a wild-eyed skeleton with collarbones that jutted like sticks. He kept flinching and darting fearful glances over his shoulder.

The Egyptian boy took a step toward Hylas. "Get out," he snarled. "That's my spot."

Hylas knew better than to back down. "Now it's mine," he said, letting the boy see the obsidian shard in his hand.

The boy chewed his lips. The others waited. With a hiss, the boy snatched his rags and found another spot.

The small boy and the scared one glanced at the leader. He hawked a gobbet of red snot, then squatted and began unwinding his head-bindings.

Hylas shut his eyes. It was over for now—although he guessed that sooner or later, they'd have another go at him.

"How old are you?" the leader said brusquely.

Hylas opened one eye. "Thirteen."

"Where you from?"

"Around."

"Name."

Hylas hesitated. "Flea." A shipwrecked sailor had called him that last summer; it would do. "You?"

"Zan." He nodded at the youngest boy. "Bat." Then the Egyptian boy. "Beetle." Then the bony one. "Spit."

Spit gave a jittery snigger that bared a slobbery mouthful of broken teeth.

"What's he so scared of?" Hylas asked Zan.

Zan shrugged. "Snatcher nearly got him coupla days ago."

"What's a snatcher?"

The others gaped and Zan sneered. "You don't know nothing, do you?"

"What's a snatcher?" Hylas repeated levelly.

"Bad spirits," said Bat, clutching a furry amulet that appeared to be a squashed mouse. "They live down the pit and they follow you in the dark. They look like us, see? There can be a snatcher right next you and you won't know it."

"If it looks like you," said Hylas, "how d'you know it's a snatcher?"

"Um . . ." Bat's small face crumpled with confusion.

Beetle the Egyptian tapped the groove between his nose and his upper lip. "Snatchers got a ridge here. That's how. But you never see them for long enough to know."

"They live in the rocks," whispered Spit fearfully. "They come and go like shadows."

Hylas considered that. Then he said, "Why are you called pit spiders?"

Zan snorted. "You'll find out."

After that they ignored Hylas, and busied themselves with unwinding the rags from their heads and knees and laying them out to dry.

A wave of homesickness swept over him. He missed Issi, and Scram, his dog that the Crows had killed. He missed Spirit the dolphin, and Pirra. He even missed Telamon, the Chieftain's son who'd been his friend till he'd turned out to be a Crow.

If he cared about someone, he lost them. He always ended up on his own. He hated that.

Well so *what*, he told himself angrily. First things first, you got to get out of here.

"Don't even think about escaping," muttered Zan, as if he'd spoken aloud.

"What's it to you?" retorted Hylas.

"You'll fail, we'll get punished, then we'll punish you."

Hylas studied him. "I bet you never even tried."

"Nowhere to go," said Zan with another shrug. "Islanders too scared to help, Sea full of sharks. Nothing inland but boiling springs and man-eating lions. If they don't get you, Kreon's men will."

"Who's Kreon?"

Zan jerked his head at the stronghold frowning down at them. "Kreon owns the island. The pit. Us."

"No one owns me," said Hylas.

All four burst out laughing and beat the ground with their fists.

At that moment, a whistle shrilled and they scrambled out of the den. Hylas followed, hoping this meant food.

Hordes of slaves were fighting over provisions. The pit spiders grabbed a basket and a rawhide pail, and Hylas elbowed his way to a few gulps of vinegary water and a handful of bitter gray mush that tasted like mashed acorns and grit.

He was licking the last of it off his fingers when he heard the thud of feet and the rattle of wheels.

"Get in line!" shouted Zan.

Red dust was rising on the westward track, and fear was rippling over the hillside like wind through barley. Hylas saw slaves bowing their heads and clamping their arms to their sides; overseers tapping their whips against their thighs and wiping their sweaty jowls.

First around the bend swept a pack of hunting dogs. They had shaggy red hides and wore collars spiked with bronze. They had the hot dull eyes of beasts who'd been beaten and starved to make them killers.

Next came a band of warriors: nightmare figures in breastplates and kilts of black rawhide, with heavy spears and vicious bronze knives. Despite the heat, black cloaks flew behind them like wings, and their faces were gray with ash.

Hylas swayed. He'd seen warriors like them before.

In their midst rode a Chieftain in a chariot drawn by

two black horses. As it thundered up the track toward the stronghold, Hylas caught a glimpse of hooded eyes and a bristly black beard. Something about that face was terrifyingly familiar.

"Head *down*!" breathed Zan, elbowing him in the ribs.

In horror, Hylas stared from the Chieftain to the tattoo on his forearm. "It's not a mountain," he whispered. "It's a crow."

"Course it's a crow!" hissed Zan. "That's Kreon son of Koronos—he *is* a Crow!"

Hylas felt as if he was falling from a great height.

He was a slave in the mines of the Crows.

If they found out he was here, they would kill him in a heartbeat.

The Sun wasn't yet up when Hylas jolted awake, but already the others were preparing to head off. They hadn't bothered to wake him. They didn't care if he got a beating.

Hastily, he cut strips from his tunic and bound his head and knees, then tied another band around his hips and tucked the shard of obsidian in a fold at his waist.

Beetle told him to take another rag too. "Down the pit, pee on it and tie it across your nose and mouth. Keeps out the dust."

"Thanks," said Hylas.

"The pit" turned out to be two shafts dug into the hill. One was an arm-span wide, with a log laid across and a rope slung over that; Hylas guessed it was some kind of pulley. The other was narrower; before it, lines of men waited to climb down. Many were covered in greenish scars, and missing fingers and toes. All had bloodshot eyes and faces stony with defeat.

"Who are they?" Hylas asked Beetle.

"Hammermen," muttered the Egyptian boy. "Stay outa their way."

As they stood in line, Hylas saw warriors guarding the mines. Kreon's stronghold glared down at him. He told himself the Crows thought he was dead: drowned last summer in the Sea. It didn't help.

Noticing that there were more slaves than overseers and guards, he asked Zan why they didn't rebel.

The older boy rolled his eyes. "Pit's got nine levels, see? You try to escape, you're sent down the deepest."

"So?"

Zan didn't reply. He was tossing pinches of dust over his shoulder and spitting three times.

"It keeps the snatchers away," whispered Bat, clutching his squashed mouse. Spit was tugging at his bony collarbones and sweating with fear. Beetle was muttering a charm in Egyptian.

Hylas asked Bat if his mouse was an amulet, and the younger boy nodded. "Tunnel mice are clever, they always get out before a cave-in. Zan's got a amulet too, a hammerman's finger."

"Shut up, Bat!" said Zan.

Ahead of them, a hammerman had noticed Hylas. It was the man with the broken nose. "You're Lykonian," he said in an undertone.

Hylas' belly turned over.

"Don't deny it, I can tell from your speech. I hear the

Crows had trouble there last spring. They were killing Outsiders, but didn't get them all."

"You heard wrong," muttered Hylas, avoiding the pit spiders' curious glances.

"I don't think so," whispered the man. "I'm from Messenia, they were hunted there too, but some got away. Why are the Crows after Outsiders?"

Messenia. That was where Issi had gone. "The ones who got away," breathed Hylas. "Was there a girl about ten summers old?"

An overseer shouted at the man to move, and he shot Hylas an unreadable look and disappeared down the shaft.

"What's an Outsider?" Zan said sourly.

"Someone born outside a village," said Hylas.

"That make you special?" he sneered.

"I'm not an Outsider," lied Hylas.

The others were taking rawhide sacks from a pile, and Zan chucked one to Hylas. Copying the older boy, he slung it on his back with his arms through the straps. Then he tossed dust over his shoulders, spat three times, and asked the Lady of the Wild Things to protect him. She felt far away in Akea. He wondered if She'd hear.

Bat climbed in first, then Zan, Spit, and Beetle.

The Egyptian boy looked almost as scared as Spit. "Watch your head," he told Hylas, "and breathe through your mouth."

"Why?"

"You'll find out."

He was struggling down a slimy rope ladder. A smell like a dung heap caught at his throat. He breathed through his mouth.

Fifty rungs . . . A hundred . . . By the time he reached the bottom, he'd lost count.

He was in a tunnel so low he couldn't stand up. It was dark, and the walls threw back the rasp of his breath. A log supporting the roof creaked. He was horribly aware of the weight of the hill pressing down. Here and there, a clay lamp on a ledge cast a smoky glimmer. Shadows leaped and skittered away. He thought of the snatchers, and crawled after the others.

As he groped around bewildering turns and sudden drops, the stink became eye watering. He sniffed his palm and gagged. He was crawling through the muck of hundreds of people.

Muffled voices reached him through the walls. He recognized Zan's, and guessed that the tunnel doubled back. "Nobody help him," Zan was saying. "He's on his own."

It grew hotter as they descended, and soon Hylas was sweating. He caught a distant sound of hammering. Nine levels, he thought. The whole hill must be riddled with holes. He tried not to think of the Earthshaker, the god whose stamping brings down mountains.

Suddenly the noise became deafening, and he found himself in a large shadowy cavern. The air was thick with dust, but here and there, little pools of lamplight glimmered in the murk. On ledges cut into the walls, naked men lay on their backs, pounding veins of green rock with hammerstones and antler picks. Boys and girls no more than five summers old flitted warily among them, collecting the fragments into piles. Hylas felt sick. The hammermen were hacking the earth's green blood from Her flesh. He was inside a giant wound.

The pit spiders had covered their mouths and noses with wet rags, and were filling their sacks with greenstone. Hylas did the same. When their sacks were full, Zan led them up a different tunnel. The straps bit into Hylas' shoulders. It was like dragging a corpse.

After an endless climb, they reached the main shaft. Two men grabbed Hylas' sack, tied a rope around its neck, and hauled. The sack rose jerkily.

Moments later, it burst and its load crashed down, narrowly missing Hylas.

"Whose sack was that?" yelled a furious hauler. He spotted Hylas. "You! You didn't check it!"

"Always check your gear," jeered Zan.

Hylas set his teeth. Zan had given him a faulty sack on purpose. All right then, he thought. Time to sort this out.

Back at the cavern, he made sure that he stayed near Zan while they gathered another load, and he stayed near as they headed for the shaft. Halfway there, Zan clutched his chest and frantically searched the ground. By the time they reached the shaft, he was shaking.

"Looking for this?" Hylas said quietly. He gave Zan the

shriveled finger, then brought his face close. "We'll keep this between ourselves," he breathed, "and I don't want to take your place as leader—but never mess with me again. Understood?"

Slowly, Zan nodded.

They did two more exhausting rounds, then an overseer called a halt. Zan must have spread the word, because the others made room for Hylas and let him share a skin of vinegar and a grimy flatbread.

Zan and Beetle ate with grim concentration, while Bat tucked crumbs in cracks for the tunnel mice. Spit ate nothing, flinching at the dark.

Under his breath, Hylas asked Zan what snatchers did to people.

"Sometimes they whisper in your ear and follow you like a shadow, till you go mad. Sometimes they reach down your throat and stop your heart."

Hylas swallowed. "And they live in the rocks?"

"Rocks, tunnels. They're spirits, they can go anywhere."

"*Sh!*" hissed Beetle with a furious scowl. Aboveground, he'd been almost friendly, but down here he was silent and subdued.

Zan peered at Hylas. "You been underground before?"

"Once," said Hylas. "There was an earthshake."

Zan whistled. "What'd you do?"

"I got out."

Zan laughed.

Hylas asked if they had earthshakes on Thalakrea, and

the older boy shook his head. "Cave-ins, smoke from the Mountain, that's all."

"*Smoke?* From a *mountain?*"

"Goddess lives inside. The smoke's Her breath, and from the fire spirits. They live in cracks in the ground, all spiky and hot."

Hylas considered that. "Does She ever get angry?"

"I dunno. But it's only ever just smoke."

At that moment, an overseer ordered them to haul greenstone from the eighth level.

A shudder ran through the pit spiders.

"Not so deep," moaned Spit. Beetle shut his eyes and groaned, and even Zan looked scared. "Right," he said. "Everybody stay close."

Zan led them down a web of tunnels to the fifth level . . . the sixth . . . the seventh.

It grew hotter and more airless. Hylas brushed past a pile of leaves and something furry and dead. He guessed it was an offering to the snatchers.

He caught an uprush of foul air, and the ground beneath him creaked. He was on a log bridge spanning a cavernous shaft. Far below, he glimpsed lamplight and toiling bodies. A face peered up at him: the man with the broken nose.

"Flea! Stay close!" warned Zan.

Hylas got off the bridge fast. "That shaft, is that—"

"The deep levels," said Zan.

"But there wasn't a ladder. How do they get out?"

"They don't. You're sent down the deep levels, you stay there till you die . . ." Zan's voice faded as he rounded a bend.

Hylas was appalled. To be trapped in darkness forever . . .

His empty sack caught on a rock. He freed it, bashed his head, and hurried after the others. "Zan! Wait!"

No reply. He must have taken a wrong turn.

As he backtracked, he heard the sound of hammering, and made for that. He fell down a drop. No, this wasn't right.

He reached a place where the walls bulged inward. This wasn't right either, but he could still hear hammering, and hammering meant people, so he squeezed through.

The hammering dwindled to one: tap tap tap.

He was in a low cavern lit by a sputtery stone lamp on a ledge. He couldn't see anyone, but the hammering was closer. Tap tap.

He edged forward.

The hammering stopped.

"Who's there?" he said.

Someone blew out the lamp.

Silence. Hylas sensed a presence in the dark.

He felt breath on his face: earthy and cold, like wet clay.

He fled. His sack snagged. He tugged it free.

Something tugged back.

Jerking the sack loose, he blundered against the wall. It

seemed to move beneath his palm. Was it rock, or flesh? His fingers touched what felt like a mouth—and above it, a ridge. He recoiled with a cry.

The darkness was so thick he could touch it, he had no idea where he was going. Then the sound of his breathing changed: He was back in a tunnel.

Somehow, he reached the place where the walls bulged, and squeezed in sideways.

A hand grabbed his ankle. He kicked. His foot struck cold earthen flesh. In panic he kicked again. The grip on his ankle crumbled like wet clay. He burst through the gap. Behind him he heard harsh angry breath.

Whimpering, he fled. Stony laughter echoed in the dark. *Snatchers live in rocks, tunnels . . . They follow you in the dark.*

"Flea!" Zan's voice sounded far ahead.

Someone crashed into Hylas. "Get *off* me!" shrieked Spit.

"You're going the wrong way," panted Hylas.

Spit grabbed him by the throat. "Get *off* me!"

He was alarmingly strong. Hylas clawed at his hands, then groped for his eyes and dug in his thumbs. Spit howled and vanished into the murk.

"Flea!" shouted Zan, much closer. "Where you *been*?"

By the time Hylas and Zan rejoined the others, Spit had also found his way back. Hylas slammed him against the tunnel wall. "What was that for?" he shouted. "I didn't *do* anything!"

"I—I thought you were a snatcher!" stammered Spit.

"Leave him alone, Flea!" barked Zan.

Hylas turned on him. "Is this a trick? We had a truce!"

"He made a mistake. Come on, we got work to do."

In grim silence they found the piles of greenstone and filled their sacks. Hylas kept Spit where he could see him. He was either extremely cunning—or the snatchers had turned him mad. Hylas didn't know which would be worse.

At last a ram's horn blew and the mines began to empty.

Hylas was exhausted, but as he hauled himself out of the shaft, an overseer chucked three waterskins at him and told him to go and fill them at the "splash."

Bat offered to show him where, and Beetle came too; he seemed like a different boy, now that he was out of the pit.

Dusk was falling and the mines were quiet, but on the furnace ridge, one hammer beat a lonely rhythm. Hylas asked who it was.

"That's the smith," said Beetle. "Sometimes he works all night. He won't let anyone near the smithy, it's guarded by slaves who can't speak. If someone comes, they warn him by beating a drum."

"Why?" said Hylas.

Beetle shrugged. "Smiths are different, they know the secrets of bronze. Not even the Crows like to cross a smith."

They skirted the hill, and Hylas saw that the island narrowed to a neck, then bulged out, like some huge humpbacked creature. At the neck, an encampment of Crows kept watch.

So no escape that way, he thought.

"That's where they keep the horses," Bat said wistfully.

Hylas didn't reply. Beyond the neck, an arid black plain stretched to the Mountain. Its steep flanks blotted out the sky, and smoke seeped endlessly from its weird, lopped-off summit.

Pirra had said once that there was only one Goddess, but Hylas didn't think that was right. The immortal who ruled this harsh land felt utterly unlike the Lady of the Wild Things, or the shining blue Goddess of the Sea he'd encountered last year.

The "splash" turned out to be three dismal pools scummed with pollen from a few dusty willows, and noisy with frogs. Proudly, Bat pointed out some swallows swooping to drink. "But I like the frogs best, 'cuz they're so beautiful."

Frogs reminded Hylas painfully of Issi; they were her favorite creature. "They're not beautiful," he snapped, "they're just frogs!"

Bat blinked.

Hylas rubbed a hand over his face. "Sorry," he muttered. "You and Beetle go back to the others. I'll manage on my own."

When they'd gone, Hylas plunged in the waterskins and watched them fill like bloated bodies. He ached all over, and his mind was full of darkness. The terror of the snatchers. That angry, inhuman breath . . .

Far away on the Mountain, a lion roared.

The swallows flew up in alarm. Hylas went still. On the furnace ridge, even the smith stopped hammering. He too was listening.

There were lions on Mount Lykas, where Hylas had grown up. They hadn't troubled him or the goats because Scram was such a good guard dog, but sometimes at night, Hylas and Issi would lie by their campfire and listen to them roar.

When a lion roars, he is telling all the other creatures whose land this really is. *It is mine! Mine! Mine!* he roars.

It is mine! roared the lion of Thalakrea.

As Hylas listened, rebellion kindled inside him. This was the voice of the mountains: wild and strong and free. It was telling him that someday, he too would be free.

The lion's roars changed to sawing grunts, then ceased, but the sound stayed with Hylas long after the echoes died.

He thought of the lion he'd encountered by the spring. He had drunk from its paw print. Maybe some of its strength *had* entered his spirit.

Shouldering the waterskins, he started back to the others.

4

The lion cub *loved* it when her father roared. He made the earth shake and he kept her safe.

She was especially glad now, because she'd had a bad sleep. In it she was being chased by savage dogs and terrible creatures who ran on two legs like birds, but instead of wings, they had horrible loose flapping hides. It was good to wake up and hear the roars. No two-legged monsters could get her now.

The lion cub stretched happily. She liked the Dark.

Then she saw that she was alone. Her father was roaring many walks away, and her mother and the Old One had gone hunting and left her behind. This made the cub extremely cross. Sometimes they let her go too, so that she could learn to hunt—but why couldn't she go *always?* She hated being on her own.

A beetle buzzed past and crashed into a thistle. The cub scrunched it up, but it tasted bad, so she spat it out.

She padded to her pool and lapped some wet, then splashed about attacking sticks. She stalked a lizard, which escaped, then sneaked up on a frog, which nearly didn't.

She had a scratch at her best scratching tree until her claws felt tingly and strong. Then she climbed the trunk, got stuck, and fell off.

She yawned.

Once, she'd had a brother to play with, but a buzzard had snatched him in its talons and flown off. The cub remembered the swish of the great bird's wings and her brother's panicky mews. She missed him. It was boring on her own.

The Dark wore on, and at last the lion cub saw the beloved gray shapes coming through the grass. The Old One was uttering soft greeting grunts, and the cub's mother was gripping a buck's neck in her jaws and dragging the carcass between her front legs.

Eagerly the cub bounded over, nuzzling the fullgrowns' faces and mewing: *Please please I'm hungry!* But her mother was hungry too, and after a hasty cheek-rub, she swatted the cub, who scampered off to her favorite bush to wait her turn.

Her father arrived, and the females withdrew to let him feed. The lion cub watched respectfully as he ripped open the carcass and gulped great juicy chunks of loin. When his belly was bulging and his chest and chin-fur dark with blood, he shook his enormous mane and ambled off to roar some more.

Now it was her mother's turn. The lion cub watched in admiration as she tore off slabs of haunch with her fangs, while the Old One—whose jaws were weaker—chewed the squidgy guts.

Finally, it was the cub's turn. Hungrily, she lapped the delicious sticky blood; then the Old One pulled out some of the buck's fur with her teeth, and the cub attacked the flank. The meat was tough, so she soon gave up and snuggled against her mother to suckle. Milk was easier, and there was always lots.

By the time she'd finished, the buzzards were circling, so she stayed near the full-growns, where it was safe. She play-hunted the Old One's tail-tuft, which the sleepy old lioness obligingly twitched from side to side. Then her mother summoned her with a soft *ng ng*, and she bounded over to be licked.

Being licked by her mother was the cub's best thing. She loved the warm mother-smelling breath, and the big strong tongue rasping dirt and tiny itchy creatures out of her fur. Most of all, she loved that she had her mother to herself.

The cub's mother was the strongest lioness *ever*, and so good at hunting that she easily killed enough prey to feed the whole pride. Her great watchful eyes shone golden in the Light and silver in the Dark; and with one swat of her paw she could fell a buck, or nudge a hungry cub to suckle.

When the licking was over, the cub curled up between her mother's forepaws. Her belly was full, and her fur was sleek and clean.

Everything (except the buzzards) existed to keep her happy and safe. The pool was there to be played in, the frogs and lizards to be stalked, and the bushes to provide places to hide. Her mother and the Old One were there to give her milk and meat, to keep her clean, and to pull thorns from her pads with their teeth. Her father was there to protect her from bad things.

No two-legged creatures with flapping hides could *ever* get near her.

<hr />

The Dark became the Light, and the Great Lion in the Up changed color. Like all lions, He was silver in the Dark, but when the Light came, He turned gold. Now His mane shone so bright that it hurt to look.

The cub loved the Light, when the whole pride snoozed together, but this time she couldn't sleep. Her belly felt crawly, as if she'd been eating ants.

Suddenly her mother leaped to her feet with a *whuff* of alarm. The Old One rose too, and both stared tensely into the wind.

Anxiously, the cub rubbed against their legs. They ignored her.

Far away, her father roared. Then he stopped. Usually he went on much longer.

Whuff! grunted her mother. She and the Old One turned tail and raced off, with the cub bounding after them. This wasn't a hunt. Her mother smelled of fear.

Struggling to keep up, the lion cub followed their black tail-tufts through the long grass and into the prickly thickets on the Mountainside.

Far behind, she heard barking. The savage dogs had escaped from her bad sleep and were coming after her.

Then she heard a strange yowling noise. No no, the terrible two-legged creatures with the flapping hides were after her too—and now she remembered: These creatures were *men*.

Until now, she'd never been scared of men. They were just puny, timid creatures who sometimes ventured into the lions' range and left them a goat.

But these men were different. Her mother was afraid of them.

—◦—

Tirelessly, her mother and the Old One ran, and the cub labored after them.

This part of the Mountain was the heart of their range, and she knew it like the spots on her paws. She knew the black slopes where the earth was growly and hot. She knew the pools of talking mud and the hissing cracks higher up, where the fire spirits lived. Surely here they would be safe?

As they climbed a ridge, she glanced back. A long way below, she saw huge angry dogs and men with long black manes and flapping hides. The men were waving big shiny claws in their forepaws—*and they were attacking her father*.

A dog lunged at him and he bared his fangs, lashing out with his claws and sending it crashing into a rock. But more dogs were snapping at his haunches and the men were closing in. How could this be happening? Lions aren't prey. This was all wrong.

An urgent *whuff* from her mother—*wait!*—then she and the Old One went hurtling back down the slope, to help him.

Obediently, the cub hid under some thistles and made herself very small and still, as she'd been taught.

At last her mother reappeared and whiffled to her to follow. The cub saw with horror that she was panting and dragging one hind leg, and her belly was dark with blood. It wasn't the blood of prey. It was hers.

They ran for a long time, to a part of the forest that the cub didn't know.

Why didn't the Old One come?

And where was her father?

When the lion cub woke, it was the Dark again. Her paw pads hurt and she was *hungry*.

Above her in a pine tree, an owl peered down at her, then spread its wings and flew away.

The cub didn't know this place. The tree smelled of her father, but the scent-marking was old: He hadn't been here for a long time.

There was no sign of him or the Old One, but a couple of pounces away, her mother lay asleep among some bushes. With a grateful mew, the cub limped over to suckle.

She drew back in alarm. Her mother's teat was *cold*— and no milk came.

Cautiously, the cub crept nearer and patted her mother's nose.

She didn't wake up. Her eyes were open and staring, but they weren't the shining silver they should be in the Dark. They were dull—*and they didn't see the cub.*

Mewing with fear, the cub squirmed under her mother's paw and tried to *make* her move.

It didn't work. The great watchful eyes went on staring at nothing.

Frantically, the cub batted her mother's face with her forepaws. She nose-nudged her mother's flank, she licked the big gentle muzzle. *Please please please!*

Still nothing. The lioness who lay sprawled in the bushes *looked* like her mother, and smelled like her—but all the warmth and the meaty-smelling breath—all the motherness was gone.

The cub put up her muzzle and yowled. *Come back, come back.*

Her yowls sounded loud in the stillness, and horribly alone.

Trembling, she crept beneath a thornbush.

Maybe if she kept very quiet, and waited like a *good* cub, her mother would wake up.

5

Sometimes, Pirra thought her mother never slept.

When the High Priestess wasn't making a sacrifice or dealing with her priests, she was listening to the voice of the Goddess; and always the lamp in her chambers burned like an all-seeing eye.

If you wanted to escape, you had to think fast and grab your chance. Pirra knew that. But now things seemed to be going wrong.

There should have been a rope ladder hanging from the wall. It had been there yesterday—she'd seen a slave climbing over the edge to repair the outer face of the House of the Goddess—but today there was only a crow and a thirty-cubit drop.

From the Great Court, she caught the distant smells of juniper smoke and roasting swordfish, then a roar from the crowd: The bull-leaping was about to begin. The crow flew off with a startled croak, and Pirra crouched behind one of the huge limestone bull's horns that lent the top of the wall its spiky grandeur.

It had rained in the night, and the horn felt slippery and

cold. With a scowl, Pirra pondered her next move. This was beginning to look like a mistake.

And yet it had begun so *well*. She'd been pushing through the throng on her way to the Great Court when she'd become separated from her slaves. She'd seized her chance and fled.

The storeroom had been shadowy and deserted: a long way from the Feast, and heady with fumes from its man-high jars of wine. Pirra had scrambled up one, then through a repair hatch, and onto the roof. It was flat-trodden clay limed a dazzling white, and beyond it lay more roofs: a whole shining hillside of shrines, cookhouses, chambers, smithies, and workshops. Her vast stone prison.

Keeping low, she'd raced over them till she'd reached the edge of the westernmost roof. Between her and the outer wall lay a gap: a passageway without a roof. She'd jumped it, thudding onto the outer wall and grabbing one of the bull's horns.

That was when she'd realized that the ladder was gone.

Now what to do? Behind her, a nasty fall to the passage. Before her, that thirty-cubit drop, then a jumble of rocks leading down to the settlement, whose mudbrick houses huddled against the great House like calves against a cow. Beyond them—freedom.

Because of the Feast, the settlement was deserted, except for a magpie hopping about on the rocks. Perfect. But how to get down without a ladder?

Hooking one arm around the bull's horn, Pirra leaned

over. She spotted a window in the wall directly below her. If she leaned a bit farther, maybe . . .

A familiar voice shouted her name.

She glanced over her shoulder.

Userref her slave stood in the passage, frozen with horror.

"Pirra what are you *doing*?"

Furiously, she motioned him to silence, then turned back to plan her escape.

Down on the rocks, the magpie was gone. In its place stood a woman with unkempt brown hair and a startling white streak at one temple. Her tunic was ragged and dusty, but she was staring sternly up at Pirra.

Pirra recoiled, slipped, and suddenly she was clinging to the horn and her legs were dangling over the passage. Her sandals scrabbled for a foothold, but the wall's polished gypsum was lethally smooth.

"*Hold on!*" cried Userref. "I'm beneath you now, let go, I'll catch you!"

Pirra struggled to heave herself back onto the wall. She couldn't.

"Pirra! *Let go!*"

She clenched her teeth.

She let go.

"This has to *stop*," hissed Userref as he marched her back to her chambers. "Think of the trouble if the Great One found out!"

"*Trouble?*" retorted Pirra. "How much worse can it get?

In three days she's sending me to the edge of the world to wed a stranger!"

"It's your duty—"

"Duty!" she snarled.

They reached her room and she flung herself onto her bed and plucked savagely at the covering. It was fine red wool embroidered with blue swallows, and it smelled of lampsmoke and captivity.

"Yes, duty," insisted Userref. "Your mother is High Priestess Yassassara. Everything she does is—"

"For the good of Keftiu, yes I know. Last year she tried to barter me for a shipload of copper. This year it's tin. All for the good of Keftiu." She was nearly thirteen, and she'd spent her whole life shut up in the House of the Goddess. In three days, she'd be sent far across the Sea and shut up again, in a stranger's stronghold, until she died.

Userref was pacing angrily up and down. "These ridiculous attempts to escape! Bribing a water-carrier. Hiding in an empty olive jar. Clinging to the webbing under a *chariot*!"

Savagely, Pirra attacked another embroidered swallow. Userref made it sound so childish; and he hadn't even mentioned her preparations for surviving in the wild. Haunting the cookhouse to learn how to gut fish. Hoisting her big alabaster lamp over and over, to make herself stronger. Stomping barefoot on a pile of oyster shells to toughen her feet. She'd even bribed a guard to teach her about horses . . .

For what?

Her one success had been preventing her mother from marrying her off to a Makedonian Chieftain. Pirra had greeted his emissary smeared in donkey dung, with a crazy grin and the scar on her cheek picked out in henna. Her mother had punished her by forbidding a fire in her room all winter, and—which was much worse—by giving Userref twenty lashes.

"*Why* can't you accept your fate?" cried Userref. "Why can't you be content with what you have?"

Pirra glanced about her, and the familiar panic sucked the air from her lungs. The cedarwood roof beams weighed down on her and the windowless walls pressed in on all sides. The green stone floor was cold as a tomb, and the broad-shouldered columns flanking the doorway looked like tall men standing guard.

"None of it's real," she muttered.

He flung up his arms. "What does that mean?"

"This lily in my hair isn't a flower, it's just a piece of beaten gold. The octopus on that jug is made of clay. Those dolphins on the wall are painted plaster. They're not even proper dolphins, the painter got their noses wrong, he made them look like ducks. I bet he's never seen a real dolphin. I bet he never . . ." She broke off.

I bet he never stroked its flank, she thought. Or held on to its fin and let it carry you out to Sea, while Hylas stood in the shallows and . . .

Thinking of Hylas made her feel even worse. For a few

days last summer, she'd escaped from Keftiu and he'd been her friend. Well, sort of her friend, although they'd fought a lot. At times she'd been hungry and terrified out of her wits—but she'd been free.

"You're thinking about that barbarian," Userref said accusingly.

"His name is Hylas," snapped Pirra.

"A *goatherd*." He shuddered. Like all Egyptians, he regarded goats as unclean. "Is that why you never wear that lion claw I gave you?"

"He gave me a falcon feather, so I'm keeping the claw for him, it's only fair."

"But you'll never see him again—"

"You don't know that—"

"—and I got that claw for *you*, to keep you safe."

"I don't *want* to be safe!" she shouted.

"Well then, the next time you decide to dangle from the roof, I won't catch you, and you can break your legs!"

Pirra grabbed her pillow and flumped onto her side.

There was a furious silence.

Userref sat cross-legged on the floor beside the incense burner and tented his kilt over his knees. Frowning, he straightened the pleats in the linen. He centered the eye amulet on his chest and passed a hand over his smooth-shaven brown scalp. His fingers were shaking. He hated losing his temper. He said it was an offense against *maat*, the divine order of his animal-headed gods.

Beneath her pillow, Pirra touched the little wooden cat

he'd carved for her when she was eight. It was yellow with black spots, he called it a "leopard," and you could make its jaws open and shut by pulling a thong in its belly. She was too old for it, but she loved it so much that when her mother had ordered all her playthings taken away three summers ago, she'd hidden it in the secret hollow under her clothes chest.

"It would be so much easier," said Userref quietly, "if you simply *accepted* your fate."

"Like you? You told me once that to live outside Egypt is to be only half alive."

He sighed. "Better half alive than dead. Your mother won't pardon you again. You know that."

His handsome face was severe, but as he spoke, he was stoking the incense burner with his special blend of iris, terebinth gum, and snakeskin—which he said helped shed sorrows as a snake sloughs off its skin.

Pirra's eyes stung. Userref was more like an older brother than a slave, but in some ways, they would always be apart. He missed Egypt so much that he shaved his head in mourning, and his greatest fear was that he would die in a foreign land, because then he wouldn't meet his parents and brother in the afterlife. And yet he'd never once tried to escape. His gods had decreed that he would be a slave on Keftiu, and he must obey their will.

The heady fragrance of incense stole through the chamber. Userref met her eyes and smiled. "I'll be with you in Arzawa," he said. "I'll look after you. I always do." As he spoke, he gripped his eye amulet. Pirra knew this was his way of taking an oath.

"I know you will," she said.

What she couldn't tell him was that she too had made an oath.

She had sworn that she would not let herself be taken to Arzawa. That somehow, whatever it took, she would escape.

6

It was still dark when Pirra woke up.

The lamp by her bed gave off a smoky glow and a whiff of jasmine. Mice scurried in the roof and she heard the distant click of loom-weights.

Curled on her side, she clutched the little lizard-skin pouch that held her falcon feather and the lion claw. She wondered what Hylas was doing, far to the north across the Sea. Maybe he'd found his sister. Even if he hadn't, at least he was free.

"Mistress?" Silea poked her head around the door-hanging.

"Go 'way," muttered Pirra. "I'm asleep."

"Nonsense." Silea bustled in with a pile of clothes. "Up, now! We want you looking your best for the Feast."

Pirra glanced with dislike at her chief slave girl. Silea took orders from the High Priestess, for whom she also spied.

Another girl brought a tray of walnut cakes and barley milk, with a pellet of frankincense for Pirra to chew to clean her teeth. A third girl combed her dark hair and twisted it into coils, while Silea none too gently got her dressed. A shift of fine saffron wool, a split blue overskirt embroidered with flying fish, a tight scarlet jacket, and a tasseled belt of gilded lambskin. Her feet were still hennaed from yesterday, so Silea just re-did the dots on her palms and forehead, which Pirra was always rubbing off.

As Silea wielded the tiny ivory wand with sharp little jabs, Pirra wondered whether the slave girl had told the High Priestess of her mistress' failed attempt to escape— or was keeping it quiet, since it reflected badly on her. Either way, she was in a rotten mood.

On impulse, Pirra snatched the wand and hennaed in her scar. There. Her bronze mirror showed her a stark red sickle that cut across her cheek like an open wound.

Silea's plump face puckered with outrage. "The Great One *won't* like that."

"That's the point," Pirra said drily. "And don't pretend you're annoyed, you love it when I get into trouble."

"Oh *mistress*!" chided Silea, opening her eyes wide.

"Oh *Silea*!" mimicked Pirra.

The Feast of Blue Swordfish was in its seventh day, and Yassassara would be conducting the rites in the Great Court. Pirra sent the others ahead, saying she'd follow later with Userref. Silea didn't like that, but Pirra gave her one of her stares, and not even Silea was brave enough to insist.

Shortly after the slave girls had gone, Userref came in. He crossed his arms on his chest and eyed Pirra with suspicion. "You're not going to try anything else, are you?"

"Of course not," said Pirra; but her mind was darting like a trapped sparrow. Two more days till she was sent to Arzawa—and she'd run out of ideas.

Instead of making for the Great Court, she headed for the Court of Swallows, where the common folk gathered.

"What do you hope to find there?" said Userref.

"I don't know." She only knew that she couldn't face her mother. Whether or not Silea had told her, Yassassara would know by now. She always did.

Sacrifice was over for the morning, and the Court of Swallows was noisy with peasants bartering their wares and consulting the cheaper seers. There was a smell of sweat and sesame, dust and honey and blood.

A woman hawked wine from a wineskin, with a stack of rough clay beakers in the crook of her arm. A fisherman roasted octopus over an olive-kernel fire and kept an eye on a pail where more waited their turn in a squirming mass. An old man guarded his little earthenware bulls from a gaggle of slack-jawed children. "They're not toys," he snapped, "they're offerings. No touching if you don't pay, and I only take almonds or cheese."

Three peasant girls stood gossiping in their feast-day best. When they saw Pirra, they fingered their necklaces of painted limpets and gazed enviously at her gold collar and the green jasper lilies in her ears. She wondered what they'd say if they knew that *she* envied *them*. They could walk out of the gates whenever they liked.

Suddenly, she felt eyes on her.

In a corner beneath a rickety reed shade, a woman sat cross-legged on the ground, watching her. With a shock, Pirra recognized the white magpie streak in her hair.

Almost against her will, Pirra went over to her. Userref followed, clicking his tongue in disapproval.

Close up, the woman appeared to be just another wandering seer. The Sun had burned her the same dusty brown as her tunic, and her sandals curled up at the ends, like a donkey's untrimmed hooves. On a wovengrass mat she'd scattered some bunches of wilting herbs, but she had no takers and she didn't seem to care. Her face was slatted with shadow and sunlight—it was hard to tell if she was young or old—and her forearms were ringed with small round scars that looked like burns.

She stared at the scar on Pirra's cheek. "How did you get that?" she said baldly.

"How *dare* you!" cried Userref. "This is the daughter of—"

"It's all right," said Pirra. Then to the woman, "What's your name?"

"Hekabi." She spoke Keftian with an accent Pirra couldn't place. "Your mark. How?"

Pirra blinked. "I did it last summer. I burned it to stop my mother wedding me to the son of a Lykonian Chieftain."

"But *how* did you burn it?"

"What does that matter?"

"Fire always matters, mistress. The question is, what does it mean?"

Despite herself, Pirra was unsettled. She told herself this was just some cheap seer who talked in riddles to seem wiser than she was; but this woman was better at it than most.

Brusquely, Pirra asked her where she was from.

"The White Mountains," she replied.

That might explain the accent, but not the attitude. The White Mountains were far away at the other end of Keftiu, and few people lived there. Those who journeyed to the House of the Goddess were awestruck and humbled. This woman was neither.

"What are you doing here?" said Pirra.

"Visiting my cousin."

"Who is?"

"A seal-cutter."

Pirra concealed a surge of excitement. The seal-cutters' workshop was built into the western wall—she'd had her eye on it as an escape route—but the seal-cutters were notoriously reserved, and she'd never managed to gain their trust. This could be her chance.

"So what does a rich young mistress want from Hekabi?" said the woman. "A smoke reading? A telling of the spirits through Hekabi's seeing-stone?"

"I don't want anything," said Pirra.

"Ah but you do. Yesterday. I saw you on the roof." Her brown eyes were uncomfortably bright. "The seeing-stone, yes." She nodded, as if Pirra had made her choice.

Userref touched Pirra's shoulder. "What are you *doing*?" he said in Akean, so that the woman wouldn't understand. "The Great One won't like you meddling with a common seer—"

"That's why," snapped Pirra, also in Akean.

By now, a handful of peasants had gathered to watch, and they stirred expectantly as the woman set before her a round shallow dish of burnished black stone. Pirra was surprised. The stone was obsidian: rare on Keftiu, and not something a traveling seer would own.

First, the woman filled the dish with water from a greasy skin. Then from a goathide bag she took a nut-sized pellet of searing yellow. She crumbled it in her fingers and rubbed the yellow powder over her palms. "The lion rock," she murmured.

Sulfur, thought Pirra. She'd seen it once in a priest's medicine pouch. It was used to ward off bad spirits and fleas.

Rocking and chanting under her breath, the woman took three lumpy gray pebbles from the bag and cast them into the water. They didn't sink, but bobbed to the surface.

Gasps from the peasants. "They *float*! What power has she, that she can make stones float!"

Pirra crossed her arms, unimpressed.

The woman drew another stone from her bag. It was round and flat, of white marble with a hole in the middle.

"My seeing-stone," she said with a sly smile. "The spirits gave it me."

Putting the stone to her eye, she peered through the hole at the floating pebbles. "Ah . . . they do the bidding of the spirits . . ."

"Pirra," said Userref, "you really can't—"

"Yes I can," she retorted. Then to the peasants, "Get back, all of you! I must be alone with the seer. You too, Userref. Out of earshot."

Grumbling, the peasants did as they were told, but Userref stood his ground. "What are you planning?"

"Nothing," lied Pirra. "Now do as I say. That's an order."

He didn't move.

"Userref. I mean it."

They locked gazes. He put his hands on his hips and shook his head. Then he heaved a sigh and moved away.

When everyone was well out of earshot, the woman put the seeing-stone to her eye once more and peered at the floating pebbles. "Three will come together," she murmured. "Yes. That's what my seeing-stone tells me."

"Three what?" Pirra said coldly. "When? Where?"

"That the spirits don't tell."

Pirra knelt and leaned closer. She caught the woman's smell of dusty hair and roadside thyme. She whispered in her ear: "Help me escape, and I'll give you enough gold to last your whole life."

The woman met her eyes and slowly shook her head.

Pirra licked her lips. "Then do it because I ask it. I'm desperate."

Again the woman shook her head.

"It would be *easy* for you!" breathed Pirra. "You're kin to a seal-cutter, you could share the gold with him; he could help me get out through his workshop and down the wall—"

"No," said the woman.

Pirra clenched her fists.

Twenty paces away, Userref was staring at her in consternation. She leaned even closer. "Then what about this," she hissed. "You're a *fake*. Those pebbles float because they're pumice. Peasants don't know that, but I do. And you made that 'seeing-stone' yourself, I can see the chisel marks." She paused to let that sink in. Then she added, "My mother—High Priestess Yassassara—deals harshly with fakes."

The woman recoiled. Her gaze hardened. "You're bluffing," she spat. "If that was true, she'd have to punish half the wisewomen here." But beneath her sunburn, she'd turned pale.

Pirra gave her a thin smile. "Do you want to take that risk?"

Midnight in the seal-cutters' workshop, the woman had said.

It was nearly midnight now, but Userref had only just fallen asleep outside Pirra's room, and she was still trying to retrieve her gear from its hiding place.

Teetering on the lamp pedestal, she groped for the gap behind the roofbeam. At last she grabbed the calfhide bag.

The lamp tipped and she leaped for the bed, catching the pedestal a heartbeat before it hit the floor. The bed's latticework creaked. Behind the door-hanging, Userref murmured in his sleep.

Pirra held her breath.

He went on sleeping.

The bag held everything she'd collected over the winter and hidden from him and from her slave girls' prying eyes. Shakily, she emptied it and put on her disguise. A rough peasant tunic, a belt and knife-sheath of stained goathide, a plain bronze knife, a hairy cloak that stank of the weaver-woman who'd sold it to her for two carnelian beads. The sandals must stay in the bag; their cracked oxhide would be too noisy on the polished floors of the House of the Goddess.

Next came a handful of earth filched from the pot of the sacred olive tree in the Great Court: Pirra smeared it on every bit of her that showed, especially her scar. She'd already covered the amethyst sealstone on her wrist with clay, and the falcon feather and lion claw were safe in the pouch at her neck.

Recently, Userref had warned her that she'd reached the age when men looked at her. *Even if you did escape*, he'd said, *you couldn't go wandering on your own*. Well then, I'll be a boy, thought Pirra as she hacked her hair to shoulder length. She would take the cuttings with her, so that her mother couldn't use them in a charm to track her down.

With pounding heart, she stuffed everything back in the bag: a block of pressed figs wrapped in vine leaves, some dried lambs' tongues, eight salted and slightly mouse-eaten mullets; and two bundles of gold bracelets wrapped in linen to stop them clinking—one to pay the wisewoman, the other for herself.

There. Hylas would have been impressed. Or maybe not. He was used to living by his wits.

Again Userref stirred in his sleep. Pirra's heart twisted. She would never see him again. And she couldn't even say good-bye.

On impulse, she placed the little wooden leopard on her pillow. Would he understand how much she would miss him?

Quietly, she drew aside the door-hanging.

He lay as he always did, across the threshold. Pirra saw that he'd smeared some of his precious green *wadju* on his eyelids, to help him dream of Egypt. She hoped it was working.

Farther along the passage, her slave girls were snoring. At her evening meal she'd drunk little, and drugged the rest of her wine with poppy juice, knowing they'd finish what was left. She hoped she hadn't overdone it.

It was still early spring, and a chill breeze was moaning through the House of the Goddess. The passages were dark, except for the odd guttering lamp. She groped past chambers where people muttered in their dreams, and nearly trod on a sleeping slave. A sliver of darkness slunk toward her, and a cat's furry warmth brushed her calf.

Moonlight silvered the Great Court and the olive tree in the middle. Keeping to the shadows against the walls, she made for the far corner. The olive tree watched her go. Silently, she begged it not to betray her.

Footsteps echoed through the Great Court.

Pirra froze.

A priest emerged from a doorway, horrifyingly close.

Rigid with tension, she watched him make for the Hall of the Double Axe. She heard the faint rattle as he parted the beaded hanging and disappeared inside.

It was past midnight when she reached the workshops in the western wall, and she was terrified that the woman had gone.

In the darkness, she banged her shins against a pile of copper ingots, and nearly sent a shelf of clay jars crashing to the floor. Her heart jerked. Eyes glared at her from a corner. She breathed out in relief. The rock-crystal gaze of the ivory god followed her as she crossed to the seal-cutters' workshop.

It was empty. Had she missed her chance?

A shadow detached itself from the blackness, and in the gloom she made out the white magpie streak.

"You're late!" whispered the woman.

"I couldn't get away! I brought the gold—"

"Not now. There's an olive press in the next room. My cousin left rope. We tie it to the press and climb out. He'll untie it before dawn, to cover our tracks."

By the faint light from a small window, they found the press—two massive grooved stones—and a thick coil of rope.

Pirra peered out of the window. The night wind blew cold in her face, and she couldn't see the rocks below. "How do we know the rope's long enough?" she breathed.

"We don't," muttered the woman.

<hr>

The rigging creaked and the sails snapped as the black ship sped across the waves. Huddled in the prow, Pirra drew her scratchy cloak around her and felt the salt spray stinging her face.

Freedom.

Where would she go? How would she survive in the

White Mountains, far from everything she knew? She felt frightened and exhilarated. It was too huge to take in.

The rope *had* been too short, and she'd nearly broken her ankle jumping onto the rocks. The settlement dogs had sniffed her suspiciously, but Hekabi had brought scraps to keep them quiet.

After walking through the night, they'd reached the gray Sea and a ship rocking in the shallows. The captain was expecting them, and they'd set off along the coast.

Hekabi said that if the wind kept up, they should reach the White Mountains by the following dusk. To throw off pursuit, she'd laid a false trail, and if that failed, she knew secret places in the Mountains where no one would find them.

The stars faded and a red slash appeared on the eastern horizon: The Goddess was walking across the Sea to wake the Sun. Pirra cut a sliver of dried mullet and threw it over the side for an offering, then cut another piece for herself.

She stopped in mid-chew. The Sun was in the wrong place. If they were heading west, it should be behind her.

She glanced over her shoulder. Her eyes widened. Keftiu had dwindled to a black line on the edge of the Sea.

She lurched along the deck to where Hekabi stood staring across the waves. "We're heading *north*!" she cried.

"Well spotted," Hekabi said drily.

"You said we were going to the White Mountains!"

"I lied."

"But I *paid* you!" shouted Pirra.

The brown eyes studied her with amusement. "I needed gold to buy my passage. Now you're just a nuisance I'll have to put up with for a while."

Pirra's outrage turned to unease. She seemed to have swapped one form of captivity for another. "Where are you taking me?" she said.

Hekabi turned back to the horizon. The red dawn lit the strong planes of her face, and the wind whipped her strange streaky hair across her cheeks. "There is a ring of islands with hearts of flame," she told the waves. "Once long ago, the Lady of Fire tore off Her bright necklace and flung it across the great green Sea . . ."

"*Wh-at?*" said Pirra. "The Obsidian Isles? But that's halfway to *Akea*!"

"The 'Obsidian Isles' may be what you Keftians call them," said Hekabi with an edge to her voice, "but we who live there simply call them the Islands." She paused. "Ten years ago, warriors came from Akea. They went from island to island till they found what they wanted."

Pirra's belly tightened. "You mean the Crows."

"The warriors of Koronos. Yes."

It was Pirra's turn to stare out to Sea. Last summer, she'd narrowly escaped being wed to the son of a Crow Chieftain. Then another Crow Chieftain had beaten her up and nearly killed Hylas.

"On the island where I was born," said Hekabi, "the Crows found what they wanted." Her hands tightened on the side of the ship. "They dug deep into the earth, wrenching the greenstone from Her entrails, calling the island *theirs*."

Pirra swallowed. "The copper mines. Is that where we're going?"

Hekabi nodded. "My poor, devastated homeland. Thalakrea."

8

Hylas had lost track of how long he'd been at Thalakrea.

Twice he'd tried to escape by creeping past the guards at the Neck under cover of darkness. Twice Zan had caught him and beaten him up. "Try that once more," the older boy had warned, "and I'll have to turn you in."

Then a spate of accidents had made Hylas forget about escape. A rope had snapped, sending a sack plummeting down the shaft and breaking a man's leg. A falling rock had nearly brained another, and a spilled lamp had set fire to a pile of ropes, badly burning three hammermen.

Fear is catching underground. Soon Hylas was flinching at shadows. Did that rock move? Was that a shadow, or a snatcher?

Once, he dreamed he was back on Mount Lykas, wading through crystal streams and cool green bracken. Issi was there. As always she was plaguing him with questions. *Where are the frogs, Hylas?* But when he woke, the dream felt as if it had happened to someone else: to Hylas the Outsider, not Flea the slave.

Despite the fear, he was growing almost accustomed to the mines. He knew that overseers were called "guts," the girls who tended the lamps down the pit were "sparks,'" and the small children who sorted the greenstone were "moles."

Apart from Spit, he got along all right with his fellow spiders. Bat was cheerful and keen to help. Beetle remained silent and fearful underground, but was friendly above, although he'd been more subdued of late. Zan was clever and resourceful, and he never pried. "We all got secrets," he said with a shrug.

One night, Hylas stole a joint of smoked hog from a gut and they sat munching in the dark, swapping their stories. Zan said he was the son of a horse-breaker from somewhere called Arzawa, far to the east. Bat had been born at the mines: He *thought* his mother had been a slave and his father a gut, but was hazy on details. Beetle's father had been a rich Egyptian merchant.

"So he says," said Zan, rolling his eyes. "But then he wants us to believe that in Egypt they got horses that live in rivers, and giant man-eating lizards!"

"We do," said Beetle. "They're called crocodiles, they—"

Zan grinned and pelted him with pebbles.

Beetle sprang to his feet and went to stand at the mouth of the den.

"What's got into him?" said Hylas.

Zan shrugged. "What about you, Flea? You got any kin?"

Hylas hesitated. "My mother left me on a mountain.

That's all I know." It wasn't. He knew she had cared about him and Issi, because she'd wrapped them in a bearskin and stroked his face; but he didn't want to tell Zan, or reveal that he had a sister.

Two days later, they were crawling down to the seventh level to pick up another load when his sack snagged. By the time he'd freed it, the others had gone ahead.

As he hurried around a bend, he made out a couple of pit props a few paces in front. Between them crouched a small murky figure, gripping a hammerstone with both hands.

It took Hylas a moment to grasp that the figure was pounding at one of the props, trying to dislodge it. "Hey, you!" he yelled.

Whoever it was flung down the stone and fled, with Hylas scrambling after him.

Several frantic twists and turns later, Hylas crashed into Spit. Grabbing him by the hair, Hylas wrenched his arm behind his back. "Knocking out a pit prop? *Why?* You could've killed us all!"

Spit wriggled and squealed. Hylas jerked his arm higher. Zan and Beetle arrived and hauled him off.

"He was trying to bring down the roof!" panted Hylas.

"It wasn't me, I swear!" whimpered Spit. "May the Lady of Fire strike me dead if I lie!"

"Leave him alone, Flea," said Zan. "He says it wasn't him."

"But I saw him!"

"I said leave it!"

A few days later, Hylas jolted awake from a bad dream.

It wasn't yet dawn, and on the furnace ridge the smith's hammer had fallen silent. Hylas lay listening to the crows cawing around the stronghold. Kreon had discovered what people called his clan, and he *liked* it. He'd ordered carcasses flung from the walls to attract the birds.

Hylas got up and started putting on his rags. These days, he moved in a fog of dread. There was something terribly wrong with Thalakrea, and it was getting worse.

It was whispered that the snatchers no longer stayed underground. Someone had glimpsed a shadow emerging from the pit and slipping downhill. A boy had woken from a nightmare and felt something squatting on his chest. And last night, a hammerman had rushed screaming up the slope and thrown himself down the shaft. Even the animals had sensed that something was wrong. The pools had fallen silent: The frogs had gone.

Some said the Mountain was angry because they were digging too deep, while others blamed Kreon for killing the lion. His warriors had been seen carrying the carcass toward the stronghold to be skinned; and soon afterward, the accidents had begun.

From the ridge, the smith's hammer rang out. Hylas wished the others would wake up.

Zan and Beetle were twitching in their sleep, as if they were still hauling sacks. Bat lay clutching the balding remains of his tunnel mouse. Spit's bony knees were drawn up to his ribs and his mouth hung open: a dark void surrounded by broken teeth.

Hylas stopped binding his knees and stared at that gaping mouth. A terrifying thought had occurred to him.

He woke Zan and dragged him to the mouth of the den.

"What's this about?" growled Zan, rubbing his eyes.

"If a snatcher gets you," breathed Hylas, "it can reach down your throat—yes?"

"That's what they say. So?"

"So that means it can get *inside* you."

"They're spirits, they can do anything. Why?"

"What's he saying?" Beetle stood behind them with his arms at his sides.

Hylas motioned him closer. "The first night I came, I asked what was wrong with Spit, and Zan said a snatcher'd nearly got him." He swallowed. "I think you were wrong, Zan. I think a snatcher already has."

Beetle's face went still. Zan's scowl deepened. "*What?*"

Hylas pointed at the sleeping boy and whispered, "He's possessed. *It's inside him.*"

They didn't believe him.

Zan got angry, while Beetle retreated behind a blank, uncomprehending stare. When Hylas insisted, Zan turned on him. "Why are you always accusing him?"

"Why are you always shielding him?"

"We're pit spiders, we stick together, that's how we survive!"

"Even if he gets us all killed?"

"He won't. He's one of us. So shut up!"

In stony silence they got dressed. Hylas watched Spit waken and pluck desultorily at his rags. He was skeletally thin, and his face was wizened, like that of an old man.

Hylas pictured the evil spirit coiled in the pulsing red darkness under his heart. Who knew what it would make him do next?

9

Telamon knelt with his hands in the cold mountain stream and wondered what to do next.

He couldn't go back to his father's stronghold, not yet. And he *must not cry*. He was fourteen summers old: almost a man. And Hylas was dead.

"I've kept my promise to you, Hylas," he said as the water lifted the blood off his fingers. "I said I'd sacrifice a ram for you, and I have. Be at peace, my friend."

Long after his hands were clean, he remained kneeling by the stream, while a chill wind from Mount Lykas dried the tears on his cheeks.

For the thousandth time, he told himself that Hylas' death wasn't his fault. How could he have known that his own kin—his father's brother—would hunt Hylas like prey? It wasn't his *fault*. It was the will of the gods.

Why then did the guilt always come back?

If only he'd warned Hylas sooner. Just a single day. Then he and Issi could have gotten away, and they'd still be alive.

As Telamon was heading for home, the gods rewarded

him for making a sacrifice for his friend: His dogs flushed a boar.

He didn't have time to be scared. One moment the dogs were harrying the great beast; the next, it was crashing through the bracken toward him.

Without thinking, he dropped to one knee and jammed the butt of his spear in the earth to steady it, aiming its point at the boar and gripping the shaft with both hands.

The boar thundered closer. Its small eyes locked on Telamon's. He caught its hot rank smell and saw its lethal yellow tusks.

Suddenly it swerved and came at him from the side. He jerked the spear to meet it. The force of the beast's charge drove its chest onto the point, snapping the shaft and jolting Telamon to the marrow. The boar fell dead a cubit from where he knelt.

He gave a jittery laugh. This was his fourth boar—he had to kill twelve before he'd have enough tusks to make a helmet—but it was by far the biggest. He couldn't believe he'd killed it by himself.

He tried to stand, but was annoyed to find that his legs didn't work. He was shaking like a girl. Thank the spirits there was no one to see.

Moments later, two goatherds came down the track, idly slashing the bracken with sticks.

Telamon lurched to his feet.

The goatherds recognized the son of their Chieftain, and dropped their sticks.

Curtly, Telamon ordered them to carry the carcass back to Lapithos.

"What about our goats, my lord?" said one.

"Do as I say," he snapped.

As he strode off, he heard them snigger. The blood rushed to his face. They'd seen him shaking.

Suddenly, Telamon despised himself for his weakness. With a stab of envy, he reflected that if it had been Hylas facing that boar, *he* wouldn't have gone all shaky. Hylas was brave and tough. No one dared laugh at him . . .

Shut *up*, Telamon told himself fiercely.

By the time he reached his father's stronghold at Lapithos, he was feeling a bit better. Thestor was delighted with his son's kill, and insisted that he sit beside him on his bench. Fire, roast venison, and strong wine mixed with honey and barley meal did the rest. Telamon sat warming himself before the great round ancestral hearth, enjoying the approval of his father's warriors and the pleasure in Thestor's eyes.

His new friend Selinos refilled his cup. "I hear it's the biggest boar in Lykonia," he said with an ingratiating smile.

Telamon shrugged.

Hylas would never have flattered me like this, he thought with a pang. He'd have grinned and said, *So how many more till you can call yourself a man, eh?* Then he'd have dragged me off to the forest and we'd have roasted a hedgehog in river clay and washed it down with a skinful of barley beer stolen from the village . . .

"Your father's very proud of you," said Selinos in an undertone. "I've no doubt High Chieftain Koronos will be too." He cleared his throat. "You've not been to Mycenae, have you? Or met your grandfather? I'm sure he'll want to change that very soon."

Telamon forced a smile. Selinos came from Mycenae. Telamon suspected that Koronos had sent him to take a look at his grandson, and report back.

This pleased and frightened Telamon in equal measure. Koronos was the most powerful Chieftain in Akea. And the most feared.

The heat and noise of the feast faded, and Telamon remembered last summer, when he'd stood in this very hall with the dagger of Koronos in his hands.

Proudly, he'd told his father how he'd taken it from the dead grip of his uncle Kratos. By retrieving the most precious heirloom of his clan, he'd gained great honor. And yet, Thestor's praise had been stilted, for with him were his terrible siblings: his two surviving brothers, Kreon and Pharax, and their cold-eyed sister, Alekto.

Apart from them, the hall had been empty. Earlier, Thestor's entire household had gathered to see the dagger that held the power of the House of Koronos—but after that, they'd been sent away. None but Koronos' closest blood kin must know of the perils their House faced. None must know what the Oracle had predicted: that an Outsider could bring them down . . .

"So tell me all about it," said Selinos, wrenching him

back. "*How* did you kill such a huge beast on your own?"

"Yes, how?" cried Thestor. Then to his warriors, "Listen to this, lads!"

Dutifully, Telamon embarked on his story. But somehow, it didn't feel real.

He was walled in by secrets.

The Oracle was a secret known only to Koronos and his kin.

Thestor had kept secrets from his own son. For years, he'd told Telamon nothing about his family, the House of Koronos. They'd done dreadful things and he wanted no part of them. Only latterly had he been forced to overcome his scruples.

Even Telamon had secrets. Hylas had been his best friend, the very Outsider who the Oracle had foretold would be the ruin of his House. And that was something only his father knew.

Layers of deception, like skin . . .

"What did I tell you?" cried Thestor, clapping him on the back. "He'll be a warrior before he's fifteen!"

It was nearly midnight. Dogs nosed the rushes for scraps, and most of the drinkers—including Selinos—had dragged sheepskins off the benches and fallen asleep.

Thestor sat cradling his gold drinking cup by the fire. These days, he drank too much. His kinsmen might be far away in Mycenae, but they cast a long shadow.

He caught Telamon watching and smiled sadly. "So, Telamon," he said, squaring his shoulders. "While you were out killing monsters, a party of merchants came up from the coast. They've set out their wares in the east chamber. Why don't you go and choose whatever you like?"

Telamon was surprised and pleased. "Thank you, Father."

Thestor gave him an affectionate punch on the arm, and turned back to the fire.

The merchants were sharp-faced foreigners who sprang awake when Telamon entered the chamber. He felt pleasantly fuddled. The wine had blunted the edge of his worries.

The treasures on the blanket shimmered before his eyes. What about that silver cloak pin with the back-to-back eagles? Or the copper wrist-guard. Or the bronze knife with the green lion inlaid on the blade . . .

Suddenly, he noticed a belt of tooled leather with two square gold plaques on either side of the clasp. His wits cleared in a heartbeat. The plaques were beautifully worked with interlocking spirals formed of tiny gold beads. He'd seen them before.

One of the merchants sensed his interest. "The young lord has a good eye," he murmured. "Finest workmanship. Keftian, of course."

Telamon already knew that. Those gold squares had

once been part of a bracelet that had belonged to the girl he was supposed to wed. Pirra was her name. He remembered her standing at his side as they'd watched the flames of his uncle's funeral pyre shooting into the sky. He remembered the smell of burning flesh, and how he'd pretended to be mourning Kratos, when inside he was grieving for Hylas.

Later, the girl hadn't been wearing the bracelet, and when he'd asked why, she'd said she'd lost it; although he could tell she was lying. At the time, he hadn't thought anything of it.

But now.

"Where did you get this?" he asked the merchant.

"My lord, it was my friend . . ." He indicated his companion.

The companion was Makedonian; the other one had to translate. "He says, lord, that he was given it by some boy in exchange for passage on his ship."

Telamon swayed.

The merchant looked worried. "Is something wrong, my lord? I assure you, it was bought in good faith—"

"This boy," cut in Telamon. "What was he like?"

The merchant was puzzled.

"Tell me everything," said Telamon. "And tell *no one* else. If you disobey me, you will suffer."

Both merchants turned pale.

It was just some boy, they said. About the young lord's age, maybe a year or so less, and not so tall. Narrow tawny eyes. Strange hair, the color of barley. And a notch in one earlobe . . .

Telamon left them and staggered back to the hall. He snatched his drinking cup and stared at it. He gulped wine, splashing his tunic.

Hylas was alive.

What would Hylas do now? thought Pirra, shifting uncomfortably on the hard earth floor.

First rule of survival, he'd told her once: *Before anything, sort your day's food and water*.

Well, she had, but that didn't help much. How was she going to survive on this strange, fiery island ruled by Crows?

The hut was sturdily built of basalt and pumice, with a door that faced south, to avoid the strong north wind. It was also fugged with the smells of unwashed people and the smoky dung fire.

On the other side of the wall, Pirra heard a pig snuffling for scraps. Her belly growled. On the shore she'd seen men gutting tuna fish bigger than dolphins, but the Islanders had only offered them a porridge of chickpeas and mackerel, and sour wine mixed with terebinth that tasted like tar.

"The Crows take everything," they'd apologized. "If we protest, they send us down the mines."

Despite their poverty, they were friendly. Hekabi's

mother had shyly welcomed Pirra—"All strangers are honored guests"—then scolded her daughter for being too thin, and bustled off to make the porridge.

Merops, the village headman and Hekabi's father, had politely shown Pirra how to bow to the fire and ask its permission to sleep in the hut. Even Hekabi had unbent a little. She was younger than Pirra had thought, maybe thirty summers or so, and she seemed actually to *like* her mother. Pirra found this intriguing, as she hated hers.

The Islanders reminded her of Keftian peasants, with sunburned limbs and horny feet—although unlike Keftians, the men had beards, and their amulets weren't seashells, but beads of black obsidian and yellow sulfur. Everyone had burn scars on their arms, and they admired Pirra's scar, which they said brought good luck.

On the other side of the wall, the pig stopped snuffling. Pirra turned over. No use. She couldn't sleep.

At the doorway, she nearly trod on a small snake drinking milk from a little pottery dish. Murmuring an apology, she waited for it to finish and slither away.

It was cooler outside because of the wind, but a sulfurous whiff from the Mountain made her head ache.

Thalakrea puzzled her. So far, she'd seen no Crows—the village was on the north coast, the mines to the south—and the island was beautiful. Their ship had entered a bay of emerald and amethyst water enclosed by white cliffs banded with yellow and orange, like a sunset turned to stone. The village was set amid silver olive trees and feathery green tamarisks, and in the distance rose a great black Mountain with smoke seeping down its flanks.

A few paces from the hut, Merops sat by a fire, sharpening an obsidian blade. "Can't sleep?" he said, motioning to Pirra to sit.

He had a leather pad on one knee, and was carefully pressing a piece of antler against the blade's edge, to remove tiny flakes of stone. His face had the same strong planes as Hekabi's, although unlike his daughter, he looked as if he laughed more than he frowned.

"You were good with that snake," he remarked.

"I like snakes," said Pirra. "I made friends with one once. It used to coil around my wrist and rest its head in my palm."

He blew away stone-dust and examined the blade. "Do you regret leaving Keftiu?"

She tensed. Had Hekabi told him who she was? "No," she said warily. "But I miss Userref. He's my sl—a friend. I'm worried he'll be punished because I left."

Merops nodded. "We too fear the wrath of High Priestess Yassassara."

So he knew. "If she sends people after me," said Pirra, "will you give me up?"

He looked horrified. "Of course not! You're a stranger here, we have to shelter you, it's the law of the gods."

"I didn't mean to offend you."

He chuckled. "You didn't. But you need to learn our

ways. You Keftians worship the Sea, we worship the Lady of Fire." He bowed to the Mountain. "So we, er, never turn our back on a fire—as you did just now when you left the hut."

"Sorry."

"You didn't know."

In the moonlight, the smoke on the Mountain glowed. Pirra thought of the stories they told on Keftiu about the fabulously wealthy island that the Earthshaker had destroyed.

"It looks dangerous," she said.

"*Dangerous?* The Lady keeps us *safe*! When our Ancestors first came to Thalakrea, She took human form and told them to build a village here. She warned them that everything beyond the Neck belongs to the Wild, and is guarded by Her sacred creatures, the lions. Our Ancestors honored Her wishes—and in return, She taught them how to free the copper from the stone."

"But that smoke . . . Don't such mountains wake the Earthshaker? On Keftiu we fear earthshakes more than anything."

"So do we, but the Lady *protects* us from the Earthshaker. Never in a thousand years have we had more than a tremor."

Hekabi emerged from the hut and came toward them. "I thought you'd run away," she said to Pirra.

"Where would I go?" Pirra said tartly.

Merops glanced from one to the other, then got to his

feet. "Watch the fire," he told his daughter. "And look after our guest."

When he'd gone in, Pirra said, "Am I a captive here?"

Hekabi's lip curled. "What makes you say that?"

"Was *any* of what you told me true? Have you even *been* to the White Mountains?"

"No."

"So—why were you on Keftiu?"

Hekabi hesitated. "There are others like me, who hate the Crows. We talk. We share what we've heard."

"You're taking a risk telling me that."

"Am I?" Her bright eyes pierced Pirra's.

"Is that why you came back to Thalakrea?" said Pirra. "To fight the Crows? Where do I fit in?"

Hekabi shrugged. "I needed gold to get home. You needed to escape."

Pirra chewed her lip. She had more gold hidden in her pouch; maybe she could buy passage off the island. But where would she go?

Hekabi woke the fire with a stick, loosing a flurry of sparks. "Tomorrow I'll show you what the Crows have done to Thalakrea. The forests they've cut down for their furnaces, the holes they've dug in Her flesh. You Keftians don't realize what it costs to make all your bronze tripods and your mirrors . . ."

"Why are you angry with Keftiu?" said Pirra. "We've always been friends with the Islands. We even speak the same tongue."

Hekabi glared at her with sudden animosity. "Would friends have stood by and watched us overrun?"

"What could we have done?"

"Has the High Priestess no power?"

"Of course! But the Crows are *warriors*. We're not."

"So that's your answer? Do nothing?"

"What's yours?"

"It's late," snapped Hekabi. "Go and get some sleep."

Afterward, Pirra lay staring at the rafters. Hekabi's outburst had unsettled her; and reminded her uncomfortably of her mother.

In her mind, she saw Yassassara standing on the topmost balcony of the House of the Goddess. She wore a skirt of Keftian purple, its folds sharply scented with oil of myrrh. Her sea-blue bodice was open at the breasts, her waist cinched with a belt sewn with green glass beads. Her arms were twined with silver snakes, and from her neck hung her great gold collar of many Suns. Her coiled black hair was pierced by bronze pins with rock-crystal heads the size of pomegranates. Her hawk-like face was painted white, her eyes and lips fierce red, and she was spreading wide her saffron talons, sending spells far out into the night to find her daughter . . .

Pirra was woken by Hekabi shaking her.

It was dark, but everyone was awake, and frightened. Then Pirra saw the warriors in the doorway.

"Kreon's sick," Hekabi said tersely. "He needs a wise-woman." She hauled Pirra to her feet. "You're coming too."

"What?"

Hekabi leaned closer. "You speak Akean, I don't. As far as the Crows are concerned, you're my slave."

Pirra made to protest, but Hekabi clamped a hand over her mouth. "You will do as I say or I'll tell them who you are. I'm sure Kreon would be delighted to learn that he has a high-born Keftian in his power. So. Will you come quietly?"

"He'll find out you're a fake," muttered Pirra as they stumbled along in the moonlight.

"Not so loud," breathed Hekabi. A few paces behind, the warriors were dark shapes in the gloom.

"What's Kreon like?" whispered Pirra.

Hekabi moved closer to her. "Greedy," she said in an undertone. "Unpredictable. He's the weakest of his father's children, and he knows it. This makes him dangerous. He works his slaves to death in the mines."

Pirra frowned. "But your father said that you Islanders also had mines."

"Yes, but *we* followed the teachings of the Lady. We never dug too deep and we always gave Her time to heal. Kreon doesn't care about that. And he calls the island *his*. No one owns Thalakrea. It belongs to the Lady." She clenched her fists. "He thinks he can do what he likes because he's a Crow, and they can't be beaten while they have the dagger."

The dagger. Something must have shown in Pirra's face,

for Hekabi was instantly alert. "You know of it?" she said sharply.

"Only that while they've got it, they can't be beaten."

But Pirra knew more than that. She knew that an Oracle had made a prophecy: *If an Outsider wields the blade, the House of Koronos burns* . . . And for a few days last summer, Hylas—an Outsider—*had* wielded it. Then the Crows had taken it back.

That was her fault. Hylas had told her to keep it safe, and she'd failed.

"What do you know about the dagger?" repeated Hekabi.

"Nothing," lied Pirra.

———

Clouds hid the Moon, and two warriors moved past them to take the lead. Pirra heard the creak of their rawhide armor, and caught an acrid taint that was horribly familiar. Last year, on a lonely hillside, a Crow Chieftain had attacked her. She remembered the ashy stench of his sweat.

"*Why* do they smear themselves with ash?" she whispered.

Hekabi's hand went to the little lump of sulfur on a thong at her breast. "They're bodyguards of the House of Koronos," she hissed. "They worship the nameless ones who haunt the dark."

Pirra caught her breath. "You mean the—the *Angry Ones?*"

"Sh!" warned Hekabi.

Despite the heat of the night, Pirra went cold. The Angry Ones came from the very fires of Chaos. They were drawn to darkness and burned things, and they hunted those who'd murdered their kin. They were relentless. They didn't care who got in their way. Once, Pirra nearly had, and now they haunted her nightmares. She remembered a shadowy gully and the leathery *thwap* of wings. A creeping horror in the dark . . .

"That's why the Crows burn their sacrifices," Hekabi said quietly. "That's why they make arrowheads of obsidian: the burned blood of the Lady of Fire, perverted for their foul rites . . ."

"But to *worship* them—*why?*"

"If they could gain the favor of the Angry Ones," said Hekabi, "think of the power . . ."

At last the sky turned gray and they reached a trio of silent pools at the foot of a stark red hill. Pirra heard the din of hammers. She saw crows circling another rocky hill on a headland, from which a squat, uncouth stronghold glared down.

The warriors halted near the pools and sat on boulders, unslinging their food pouches and easing their shoulders. Pirra watched hungrily as they drew out leather wine flasks and mouthwatering slabs of dried tuna.

A gang of boys was filling waterskins. They were painfully thin and covered in red dust, with the cropped hair of slaves. Pirra guessed they were from the mines.

Hekabi told her to go and fill the waterskins, but she refused; she wasn't going near the warriors, or those slaves. Hekabi leaned closer. "Shall I tell them who you are?"

Pirra glared at her. Snatching the skins, she stalked off.

To her relief, the warriors were too hungry to notice her, and she found a spot some distance from them and the slaves.

As she knelt by the shallows, she saw one of the boys edging toward the warriors. When the nearest man opened his food pouch, the boy sidled closer. When the man glanced up, the boy stopped and tended to his waterskins.

Now the warrior was sharpening his knife on a whetstone.

What happened next was so fast that Pirra didn't even see it. One moment there was a chunk of tuna jutting from the man's pouch; the next, it was gone, the sack's contents were deftly rearranged so that he wouldn't notice, and the boy had shot under the willows and was gobbling his prize with the ferocity of a wild beast savaging its kill.

Pirra froze.

The boy was Hylas.

He seemed to sense her staring, and lifted his head. For one astonished heartbeat, his tawny eyes widened. Then he went back to demolishing his fish. He was pretending he hadn't recognized her, but he had.

Squatting with her waterskin, Pirra sidled closer. "Hylas, it's me!"

"Shut *up*!" he hissed.

She remembered that the Crows knew his name; he'd be using a false one. "Sorry. I—"

"I thought you were safe in Keftiu! How'd they get you too?"

"What? Oh—no, I'm not a slave, I just look like one. I escaped from Keftiu. I thought I'd ended up here by chance—but not anymore . . ." She was gabbling. But it was so incredibly good to see him.

On the other side of the pool, an older boy with a hook nose and a scowl shouted at someone called Flea to hurry up. Hylas shouted back that he was coming.

"Did you find your sister?" whispered Pirra.

"Does it look like it?"

"What happened to your earlobe?"

"I got a man to cut it off."

She winced. "Was that so they wouldn't know you're an Outsider?"

"*Sh!*" He cast about him. "Shouldn't have bothered," he added. "Nobody'd recognize me like this."

He was right. He'd been skinny before, but now his shoulder blades jutted like knives, and she could see every one of his ribs. He was caked in red filth, and his back was covered in weals. Only the way he moved had alerted her, and his straight nose that made an unbroken line with his brow.

"Stop staring," he muttered.

She bristled. "You must be a bit glad to see me. And thank you, yes," she added tartly, "I did manage to escape from the House of the Goddess, and it was actually quite hard."

He snorted a laugh, and was suddenly much more like himself. "So how'd you do it, then?"

"I bribed a wisewoman. That's her over there. She said we were going to the White Mountains, but she lied." She gulped. "I'm *so* glad to see you."

He frowned, but she could tell he was pleased. "What," he said, "stinking like a dung heap and crawling with lice?"

"Well, I bet I don't look much better."

He flashed her a grin. "You're right about that. Bit of a change from gold spangles and Keftian purple."

She laughed, and smoothed her tunic over her knees. "I got it from a peasant. Do I look like a boy?"

"No. You haven't got a hope of looking like a boy."

"Oh," said Pirra, oddly pleased.

Hylas splashed her.

She splashed him back. "You're a *really* good thief," she said enviously.

He shrugged. "Lots of practice. You're going to need to learn how."

"But you did take a chance stealing from a Crow. What if he'd recognized you?"

"He wouldn't. I'm a slave. Nobody looks at slaves."

The Sun was rising, and farther off, the other boys had filled their waterskins.

"I'll help you escape," said Pirra.

He threw her a strange, lost look. "You can't. I tried twice. Got as far as the Neck over there. Zan tracked me—"

"Who's Zan?"

"Pirra, *listen*! I'm a slave, see? A pit spider. That means I go down the pit every day and don't come out till dark. Down there it's not just rockfalls you got to watch out for, it's snatchers. And one's got into Spit and he's . . ." He could see that she had no idea what he was talking about.

One of the warriors ambled to the pool's edge not five paces away from them. Hylas retreated farther into the willows, and Pirra bent over the water.

The warrior dipped in his head, then returned to the others, wringing out his long black hair.

"Spit's what?" prompted Pirra. The Crows were ready to move off, and Hekabi was beckoning.

"Can a spirit get inside a person?" Hylas said abruptly.

"What? Yes, sometimes. It sends them mad. They bring people like that to the House of the Goddess to be cured. It doesn't always work."

"That's what's happened to Spit, but the others don't believe me." His jaw tightened. "I watch him all the time. And I've learned the places where there are beams propping up the roof. They'll be our only hope if he tries anything. Although what good will that be if the tunnel caves in and we're trapped?"

He was talking to himself; she couldn't follow. "What do you mean, if he tries anything?"

He swallowed. "He's going to bring down the mine."

Pirra's spine prickled. Hylas was scared. It took a lot to frighten him.

Hekabi was coming to fetch her, looking annoyed.

"I have to go," she said.

Hylas jerked his head at the warriors. "Do they know who you are?"

"Of course not!"

"So where are they taking you?"

"Kreon."

"*Kreon*? What's he want with you?"

"Not me, Hekabi. I'm supposed to be her slave."

He was struggling to take it in. "Whatever you do, keep your head down and don't say anything! Someone might remember what you look like."

"Thanks, I'd managed to think of that myself." She gave him a wry smile, but he didn't smile back.

"I mean it, Pirra, keep your head down. It's not just clothes that make a disguise. You still hold yourself like the daughter of a priestess. And you're too clean. You're poor now. Act like it."

Pirra scooped a handful of mud and rubbed it over her face and hair.

"Better," said Hylas.

"I will help you escape," she said fiercely.

Again that strange, lost look. "Don't even try," he warned. "You'll only put yourself in more danger than you are already."

"That's my choice, not yours. We'll find a way off this island. Then I can finally give you that amulet I've been carrying around since last summer."

Hekabi was almost within earshot.

"How will I reach you?" whispered Pirra.

Hylas shouldered his waterskins. At the last moment he turned and breathed one word: "*Hedgehog.*"

"So who *was* that?" said Zan as they dragged their empty sacks down to the deep levels.

"I told you," said Hylas. "Just some slave I met once."

"Oh yes? Is she your girl?"

"No!"

"Fine. Then you won't mind if I—"

"Yes I will, you stay away from her."

"Why? She'd be quite pretty cleaned up—"

"Zan!" Hylas gave him a shove.

Zan laughed. "All right, all right. So if she's not your girl, what'd she want?"

"She's scared. They're taking her to Kreon. I told her I couldn't help."

"You're right about that," said Zan.

They went deeper, and the older boy became more subdued. Ahead of them, Spit began to whimper. Beetle swung his head from side to side, peering into the dark.

Mice scurried along the floor and a bat flickered past Hylas. He hardly noticed. Pirra was here, on Thalakrea. *Pirra*. Shock, joy, anxiety, fear—all churning inside him. He hated thinking of her in Kreon's stronghold. She was clever, but she hadn't grown up living by her wits. She'd need help getting out of there.

All of which should've made him angry. Now he had to think about her as well as himself. And yet—somehow, that didn't matter. He was no longer alone.

They reached one of the shafts that opened onto the deep levels. The greenstone was piled near it amid coils of rope, and the men who'd hauled it up from below were heading back to the upper levels. Hylas loaded his sack and tried to forget about Pirra. He had enough to worry about, staying alive down here.

This was one of the better places in the mines, where the roof was strengthened with beams; and the men had a lamp, so he could keep an eye on Spit.

Spit had grown even thinner and more like a skeleton than ever. Sometimes, Hylas almost felt sorry for him. Then he would remember the snatcher inside him, and what it might do.

"What's Kreon want with a wisewoman?" Bat asked Zan as they filled their sacks.

"He gets these terrible pains in his head," said the older boy. "That's what I heard."

"Maybe he'll die," Bat said hopefully.

They sniggered. Hylas didn't. If Kreon died, the wisewoman would be punished—and so would Pirra.

"Pains in his head," repeated Zan. "Maybe some spirit's sticking its knife in his ear, eh?"

"It's 'cuz he killed that lion," said Bat with feeling. "He shouldn't of, it done nothing to him."

"You and your animals," teased Zan.

Hylas stopped listening. *I'll help you escape,* Pirra had said. She'd been so certain. That was only because she didn't know what the mines were like, but it still helped. And she'd called him Hylas. It had been a shock hearing her say his name, but a good one. For the first time in a moon, he felt like himself: not Flea the slave, but Hylas of Lykonia, who was going to escape and find his sister.

A bat brushed his ear, bringing him back to the present.

"Come on, Flea," called Zan. "Time to get moving."

As he started after them, mice scurried over his hands, and he shooed them away.

Lots of mice: a river of tiny furry bodies and scratchy little feet. It struck him that they were all scurrying the same way.

The bats too were all flying *up* the tunnel.

He stopped. What had they sensed?

Beneath his palms, he felt a tiny shudder in the rock.

He went cold. "Zan!" he yelled. "Bat! Beetle! Get back here!"

"What?"

"Get back here under the beams, quick! *It's caving in!*"

There was a roaring in his ears and the lamp snuffed out.

Then the darkness slammed down.

"**Z**an? Can you hear me?"

"*F-Flea?* Where are you?"

"Down here by the shaft. You?"

"Uh . . . Tunnel's blocked. I can't see a thing."

"Me neither. Are the others with you?—Zan?"

"Um—yes."

"There's space where I am. Can you make it down?"

"I—I think so."

"There's a gap, can you reach my hand? Got you. Can you get through? *Zan*. Answer me. Can you get through?"

"M-maybe."

"Right. Bat, you first, you're the smallest. He's through, Zan. Get behind me, Bat, and mind the shaft. Beetle, you're next. It's Flea, I've got you. Your turn, Zan."

"N-no, Spit's next."

"*Spit?*" Hylas hadn't reckoned on Spit being there; he was the one who'd caused the cave-in by knocking out the prop.

"H-help me," stammered Spit.

In the dark, Hylas felt bony fingers clutch his through

the gap. He hesitated. He was trapped eight levels down with a mad boy possessed by a snatcher. But this was no time for a fight. Quickly, he pulled Spit through, followed by Zan. The five of them huddled together, their breath loud in the dark.

"What do we do now, Zan?" said Bat in a small voice.

Zan didn't reply. Hylas could feel him shaking. He was supposed to be the leader, but instead he was frozen with fear.

Hylas said, "What do you think, Zan? The main tunnel's blocked; any chance we could dig our way out?"

"None," said Zan curtly.

"Right. So we find another way. Help me feel for gaps." The older boy seemed to get a grip on himself, and together they started groping in the dark.

"How did you know it was going to cave in?" said Zan in a low voice.

"What?" said Hylas.

"You warned us just before it happened. How'd you know?"

"Ask Spit," muttered Hylas. "He got us into this."

"I n-never!" stammered Spit.

"He couldn't have," said Zan, "he was right in front of me, he wasn't doing anything."

"We're wasting time," said Hylas. Then later, "I think I've found something. Can you feel a draft? Behind these rocks. Wasn't there a side-tunnel?"

Zan gasped. "Of course! It's not used, but—"

"If we could clear the entrance," said Hylas, "it might be a way out."

A cold hand clutched his shoulder. "It's no use," said Beetle.

Angrily, Hylas shook him off.

"It's no *use*," Beetle repeated.

From below, a man's voice rang out. "Who's up there? Let down the rope!"

They froze. They'd forgotten the men in the deep levels.

Hylas crawled to the shaft and peered down. A man holding a rushlight peered up at him. He was filthy and gaunt, but Hylas recognized the man with the broken nose.

"Let down the rope," he ordered.

Hylas grabbed it, but Zan held him back. In the glimmer from below, his face was clammy and pale. "*What if that's not really a man?*" he breathed. "*What if it's a snatcher?*"

Again Hylas peered down the shaft. The man with the broken nose had been joined by three others. All were wild-eyed and covered in grime. They didn't look human. Did those matted beards conceal the telltale ridge?

"We can't leave them to die," he said.

"What if Zan's right?" whispered Spit, his eyes bulging with terror.

Hylas swallowed. He called down to the man with the broken nose. "What's your name?"

"Periphas. What's yours?"

"Where are you from?"

"What does that matter? Throw down the rope!"

"Answer me!"

"Messenia, you know that! Now the rope!"

"That proves nothing," hissed Zan.

"You're right," said Hylas, "but we *need* them. We can't clear this tunnel on our own. We'll just have to risk it."

<hr />

When you're underground, time doesn't exist. Hylas had no idea how long it had been since the men had climbed out of the shaft.

Only four survivors from the deep levels; although from glances exchanged between them, Hylas guessed that an overseer *had* survived, and been swiftly finished off.

They weren't snatchers. At least, he didn't think they were, but they worked with the strength of ten men, while he and the others helped as best they could.

At last the entrance to the side-tunnel was clear. It led upward; they felt a faint draft that was slightly fresher.

From the deep levels, the men had salvaged three rush-lights, two coils of rope, and a full waterskin. Periphas, who seemed to be the leader, allowed everyone a mouthful of water, then they headed off. The men went first to clear the way, followed by Zan, Bat, Spit, and Beetle. Hylas volunteered to go last, with a rushlight, so that he could keep an eye on Spit.

It was painfully slow going, as they had to keep stopping to clear rubble and listen for more cave-ins. Soon Hylas' rushlight was nearly spent.

He began to regret having offered to go last. Ahead

of him he heard Beetle's harsh breathing, and the others shuffling forward. Behind him—what?

He pictured the angry ghosts of dead hammermen crawling out of the shaft, and snatchers emerging from the walls and silently following. He thought of cold earthen fingers stealing down his throat, squeezing his hot fluttering heart . . .

In front of him, Beetle came to a sudden halt.

"Why'd you stop?" said Hylas. The glimmer of the others' light was moving ahead.

"It's no use," said Beetle, shaking his head.

"Stop saying that!"

The others rounded a bend and their light blinked out. Hylas' own was nearly spent. He called to them to wait, but they didn't hear.

"It's no *use*," repeated Beetle.

Hylas grabbed his shoulder and shook him. "I'm not leaving you, so get moving!"

Beetle turned his head and stared at him. In the rushlight's dying glimmer, his eyes were unblinking and strangely dull. His flesh felt clammy. Hylas snatched his hand away.

The light died.

In the dark, Hylas felt Beetle's breath on his face. It smelled of clay. Horror washed over him. Everything fell into place. Beetle was friendly aboveground, but surly and silent down the pit: like two people in one body.

"It's not Spit who's possessed," whispered Hylas. "It's *you*."

13

The thing that had stolen Beetle's body slammed Hylas against the rocks. His nostrils clogged with the smell of earth. Cold fingers crawled up his chest, feeling their way like spiders toward his mouth . . .

With a huge effort he shook his mind free, pushed Beetle off, and fled.

Stony laughter echoed behind him, and he heard the earthy flap of feet.

He hadn't gone far when the ground beneath him creaked. He felt the roughness of wood and an uprush of hot foul air. He guessed he was on the log bridge that spanned the other shaft over the deep levels. As he blundered across, he glanced over his shoulder.

All was dark—and yet somehow, he sensed what was there. He knew that on the other side of the bridge, there were *two* tunnels: the one he'd just left, and beside it another, a gaping mouth guarded by stone teeth jutting from the floor. And among them, flitting like half-seen shadows, were the vengeful spirits of the earth. In his mind he saw hair like spun dust, and eyes of lightless clay;

earthen fingers groping for the tremors that betrayed the movements of their mortal prey.

Hylas backed away, loosing a trickle of pebbles.

The darkness tensed. They knew where he was. Now they'd found the bridge. They were surging across.

He raced up the tunnel. Beneath the noise of his flight and his urgent breath, he caught a whisper of voices. *Lone . . . sss . . . leave . . .*

Some mad impulse made him wheel around. "What do you *want*?" he cried.

Dark against dark, they swayed, their lipless mouths snapping at his words.

"What do you want?" he said again.

Leave . . . lone . . . sss . . . leave . . . sss

"But how *can* we leave?" he shouted. "You won't let us out!"

Sss . . . leave . . . lone . . .

Suddenly the sounds came together in his mind and he grasped their meaning. He knew what they were trying to say.

A man was calling him, somewhere close.

Hylas lurched around a bend and thudded into him. Panting with terror, his fingers groped a matted beard and a broken nose—and below it, not the ridge of a snatcher, but the groove of a mortal man. "They're behind us," he gasped. "I think I—"

"Come on," muttered Periphas, "it's not far to the others."

"I think I know what they want!"

"He's lost his mind," said Zan. "It can't be Beetle!"

Murmurs of agreement from the others.

"It is," insisted Hylas. "He's the one who's possessed, not Spit. It was him all along."

They were in a low echoing cavern, faintly lit by their final rushlight.

"How do we know *Flea's* not the snatcher?" said Zan. "How do we know he didn't kill Beetle, and it was *him* all along?"

Hylas set his teeth. He knew that Zan was ashamed of his earlier failure, and desperate to reassert himself. "It's Beetle," he said. "There's a snatcher inside him. It made him bring down the roof, and it'll do it again."

"It's true," said Spit.

All eyes turned to him.

His skull-like face was shiny with sweat, but for once he was looking them in the eye.

"Why didn't you *tell* us?" said Hylas.

"I couldn't," said Spit. "Beetle—the thing inside him—it said it'd kill me. It said such terrible things. I've been so frightened—"

"None of this matters now," cut in Periphas. "What matters is getting out."

"That's what I'm trying to *tell* you," said Hylas. "We've got to give them what they want—or they'll never let us go!"

"And what's that?" demanded Periphas.

Hylas took a deep breath—and told them.

Snarls of disbelief.

"Now we know he's mad!" said one of the hammermen.

"I say we kill him and give him to the snatchers," said another. "Maybe then they'll let us go."

Periphas was staring at Hylas. "We're seven levels down, with who knows what ahead—and you want to make it *worse?*"

"It's the only way," said Hylas. "Look. I know I can't prove any of this, but I also know I'm right. This is what they've been trying to tell us. Don't you see? They want the deep levels. If we can't make that happen, they'll never let us out."

Out, out, out . . . His voice echoed through the cavern.

"He's right," whispered Spit. "Can't you feel them? They're here in the walls, listening to everything we say . . ."

The others glanced at one another, then at Periphas.

He licked his lips and rubbed a hand over his beard.

Hylas crawled back down the tunnel with one end of the rope over his shoulder and the last rushlight clamped between his teeth: back toward the bridge, and the angry spirits of the earth.

This was the price the others had exacted for doing what he said. They would wait in the cavern, gripping the other end of the rope—which was actually the three ropes, knotted together—while he found his way to the main prop on this side of the bridge, and tied the rope around it. Then, when he'd rejoined the others, they would pull as hard as they could, and yank out the prop.

If it worked, it *might* bring down the roof without killing them all—and seal the deep levels forever.

The murmurs of the others faded behind him as he reached the bridge. All was eerily still. Shadows shrank from his rushlight and hid behind the stone teeth on the other side. No sign of snatchers—or Beetle—but Hylas could feel them watching.

He found the pit prop, a sturdy log supporting the tunnel roof near the bridge. It looked immovable. He prayed it wasn't.

Jamming the rushlight in a crevice, he passed the end of the rope around the prop.

At the corner of his vision, one of the stone teeth seemed to move. He forced himself not to look.

The braided rawhide was thick, and his hands were slippery with sweat. He struggled to tie a knot.

Laughter like falling stones echoed around the walls.

"We're doing what you want," he panted. "We're giving the deep levels back to you . . ."

The laughter sank to an angry hiss.

"Flea?" called Periphas. "Have you done it yet?"

"Nearly," he called back. There. That *had* to hold.

Another hiss from across the bridge. He saw a figure crouching in front of the stone teeth. It was Beetle. He was *beckoning*.

"Flea come *on*!" shouted Periphas.

Hylas froze. Was that a draft gusting from between the stone teeth, cooling his sweat-soaked skin? Were those mice scurrying between them? And what was that dim light filtering through?

In the gloom, Beetle's face was empty of expression; but he was still beckoning. *This way* . . .

Hylas caught his breath. That light . . . Was it the gray glow of the spirit world—or daylight? Was Beetle playing one last lethal trick—or showing him another way out?

His mind raced. If he returned to the others, they would make it to the surface, but they'd be back at the mines: They'd still be slaves. This other tunnel headed *away* from the mines. If it led anywhere, it might just lead him to freedom.

"Hylas . . ." whispered Beetle. And for a moment, his expression changed and he was a boy again. "This way, Hylas," he urged. "*Freedom* . . ."

Hylas glanced from him to the rope. Then he shouted to Periphas: "Pull!"

"*What?* What about you?"

"Pull! Pull!" yelled Hylas.

The rope snapped taut against his thigh. The wooden prop creaked. He crawled across the bridge toward Beetle.

As he reached the stone teeth, the wooden prop creaked—tilted—and fell with a crash. Rocks thundered onto the bridge behind him, snapping it in two and sending it hurtling into the shaft.

The stone teeth juddered as he squeezed between them. Beetle was gone. The last of the mice were streaming up the tunnel.

It was endless and steep, and Hylas climbed till his breath was sawing in his chest.

Far above, he saw a dazzle of light.

From below came a deafening roar—then a *whump* and a rush of air blasting him forward. Through the noise and the billowing dust, he thought he heard shrill laughter. Glancing down, he seemed to glimpse shadowy figures whirling and twisting in a wild gleeful dance. The snatchers were reclaiming the deep levels.

Wheezing and coughing, Hylas crawled toward the light.

14

As the Light grew stronger, the lion cub finally understood that her mother wasn't going to wake up. Her face was crusted with flies, and when her fur moved, it wasn't her, it was maggots. This made the cub feel shaky inside.

Leaving the trees, she padded into the open, where the whispering grasses arched over her head and the Great Lion shone fierce in her eyes.

She heard a whooshing of wings. *Buzzard.*

She shot under a bush.

It wasn't a buzzard, it was a vulture.

The cub never used to be scared of vultures. Vultures don't hunt lion cubs, and they can be helpful, as their squawks tell lions where to find carcasses; but now, the cub was scared of everything.

Cowering beneath the bush, she watched the vulture rip her mother's belly with its beak. Another vulture lit down. Soon her mother had vanished beneath flapping, squabbling birds.

Miserably, the cub huddled under the bush, waiting for

her father or the Old One to fetch her. It grew hotter. Flies crawled in her eyes, and although she lashed out with paws and tail, they never gave up.

At last it came to her. Her father and the Old One weren't coming back. The terrible men and their dogs had gotten them too. *She was on her own.*

This was so frightening that the lion cub put up her muzzle to cry. But there was no one to hear her.

She would have to go against everything she'd been taught, and set off alone.

She would have to look after herself.

———

Flies tormented her as she plodded along, and twice, as she watched anxiously for buzzards, she nearly fell down a hole.

She'd left the Mountain behind, and was in a dangerous place of sharp black rocks and thorny scrub; but something made her keep going.

She found a boulder and scrambled on top to catch the smells. She smelled *wet*. Somewhere close.

Eagerly, she bounded over the rocks. There: a small shining pool!

Mewing with delight, the lion cub lapped till she was full, then rolled so that she was beautifully muddy and cool. Thorn trees murmured encouragingly, and she heard the squawks of more vultures, not far off.

They were fighting over a dead deer. Greatly daring, the cub charged, snarling and swiping with her paws. To her astonishment, the vultures lifted into the Up.

The meat was tough, and the lion cub was too tired to tackle it for long. She would eat more when she'd had a sleep.

She woke from a sleep in which she'd heard the Old One calling to her. It was Dark. For a moment she thought she still heard those faraway grunts; but it was only the wind.

Her spirit sagged. Foxes and vultures had made off with the deer carcass, and the pool had dried up.

She prowled about, trying to hunt. She snuck up on a weasel, but it was too fast. A hedgehog was better, but when she pounced, it rolled into a ball and refused to be eaten. All she got was a prickle in her forepaw, and when she tried to pull it out with her teeth, it broke, leaving the point in her pad.

She was so hungry it hurt. Worse even than that, she was *lonely*.

In the blackness of the Up, the Great Lion shone silver, surrounded by his glittering females and his many cubs. His was the greatest pride of lions ever, but it was so far away that it only made the cub lonelier.

She missed her mother. When she was small, her mother would carry her in her jaws, sometimes putting one huge, comforting paw under her bottom; and the cub would bob along, washed in warm meaty breath . . .

It was beginning to get Light. Wearily, the lion cub hauled herself to her feet. She found a stick and did some scratching, but her pad hurt from the hedgehog prickle, so she stopped.

Suddenly, she sensed danger. She sped under a bush.

This time, it really *was* a buzzard. The cub watched it settle in a thorn tree just a pounce from where she hid. It knew she was here.

She was trapped. She'd scared off those vultures by pretending to be a full-grown, but that wouldn't work with the buzzard.

The lion cub was beginning to lose hope when suddenly the buzzard spread its wings and flew away.

Something had startled it. Could it be a lion? *Could it be her father, come to fetch her?*

Then, on the wind, the cub caught a strange smell that was horribly familiar. Fear tightened her pelt.

It wasn't a lion who'd scared off that buzzard.

It was a human.

15

Hylas chucked another stone at the buzzard. "Go away!" he croaked. He couldn't risk it telling the Crows where he was.

In the distance, Kreon's stronghold glared down at him. Did they think he'd been killed down in the pit? Or had they found his trail and were coming after their runaway slave?

The cave-in and the snatchers were an evil blur. He'd emerged from the tunnel to find himself on the Neck, so close to the guards' camp he could hear them breathe. He remembered waiting till dark, then creeping up a gully and collapsing.

After that, nothing till dawn.

Had Zan and the others gotten out alive? And what had happened to Pirra? He'd been leaving signs for her as he went, but how would she ever escape from Kreon's stronghold?

From the Neck, he'd stumbled across a blistering plain of thornscrub and poisonous oleander. Instead of earth, there was brittle black rock: It looked as if it had once bubbled like mud, until a god had turned it to stone.

The Sun was punishingly fierce, even though he'd used his knee-bindings for footcloths and to cover his head. He was thirsty, but when he came upon a spring, he was startled to find that the water was *hot*, and so salty he spat it out. His spirit quailed. Thalakrea didn't want him. *Here's water, but you can't drink.*

The Mountain loomed over him. Its lower slopes were green with thickets of prickly broom, and above them rose naked black cliffs. Smoke seeped endlessly from the weird, lopped-off summit. Hylas thought of fire spirits and the terrible Goddess who lived inside. But behind him in the distance, Kreon's stronghold still glared down at him. He *had* to get into those thickets. Silently, he begged the Lady of Fire to let him.

Soon afterward, he killed a lizard with a rock. It was barely a mouthful, but he took it as a sign that She'd granted him leave. He tucked the lizard skin in his kilt—he'd find a use for it later—and felt a bit better. Come on, Hylas. The gods help those who help themselves.

As he walked, he sensed eyes on him, and glimpsed a flash of lion-colored fur. It was a relief when it turned out to be a tussock of grass.

At last he reached the thickets, and Kreon's stronghold disappeared from view. In places, the broom grew as tall as trees, with gnarled roots and gullies where he could hide. Again he fancied he was being watched. Again it was nothing.

He came to some straggly pines and the bones of a

lioness, picked clean by scavengers. This was good. Lions need prey, there must be *something* here to eat.

He followed a trail up a shoulder of the Mountain, hoping it led to another spring. It didn't. He was now *above* the thicket, on a windswept ridge.

A lonely wild pear tree clung to life amid great drifts of black obsidian pebbles. Scattered among them were marble hammerstones. It looked as if people had been coming here for years, to hack the obsidian from the ridge and make their weapons. Hylas found this encouraging. Now it was his turn.

Back in Lykonia, he'd made weapons of flint. Obsidian was sharper and more brittle, shattering into vicious slivers; but it broke cleanly, and soon he'd shaped an axehead the length of his hand. As he worked, he sensed the ghosts of those long-dead weapon-makers watching with approval. Maybe they'd been Outsiders like him, used to living in the wild.

For a shaft, he hacked a branch off the pear tree—muttering a hasty apology to its spirit—then gouged a slot in one end and jammed in the axehead. A clump of fireweed near the thicket would do for twine. Slitting the stems with his thumbnail, he chucked the pith and twisted what was left into cord, which he wound securely around the axehead.

There. Sunlight glinted on the axe's vicious black edges, and his spirits rose. It was good to have a weapon again. Now he was a hunter, not a slave.

He still had the lizard skin, so he decided to make a slingshot. With a shard of obsidian, he trimmed the hide to an oblong, then scraped it clean to make a pouch for holding a stone. He cut slits in either end, then threaded through another length of fireweed twine, tying a knot at one end for a handy grip, and a loop at the other, to slip over his thumb.

The slingshot made him feel even more like himself: He couldn't remember a time when he *hadn't* known how to use one.

The Sun was getting low. To the west, he spotted another ridge jutting from the Mountain, this one covered in trees. Leaving a few more signs for Pirra, he started down toward it. He passed a clump of rue and rubbed some on his limbs, to mask his scent and keep off the flies; he didn't want them settling on his skin, then carrying his smell to the prey.

It was cooler under the pines and the air smelled fresh and sweet. He munched goosefoot leaves and crunchy little bulbs of tassel hyacinths. He saw the shiny pellets of wild goat, and a patch of flattened grass where a hare had rested.

He found another hot spring, ringed by vivid orange mud. The water wasn't as hot as the last spring, and it tasted all right. He drank greedily, and strength coursed through him. Maybe Thalakrea wasn't out to get him. Maybe he just had to learn its ways.

The hare lolloped out of the brambles twenty paces away.

Hylas froze.

The hare was young and foolish. It sat up with its back to him and its paws on its belly.

Not daring to breathe, Hylas swung his slingshot and let fly.

—※—

He couldn't risk a fire in case the Crows saw the smoke, so he ate the hare raw, drinking the blood and gobbling the sweet slithery liver. He chewed the knobbly little heart and as much meat as he could, but it was the first he'd had in moons, and he soon felt sick.

Hastily, he thanked the hare for letting itself be eaten, and sprinkled dust on its nose to help its spirit hop off and find a new body. He set its forepaws on a boulder as an offering for the Lady of the Wild Things, its hind paws for the Lady of Fire, and stuck its tail in a bush for the long-dead stoneworkers on the ridge; they were the closest he'd ever gotten to having Ancestors of his own.

He slung what was left of the carcass over a branch, to tackle tomorrow. Right now, he barely had enough strength to wash his hands.

The hot water stung, but it felt good. Maybe it was a magic spring. On impulse, he slid all the way in.

In his whole life, Hylas had only ever bathed in cold lakes and streams, and being in *hot* water felt incredibly strange. But he could feel it healing his cuts and soothing his knotted muscles; washing away the grime of the pit and the last traces of Flea the slave. When he climbed out, he was Hylas the Outsider. He was *free*.

He was also dizzy with fatigue. He cut an armful of ferns, dragged them under a rocky overhang, and curled up.

Tomorrow he would make needles from the hare's bones and thread from its sinews, then sew a waterskin and a kilt from its hide. After that, he'd work out how to rescue Pirra . . .

A knife, he thought hazily. You forgot to make a knife.

An image of the dagger of Koronos floated into his mind. He saw its lethal bronze blade in all its savage beauty, and his fingers tightened to grasp its hilt. He'd only possessed it for a few days last summer, but it had made him feel stronger and less alone. He wished it were with him now.

Gradually, his thoughts loosened. He was dimly aware of the song of the night crickets and bubbling of the spring . . .

Was that something larger making its way through the ferns?

Not big enough to be dangerous. Probably a badger or a fox.

The ferns rocked him to sleep on a cool green-scented Sea.

16

The lion cub didn't know what to make of the human. He was different from the ones who'd killed her mother and father. He was half-grown, and he had no dogs and no terrible flapping hide. *And* he'd scared off the buzzard.

This made the cub wonder if he might be the one who was supposed to look after her. She'd thought it would be a lion; but somehow, this human felt right.

All through the Light, she'd padded after him: past the hot wet and into the thickets, past the bones that had been her mother, up the ridge and down to the forest. They'd wandered for *ages,* and her bad paw hurt a lot. Why did he walk when it was glarey and hot, then sleep through the beautiful cool Dark?

Now he was whiffling in the ferns, so she crept out from under the bushes.

She was encouraged to find that he'd left his kill for her, and even playfully hidden some of the bits. The paws and tail were too furry to eat, so she had a wonderful game of toss-and-catch before drowning them in the hot wet.

Then she attacked the carcass, which he'd slung over a branch. In one huge leap she caught it in her jaws, then pretended it was trying to get away, and pounced. Like a full-grown lioness hauling her kill, she dragged it about between her front legs. When she got bored, she ate as much as she could, and clawed the rest to shreds.

After this, she climbed on a log and lay with her legs on either side, to have a nap. At last she was sure about the human. He was definitely the one.

Hylas knows he is dreaming, and he doesn't want it to end. He's with Issi on Mount Lykas, playing bears and wolves. She's the wolf and he's the bear, and as usual she's cheating, wielding her slingshot with deadly accuracy and pelting him with chestnuts.

"Wolves don't use slingshots!" he shouts.

"Neither do bears!" she yells when he pelts her back.

Now Pirra is with them too, and she and Issi are ganging up on him, chasing him through the bracken with wild wolf howls as they hurl pebbles and sticks. He's laughing so hard he can barely run. Then he has an idea, and doubles back to sneak up on *them*.

He bursts out with a roar, and now *they're* running away, squealing and sputtering with laughter. He glimpses a flash of fair hair, that's Issi up ahead. He pushes through the undergrowth, he's gaining on her—

Hylas woke up.

Moonlight slanted through the pines. He heard the

night crickets and the bubbling spring. Dejection crashed over him. It had felt so real.

Was Issi trying to dream to him? Was Pirra? Or was it one of those false visions the gods send to make fun of a mortal?

Sometimes, down the pit, he had imagined what it would be like if he and Pirra ever got back to Mount Lykas and found Issi. At first, Issi would be wary of Pirra, but they'd soon become friends. And Pirra would like the mountains, and he would show her all his favorite places . . .

Scowling, Hylas turned onto his side. Issi was far away, and Pirra was trapped in Kreon's stronghold. He didn't know what to do. If he managed to escape Thalakrea and went after Issi, then Pirra would never get free. If he went back to rescue Pirra, he might lose his chance of finding Issi.

In the forest, an owl uttered a wavering *oo-hoo*. Much closer, something heavy fell with a thud.

Hylas was instantly alert. Reaching for his axe, he crept out into the moonlight.

His camp had been wrecked. Every part of the hare's remains—even the offerings—had been savaged. What hadn't been eaten had been shredded, flung about and trampled into the mud.

A scavenger would have eaten what they could, then hidden the rest. This devastation must be an attack by some bad spirit . . .

At the corner of his vision, he caught movement. There, behind that log.

The lion cub wasn't much good at hiding. Its bottom stuck out, but because it couldn't see Hylas, it seemed to think that *he* couldn't see *it*.

"Shoo!" shouted Hylas, waving his axe. "Go on, shoo!"

For a heartbeat, the lion cub stared at him with big moon-silvered eyes: caught red-pawed in the ruin of his camp. Then it turned tail and fled.

The lion cub didn't understand what was happening. The human was barking and waving his forepaws. He seemed *angry*.

Or was it a game?

It didn't appear to be; he was chasing her with a stick.

Bewildered, she sped for the safety of the thickets.

As she left the trees, she glanced back to see if he was still chasing.

She stumbled. Suddenly there was no more ground beneath her paws and she was falling into the dark.

Hylas burrowed into the ferns and willed himself to sleep.

No use. Those faint, despairing yowls wouldn't let him.

"Oh, shut *up*," he muttered.

More yowls. That lion cub sounded desperate.

Then it stopped, and that was worse.

With a snarl, Hylas sat up.

As the sky turned gray, he tracked the lion cub through the forest. It occurred to him that where there was a cub, there would also be a lioness—but then he remembered the skeleton he'd found the day before. That must have been its mother; Kreon had probably killed her, as he'd killed its father.

It turned out that the cub hadn't gotten far, it had fallen down an old mine shaft a few paces into the thicket. A buzzard was perched on the edge, peering down at it. Hylas shooed the bird away.

The lion cub saw him and gave a plaintive mew. It was small, filthy, and shaking with terror.

"Well what d'you want me to do?" he said crossly. "You should've looked where you were going!"

The cub stopped mewing and stared up at him with great round golden eyes.

Hylas threw down his axe, found a fallen sapling, and shoved it down the hole. "There. Now climb out and leave me in peace!"

The cub wobbled onto the sapling and fell off. It tried again. And again. Hylas blew out. Lions aren't the best climbers, and this cub was the worst he'd seen. It didn't help that it seemed to be lame in one forepaw.

It had wrought havoc with his kill, but he couldn't leave it in there to starve, and the shaft wasn't deep. Muttering, he shinned down the sapling.

The hole was cramped, and stank of lion scat. The cub backed into a corner and hissed. Hylas grabbed it by the scruff, plonked it on the sapling, and gave its furry bottom a shove. "Go on, up you go!"

The cub lashed out, raking him with needle-sharp claws. Then it fell off again.

"You stupid beast, I'm trying to *help* you!" Picking it up, he slung it around his shoulders and gripped its paws on his chest, as if he was carrying a goat. The cub struggled and scratched. He flung it from him.

"Well it's not my fault you fell in!" he shouted. "D'you think I *want* to be down this stinking hole?"

The cub cowered under the sapling. It was snarling and lashing its tail, but its flanks were heaving and it was trembling.

Hylas rubbed a hand over his face. "All right," he said quietly. "I know it wasn't your fault. I mean, it *was* your fault, but you were just hungry."

The cub stopped lashing its tail and swiveled its ears to listen.

It was about knee height, maybe three or four moons old. Like all lion cubs, its paws were too big for the rest of it, and the fur on its belly, legs, and haunches was paler, with fuzzy dark spots. Its pads weren't black, like a full-grown lion's, but a tender light brown. The tip of its nose wasn't black either, it was a freckly pink, and just above was a long, bloody scratch. And lion cubs should be plump. This one was so thin Hylas could see its ribs.

"All right," he said again. Squatting on his haunches, he started talking in a low, soothing voice: Speaking nonsense, but letting the cub hear from his tone that he meant no harm.

After a long wait, the cub edged closer and sniffed his toes. He kept talking.

It tried to take his heel in its jaws. He flinched. It drew back. He kept talking.

The Sun rose and the song of the crickets changed. Hylas kept talking.

A little later, the cub approached and sniffed his knee. When he didn't move, it rubbed its cheek against his shin. It licked his hand. Its tongue was surprisingly rough, but he stayed still, letting it become comfortable with his taste and smell.

At last, the cub rested its head on his knee. Gently, he stroked behind its furry ear. It slitted its eyes and began to purr. Slowly, he gathered it up in his arms. It squirmed and scratched his chest a bit, but he could tell it didn't mean to hurt him, it just hadn't learned to sheathe its claws.

Awkwardly, with the cub in his arms, he climbed out of the hole. "There," he panted, setting the cub on the ground. "Now you really are on your own. I can't look after you, I've got to go and find Pirra."

As he started back for camp, the cub limped at his heels.

He shooed it away. It darted into the thicket. But as he entered the trees, it reappeared.

Hylas stopped and stared down at the small bedraggled cub, and something shifted painfully in his chest. It was all on its own, and too small to hunt for itself.

"Oh all right," he said.

The lion cub reached his shelter before he did. It sniffed the ferns where he'd lain, turned around twice, then flumped down and fell asleep.

17

Telamon felt a surge of pride as he galloped toward Mycenae. We're not crows, he told Hylas in his head. We're *lions*.

The trail was wide enough to take two chariots abreast, and it climbed in a sweeping curve to the great citadel on the hill with the mountains at its back. Mycenae, rich in gold. The very heart of his clan.

Telamon rode across the bridge that spanned the ravine, and past the huddled gravestones of conquered Chieftains. Ahead he saw the massive gates with the lions painted above. He told himself that he belonged here. He almost believed it.

It was only a few days since he'd learned that Hylas was still alive, but it felt like moons. That first shock, joy, unbelievable relief—that he *hadn't* killed his friend—had swiftly curdled to bewilderment and pain. His long winter of grief had been for nothing. Hylas and the Keftian girl had been making fun of him all along.

His horse shied at the gravestones, and he checked it savagely.

When he thought how he'd wept in front of Pirra, he burned with shame. She must have known that Hylas was still alive. Had they enjoyed fooling him? Had they put their heads together and laughed?

Somehow, he couldn't quite believe that Hylas was capable of such betrayal. But what about Pirra, with her clever black eyes that missed nothing, that seemed to spy out all his weaknesses and fears?

Again the horse shied, nearly throwing him off. Angrily, he yanked its head around and dug in his heels, forcing it to skitter in tight circles until it halted, trembling and subdued.

"There," he muttered. "Now you know who's master."

The guards at the gates sprang aside as he clattered into the courtyard. Tossing the reins at a slave, he strode toward the doorway.

Behind him, the horse was blowing hard and its flanks were heaving; Telamon heard the slave cluck his tongue in disapproval. He spun around. "What was that?" he snapped.

The slave turned pale. "Nothing, my lord."

Telamon nodded. "Keep it that way."

As he entered the lamplit passage, more slaves scattered. He tried to take pleasure in the storerooms on either side, crammed with wine and barley and wool; in the armory piled with bronze weapons and armor. Again he told himself that this was where he belonged.

His father didn't think so. When he'd received the message

summoning Telamon to Mycenae, Thestor had refused to let him go.

"Why?" Telamon had demanded. "He's my grandfather, and I've never even seen him!"

"You don't know them as I do," Thestor had growled.

"Then let me make up my own mind."

In the end, Thestor had given in, as he usually did these days, but Telamon had felt obscurely guilty. He hadn't told his father the real reason he needed to leave Lykonia: That every rock and tree reminded him painfully of Hylas.

That first night at Mycenae . . .

He had sat on a bench among the warriors, stunned by the grandeur of the vast painted hall. Slaves had brought roast oxen and venison, and poured rich black wine mixed with crumbled cheese and honey. On the walls and pillars, Ancestors hunted boars and leaped from ships to slaughter their enemies. Everywhere, he'd seen the glint of gold. Compared to Mycenae, Lapithos was a peasant's hut.

He'd been relieved to learn that Pharax and Alekto had gone to join their brother on Thalakrea—but that still left his fearsome grandfather, Koronos.

The High Chieftain sat like a spider on his great marble throne, drinking little and eating less. He was old, but when he spoke, hardened warriors blanched. Telamon had been horrified when Koronos had ordered him to tell how he'd retrieved the dagger.

The hall had fallen silent. Haltingly, he'd begun, and Koronos had stared fixedly over his head. His gaze hadn't wavered when Telamon related the death of his firstborn son, Kratos; and when the tale was finished, he'd raised his gold cup to his lips with a steady hand and said stonily, "I can beget more sons."

When the ordeal was over, Telamon had been glad that the talk had turned to the mines: something about a rite at the dark of the Moon, although by then he'd stopped listening.

So he'd been startled when, as Koronos rose to leave, he'd addressed him again. "We're needed on Thalakrea, grandson. Will you come?"

What made it so frightening was that Thestor had foreseen this, and expressly forbidden him to go. Koronos must know that. He knew everything. He was making Telamon choose.

The silence in the hall had gone on forever. Telamon had tried to speak, but his throat was too dry.

"Think on it," the High Chieftain had commanded. "Decide soon."

For two days, Telamon had agonized; but now, as he strode toward the hall, he suddenly knew what his answer would be. It was as if the gods were whispering in his head. *Hylas is nothing to you now. You are of the House of Koronos.*

Telamon saw himself crossing the Sea in his grandfather's splendid black ship. He saw the stronghold of his uncle Kreon rising above the waves. Yes. He would go to Thalakrea.

On Thalakrea, he could put Hylas behind him once and for all.

For two days Pirra had been imprisoned with Hekabi
in this windowless cell, listening to the crows cawing
about the walls and wondering if Hylas was dead or alive.

Soon after they'd reached Kreon's stronghold, word
had arrived of the cave-in. Shouts, uproar, a man bellow-
ing like a raging bull. Later, Pirra had glimpsed a slave
dragged into the next-door cell. It was the hook-nosed
boy she'd seen at the pools. She'd caught snatches as they
questioned him. "Pit spiders killed or buried alive . . .
Beetle, Flea." She'd fought to conceal her horror.

"Are you going to eat that?" said Hekabi.

Pirra stared at the bowl of mashed acorns and shook
her head.

She kept telling herself that if that boy could survive the
cave-in, then so could Hylas.

"You should eat," mumbled Hekabi with her mouth
full.

"How much longer?" said Pirra. Their cell stank of
urine, and she could feel things crawling in her hair.

Hekabi shrugged. "He makes us wait to show his power."

He hardly needs to do that, thought Pirra.

Everything about this stronghold shouted power. It was ringed by double stone walls each an arm-span thick, and could only be reached by a dizzying flight of steps hacked out of the raw red rock. It turned out that Kreon's chariot was merely for show; the trail ended at the foot of the hill.

Pirra remembered trudging up the steps in the noonday heat and the stink of burned flesh. She'd climbed past the charred remains of snakes: Were they offerings to the Angry Ones? And she'd shrunk from something that had once been a man. His empty eye sockets glared at the Sun, and his rib cage was black with crows, jostling and heaving like a dreadful mockery of breath . . .

A warrior strode into the cell. With a start, Pirra recognized Ilarkos, the second in command of the Crow Chieftain who'd beaten her up last summer.

To her relief, he didn't recognize her. "On your feet," he said. "It's time."

⸺

"He hates light and has a horror of snakes," said Ilarkos as he led them through a maze of passages. "Which makes what you're planning—"

"Did you get it?" said Hekabi.

He signed to a slave, who handed her a lidded basket. "This is a mistake," he muttered. "You'll end up like the last seer."

"What happened to him?" said Hekabi.

"You passed him on the steps."

Pirra's belly turned over. But how *could* Hekabi cure Kreon, when she was a fake?

"I hear he has visitors from Mycenae," said Hekabi.

"How do you know that?" Ilarkos said sharply.

"People talk."

Pirra realized that Hekabi was speaking Akean. "I thought you didn't speak Akean," she whispered.

Hekabi's mouth twisted. "You must have misheard."

"So why make me come?"

The wisewoman didn't reply. She seemed undaunted by the prospect of meeting Kreon. In fact, she seemed excited: as if she *wanted* this.

They reached a doorway covered by a scarlet hanging and flanked by two hulking guards. Hekabi handed the basket to Pirra. It hissed. Pirra was so startled she nearly dropped it.

"They're only grass snakes," murmured Hekabi, "they won't hurt you."

"*What?* But he said—"

"Do as I say, and you'll be all right."

Voices reached them through the hanging. "I don't need your help," growled a man.

"I don't care," said another. "You've angered the Mountain, brother. There's only one power strong enough to put that right."

"Thalakrea is mine! *I* will decide!"

"Our father will decide," a woman said coldly.

"Get out," said the first man. "Both of you!"

"For now," said the woman.

The hanging twitched, and two people swept into the passage. Ilarkos yanked Pirra and Hekabi out of the way. "Stand aside for the lord Pharax and the lady Alekto."

Pirra saw at once that Pharax was a man who lived to fight. His tunic was plain oxblood wool, with a sword-belt across his chest. His powerful limbs were ridged with scars, and his left shoulder was calloused from carrying a shield. His dark gaze slid over her as if she were a piece of meat.

Alekto was young. She wore a tight-waisted silk robe zigzagged in black and yellow, and her face was perfect and without blemish; she reminded Pirra of a beautiful wasp. Her dark eyes flicked to Pirra's scar and she shuddered with disgust.

When they'd gone, Ilarkos wiped the sweat from his brow. Then he squared his shoulders and drew aside the hanging. "I've brought the wisewoman, lord. Do you still—"

"Bring her in."

Ilarkos pushed Hekabi inside, then Pirra, with the basket of snakes in her arms.

The chamber was shadowy and choked with smoke. Pirra made out a reed screen covering the window, and a bronze brazier giving off a red glimmer and a reek of charcoal. On the walls hung bronze axes and spears. Armor glinted in a corner: greaves, breastplate, wrist-guards, an oxhide shield as tall as a man; a boar's-tusk helmet crested with black horsetail.

Kreon was pacing angrily up and down. He was as big as a bull, with the pelt of a lion slung across his shoulders. Through his long dark warrior's braids, Pirra caught the restless glitter of his eyes.

"Well?" he snapped.

"I've come to rid you of the pain," Hekabi said fearlessly.

"They all say that," he retorted.

"The difference is, I can."

Kreon ground his knuckles into his temples. "Snakes," he snarled. "Crawling in my head, scraping my skull with their fangs . . ."

"I can banish them," said Hekabi.

"Then do it," he said thickly.

Crossing to the window, Hekabi tore aside the screen. Moonlight flooded in, and Kreon flinched. "I should have you killed for that!"

"But then you'd never be cured." In a tone that brooked no opposition, she told Ilarkos to have the brazier removed and another brought that didn't smoke.

Ilarkos looked to Kreon, who gave an irritable nod.

With the night wind gusting through the window and a clean pinewood fire brought in, the haze cleared and everyone breathed easier.

Kreon flung himself onto a bench strewn with black sheepskins, and peered suspiciously at the basket in Pirra's arms. "What's that?"

"Snakes," said Hekabi.

"*Snakes?*" He leaped to his feet. "What *is* this? Get them out!"

Ilarkos made to obey, but Hekabi stopped him with a glance. "You dreamed that a snake bit you," she told Kreon.

He blinked. "How did you know?"

She didn't, thought Pirra. Most people dream of snakes from time to time.

"That's why you have pain," said Hekabi. "They're nesting in your skull. My slave will perform a snake rite to drive them out."

Pirra stared at her in horror.

"Do it," Hekabi told her in Keftian.

Shakily, Pirra set the basket on the rushes. Its contents rustled and hissed. She took off the lid. Hekabi was right, they were grass snakes, but they didn't enjoy being confined.

"This had better work," threatened Kreon, "or you'll both be feeding the crows."

"Do it," Hekabi told Pirra again.

Her blood roared in her ears. Swiftly, she grasped two snakes behind their heads, as she'd seen her mother do, and held them up. She felt their soft coils wrapping around her arms. Their tiny tongues flickered like black lightning. Kreon watched every move, his terror and loathing coming at her like heat from a fire.

"Approach the Chieftain," commanded Hekabi.

With her arms raised, Pirra took a step toward the Chieftain, who sat hunched on the bench, gripping his knees.

Close up, Pirra saw that his beard and his long greasy hair were entwined with bronze wire. She saw ash crusting his cheeks. She caught the rank smell of his fear. But his red-rimmed eyes stared as if she didn't exist. He saw only the snakes.

Hekabi circled the chamber, strewing herbs. "To banish the dream snakes," she said calmly, "we need to know why they came." She caught Pirra's eye. *Stay there.* "The spirits tell me that you've dug too deep. You've offended the Lady of Fire."

Kreon snorted. "We worship powers not even She can withstand." But a thick vein was throbbing in his temple.

"The spirits send me a vision of a dagger," said Hekabi.

He licked his lips. "My father's bringing it to hallow the rites at the dark of the Moon. The Angry Ones will bend the Lady to our will. Then at last Thalakrea will truly belong to me."

Hekabi nodded, and Pirra saw how clever she was, using the snakes to distract him, and pretending she knew more than she did, to make him talk.

"I see other hands reaching for the dagger," Hekabi said softly.

His face darkened. "My brother and sister. Plotting to take Thalakrea for themselves."

Suddenly, Pirra noticed that a snake had escaped the

basket and was slithering toward him. With her foot she tried to shoo it away.

Too late. With a cry of loathing, Kreon seized the snake, crushed it in his fist, and tossed it on the fire.

In horror, Pirra watched it twitch and go still. The snakes in her hands sensed their brother's death and became agitated. Gently, she rubbed their jaws with her thumbs, and made a silent promise to release them into the Wild.

"What else do the spirits tell you?" panted Kreon.

"They tell me that Kreon is master of Thalakrea," said Hekabi soothingly. "Kreon will seal the treaty with Keftiu—"

"Keftiu!" he spat. "We don't need *treaties*. We'll take Keftiu for our own, then all its riches will be ours."

Pirra nearly dropped the snakes.

Hekabi shot her a warning glance.

"They look down on us as savages," Kreon went on, "but who has the warriors? Who has the *power*? Soon we will—" He broke off and put his hands to his temples. "The pain. It's gone."

Ilarkos gaped.

Kreon stared at Hekabi in wonder.

"I told you it would be," she said. From her pouch, she took a goathorn vial and a shriveled root. "Rub this oil on your temples twice a day and chew a piece of this root the size of a pomegranate seed before sleep. If the snakes return, send for me again."

"You did it," murmured Ilarkos when they were out in the passage.

Pirra hardly heard him. The Crows planned to invade Keftiu. This was why they were so hungry for bronze: to make war on her people.

In front of her, Hekabi staggered and sank to her knees.

"Hekabi?" said Pirra.

The wisewoman was writhing on the floor, her face clammy and pale.

"What is it?" said Ilarkos.

"What's happening?" cried Kreon from the doorway.

Hekabi was arching her back and thrashing from side to side. Her lips were flecked with foam, her eyes rolled up into their sockets. "*I see him . . .*" she whispered in a deep voice not her own. "He crawls out of the earth . . . the red river swallows Thalakrea . . . *The Outsider lives . . .*"

"*What?*" roared Kreon. "*What* does she say?"

"She's raving, my lord," said Ilarkos. "Guards! Take them to their cell!"

"*The Outsider lives,*" rasped Hekabi.

"The Outsider is *dead*!" bellowed Kreon. "With my brother's dying breath he called to the Angry Ones and They *heard* him, the Outsider is *dead*! *Dead*!"

Dead! Dead! The echoes followed them down the passage.

Back in their cell, Pirra set the snake basket on the floor and slumped down with her hands to her mouth. The dagger of Koronos was coming to Thalakrea. The Crows were going to invade Keftiu. Hylas was alive.

With a moan, Hekabi sat up. Her face was waxen, but

she seemed herself again. "What happened?" she mumbled. "How long did it last?"

"You're not a fake," said Pirra.

The wisewoman leaned against the wall and shut her eyes. "Of course I'm not. It came on when I was your age. I fell and hit my head. That's how I got this." She touched her magpie streak.

"Why pretend to be a fake?"

"Work it out."

Pirra thought for a moment. "You needed me to believe I was *forcing* you to help me, so that I wouldn't suspect that you wanted me here all along."

"Very good," said Hekabi drily.

"You knew the Crows were planning to invade Keftiu—"

"I only suspected. Now I know."

"—and you wanted me to hear it, so that I'd tell my mother."

"And then she'll do what Keftiu should have done ten years ago. She'll rid the Islands of the Crows."

Footsteps in the passage, and Ilarkos came in, shaking his head in disbelief. "I thought he would have you killed—but he's *impressed*. He wants you to stay."

"I'll attend him whenever he likes," Hekabi said firmly, "but I won't stay here. I must be free to come and go."

Ilarkos inclined his head with new respect. "As you wish."

When he'd gone, Hekabi wiped the sweat from her face. "What did I say when I was in the trance? Tell me exactly."

Pirra hesitated. "You said the Outsider lives."

Hekabi frowned. "The Outsider . . . But who *is* that? And why does he frighten Kreon?"

Again Pirra hesitated. She moved closer to Hekabi. "There was an Oracle," she whispered. "It said, *If an Outsider wields the blade, the House of Koronos burns.* I'm pretty sure they've kept it secret. All their warriors know is that Outsiders must be killed."

Hekabi's eyes gleamed. "That boy you spoke to at the pools. It's him, isn't it? The Outsider. Don't deny it, I can see it in your eyes."

Pirra licked her lips. "You said he's alive. You said you saw him crawl out of the earth. That must mean he survived the cave-in."

"Go to him. I'll tell them I need you to gather herbs. Find him. Warn him that they know. *Find him,*" she repeated. "If he's an enemy of Kreon, then he's my friend! Now go!"

The lion cub shoved her head under the boy's forepaw and gave an impatient mew. He went on sleeping, so she climbed on his belly and flexed her claws—and he woke with a yelp.

Yawning and growling, he crawled to the hot wet. Earlier, he'd fished out the hare's paws and tail and flung them into the bushes for her to find. Now she watched curiously as he drank, not lapping like a lion, but scooping the wet in his long thin forepaws.

After this, he grabbed a stick and dug under a plant. She pushed in to sniff, but he wouldn't let her. Then he pulled out a root and ate it. The cub was impressed.

She'd been wondering why he didn't lick her clean, but now she realized that his tongue was too smooth: useless for giving one's fur a nice rasping lick. His teeth weren't much good either, and his claws were hopeless, he couldn't even pull them in and out. He had no tail, so he couldn't lash it when he was angry, and without a tail-tuft, he couldn't signal in long grass. Oddest of all, he had neither whiskers nor fur, except for a shaggy little mane that didn't go all around his face. This worried the cub. How did he keep warm?

He was sitting on the ground, talking to her. She liked his voice, it was calm and strong, so she stood on her hind legs, put her forepaws on his shoulders, and licked his nose. He yelped, but she sensed this was his way of laughing, so she licked harder. Now they were rolling about, play-fighting. The lion cub felt better than she had since her mother was killed.

After this, the boy splashed her to wash her clean, which she didn't mind, then took hold of her bad paw—which she did. He yanked the prickle out of her pad. She shot under a bush and hissed. That *hurt*.

Shaken, she watched him chewing leaves and mixing them with mud. Now what was he up to?

Talking softly, he crawled toward her and again reached for her bad paw. She snarled, but to her astonishment, he grabbed it and smeared the pad with the leafy-smelling mud. She was so startled that she forgot about biting and licked it off. The boy smeared on some more. She licked that off too. They played this game for a while until he got cross and chewed some different leaves, which tasted so awful that she left them alone.

After that she had a nap, and when she woke up, her paw was better.

Later, the boy rose to his full, tree-like height and spoke to her. The cub was instantly alert. He was going hunting, and he wanted her to go with him.

Feeling important, she trotted behind this tall furless creature who'd taken the place of her pride. He wasn't a lion, but his mane was the color of a lion's mane, and his strange narrow eyes were lion-colored too.

The cub felt in her fur that although he was not lion, there was lion in his spirit.

⁓

The day before, Hylas had trapped two partridges, and this morning a lucky shot killed a small deer.

Havoc pushed in to investigate. "No," he told her firmly.

The lion cub gazed up at him imploringly.

He snorted. "After what you did to that hare?"

With the deer over one shoulder, he started back for camp, Havoc trotting behind him.

After lots of food and sleep—much of it sprawled on top of him—she'd recovered with astonishing speed. Her belly was plump, her fur fluffy and soft. Best of all, she was learning to trust him. She would bound toward him with eager little grunts—*ng ng ng*—then flop onto her back and waggle her big spotty paws, asking to be scratched.

It was wonderful to have someone to talk to and look after. In some ways, she reminded him of his dog, Scram. She was insatiably curious, always scrambling into his lap to be part of what he was doing; always wanting attention. But she had a lion's unnerving ability to vanish in long grass, and unlike a dog, she didn't wag her tail when she was pleased, she lashed it when she was annoyed. What annoyed her most was being ignored. She *hated* that.

She was still limping a bit, so at camp he made another poultice of bitter wormwood and smeared it on her pad and on the cut on her nose. Then he tossed her the deer's guts to keep her quiet.

While she was happily getting filthy again, he butchered the carcass with his new obsidian knife. He would dry some meat and bury the rest in hot mud by the spring; no need to risk a fire with so much heat in the ground. Then he'd wash the hide, rub it with mashed brain, and sling it over a branch; it might be big enough to make a waterskin and a kilt.

All this would take time, and he needed to go after Pirra. But he wouldn't be much use to her if he died of thirst on the way.

Around dusk, he cracked open the mud and ate the juicy, tender meat. Havoc was awake, gazing up at the deerskin on its branch. Hylas could see her plotting to climb the tree, so to distract her, he wove a rough wicker ball out of fireweed. "Look, Havoc! Fetch!"

She didn't know about fetching, but she adored the ball. They had an amazing game of toss and catch around camp and in and out of the spring; then Havoc was suddenly tired, and flopped down and fell asleep.

Hylas sat chewing a deer rib, while she lay against him, her tail twitching in her dreams. Strange. A few days ago, he hadn't known she existed. Now it felt as if they'd always been together.

Havoc trotted ahead, then turned and looked back at Hylas. *Keep up.* She seemed surprisingly at ease on the Mountain, and had found this goat trail winding up its shoulder.

Hylas trudged after her. The noonday Sun beat down on him, and he was laden with the waterskin, a bundle of meat, and Havoc's beloved wicker ball, which she'd refused to leave behind.

A glance over his shoulder revealed that they'd climbed higher than he'd thought. The forest and the thickets, the obsidian ridge and the wild pear tree, lay far below.

He'd decided not to risk retracing his tracks to the Neck, so he was climbing this spur, to spy out the land from there. He might spot some way of avoiding the mines—although as yet he had no idea how he was going to rescue Pirra.

He hated to think of her shut up in Kreon's stronghold. If Kreon found out who she was, he would use her for his own ends. Hylas' mind skittered away from what those might be.

He'd climbed too far. He was on a slope of coarse black sand dotted with clumps of brittle red grass. No cover except for a rocky outcrop, and above that, charcoal cliffs rising to the summit. Smoke wafted down. He caught its rotten-egg stink.

As he neared the outcrop, the stink grew suddenly worse and the earth turned hot underfoot. He stopped.

Two paces ahead, smoke spurted angrily from a crack in the ground. It was about the size of his fist, and around it the black sand was spattered with astonishing crystals of deep, throbbing yellow. Like the droppings of some fiery creature, they formed a spiky crust around the crack—from which jetted that stinking smoke and a fierce, continuous, bubbling *hisss*.

Something Zan had said came back to him. *Fire spirits live in cracks in the ground, all spiky and hot.*

Hylas felt a blast of heat: as if some unseen spirit had swept past him out of its lair. He backed away. But to his astonishment, Havoc padded toward the crack, quite unafraid.

"Havoc, come down," he called sharply. He didn't dare raise his voice, or go and fetch her. There is a veil that separates the world of men from that of immortals, and he knew he was far too close.

"*Havoc!*" he said again.

Suddenly the wind shifted and he was engulfed in choking hot smoke. The stink was a kick in the throat. He couldn't see, couldn't breathe.

"Havoc!" he gasped, blundering down the slope.

She came bounding toward him, then turned her head, as if to follow something he couldn't see.

"What is it?" he panted.

In her tawny eyes, he glimpsed little flickers of flame— although on the Mountainside, he could see no fire. Then she sneezed and rubbed her forehead against his calf.

"We've come too high," he muttered. "We've got to go back."

That fire spirit had been warning him. This was a place for immortals, not for men.

The lion cub watched the fire spirit pass within a tail-flick of the boy—but to her surprise, he didn't see it.

Around him on the Mountainside, more fire spirits were flickering in and out of their lairs. Some were big and crackly, others silent and small. The boy didn't seem to see *any* of them.

The lion cub wondered what to do. She'd brought him here because she'd sensed that he wanted to climb the Mountain, but now she worried that he would get bitten.

Sure enough, he was just about to tread in the lair of a small fire spirit.

The lion cub raced down and threw herself against his leg. *Not that way!*

The fire spirit spat, and the boy yelped and hopped away.

After this, the lion cub stayed close and did her best to steer him out of danger.

A large fire spirit drifted in front of her, and she smoothed back her ears respectfully. The fire spirit crackled past her and shimmered into its den.

Completely unaware, the boy stumbled to some rocks and stopped to pour some wet on his burned hind leg. Feeling quite grown-up, the lion cub followed.

She realized now that although he was supposed to look after her, in some ways, *she* had to look after *him*.

Hylas finished washing his burned ankle, and smeared on a gobbet of deer fat. Havoc glanced back at the fire spirits' lairs, then padded down to lie beside him, stretched on her belly with her forelegs straight in front and her golden head held high.

"Can you actually *see* fire spirits?" he asked her quietly.

She turned her head and looked at him. Her eyes were clear tawny, marked with darker amber, like the rings in a tree. He could no longer see the tiny leaping flames.

"Can you?" he said again.

She gave a huge yawn that ended in a whine, then rubbed her forehead against his thigh.

For the first time since he'd found her, he wondered what power had brought them together. When she'd wrecked his camp, she'd eaten the offerings he'd set out. If a wild creature does that, it means they've been sent by an immortal.

But *Havoc*? This mischievous little cub, a messenger from the gods?

And yet. Hylas remembered the lion he'd encountered on the day he was taken for a slave. If it hadn't been for that lion, he wouldn't have been caught and brought to Thalakrea.

Had it *wanted* him to be caught? Had it *meant* him to find Havoc?

All he knew was that in some way, they were meant to be together.

Suddenly, Havoc sprang to her feet and raced to the edge of the rocks. She was staring east and her ears were pricked. Listening.

"What is it?" whispered Hylas.

Then he heard it too, and his belly tightened.

The baying of dogs.

20

Pirra ducked behind the wild pear tree and listened.

Wind. Crickets. No dogs. But she *had* heard them.

Creeping to the edge of the ridge, she peered down at the sweltering black plain she'd just struggled across. No men and no dogs, although in places the thorn scrub was too dense to see.

It was probably just a hunting party after wild goats, but the sweat broke out on her palms. Kreon starved his dogs to keep them savage, and they attacked anything in their path. Had they caught her scent? Or had their masters found Hylas' signs? After all, if she could find them, so could they.

Ilarkos had believed Hekabi when she'd said that Pirra must go and gather herbs. He'd even given her a waterskin and a bag of olives, with his mark on a scrap of clay, to get her past the guards at the Neck. She'd kept her promise to the grass snakes and released them, and soon afterward, in a little wayside shrine, she'd found Hylas' first sign. Among the shriveled garlands and lumpy clay bulls, he'd scratched it on a pebble: a blob with a pointy nose and spikes. *Hedgehog.*

Its nose had been pointing west, so she'd headed that way. Sure enough, she'd found another hedgehog daubed in mud near a spring spouting weirdly hot water, then another scratched on a red boulder at the foot of the Mountain. Three more in the broom thicket had led her here, to this eerie black obsidian ridge.

The Sun beat down on her, and a hot wind whipped grit in her eyes as she squinted at the plain. If there were hunters down there, they didn't seem to be coming her way.

Back on the ridge, she searched for another sign from Hylas. Nothing. Now what?

She drank a mouthful of warm goaty-tasting water and ate a couple of olives. She'd been walking since dawn, and it was past noon now. She was tired, sunburned, and footsore. With a flicker of alarm, she realized that she might be on her own out here for days; and in the stronghold, they'd taken her knife.

Quickly, she grabbed a lump of obsidian, found a stick under the pear tree, and tied the stone to the stick with a strip from her tunic, to make a club. When she swung it, it made a satisfying *whoosh*. To thank the tree for the stick, she poured a few drops of water on its roots, and it rustled its leaves approvingly.

Close by, a bird lit onto a boulder and uttered a piercing cry. Pirra went still. The bird was a falcon. She watched it preen its wings, then lift into the sky. It circled, looking down at her, then flew off with another shivering cry.

Some part of her flew with it. She thought of the falcon she'd once seen hurtling out of the Sun, and touched the pouch at her breast that held the feather and the lion claw.

Once, Hylas had said, *You're brave and you don't give up*. Come on, Pirra. He's got to be somewhere.

Reasoning that he wouldn't have climbed any farther up the Mountain, she decided he must have gone either *west* toward that forested spur, or *south* to the coast. He was good at catching fish, so she guessed he'd headed south.

She found a trail leading downhill through the thicket. A startled bleat told her it was a goat trail. Fine. Goats would know a way down.

Apparently not. The trail turned dangerously steep and ended at the edge of a cliff. The Sea churned sickeningly far below.

From here, Pirra saw that the forested spur in the distance ran down to a white beach. She'd been wrong. Hylas must have gone *west*. That falcon had been trying to tell her: It too had flown west.

As she scrambled uphill, she realized that she was on a different trail, because this one veered down again and ended in the strangest cave she'd ever seen. Its walls were chalky white, banded with violent orange, and deep within bubbled a pool of warm, thin, stinking green mud.

The sulfurous smell caught at her throat. Uneasily aware of the Goddess in the Mountain, she stayed just long enough to make sure there were no hedgehogs scratched on the rocks.

This time, there was no mistaking the baying of dogs.

Gripping her club, Pirra raced uphill. Through a gap in the broom, she spotted the pear tree, and made for that.

Having regained the obsidian ridge, she crept toward the boulders at the edge.

There. Far below, and horribly close to the red rock where she'd found Hylas' sign, were three Crow warriors and several vicious dogs. The men wore black leather tunics and ankle-high boots; each had a quiver on his back and a dagger at his hip, with a bow as tall as himself slung over his shoulder. The dogs were milling about with their noses to the ground.

Pirra had scratched Hylas' sign off that boulder; but what if they came after her? Somehow, she doubted that Ilarkos' mark would guarantee her safety—especially if the dogs got her first.

Suddenly they burst into a frenzy of barks, then hurtled north, with the men running after them: *away* from her. Pirra glimpsed their quarry bounding through the scrub. A deer. She willed them to keep going.

But now to her horror, two dogs were racing back.

She forgot to breathe.

Once again they were circling the red boulder, sniffing eagerly. One lifted its head and uttered a blood-chilling howl. Then both started up the slope.

They had caught her scent.

21

Hylas saw the Crows far below him on the plain. He saw two dogs racing up the slope. He saw a figure on the ridge. No no no. It was Pirra.

Scooping Havoc into his arms, he scrambled downhill. Havoc sensed it wasn't a game and didn't struggle, but she was frightened, and dug in her claws.

By the time he reached the ridge, Pirra was gone; she must have taken cover in the thicket. He shoved Havoc in the highest fork of the pear tree, where she clung on shakily.

"*Stay*," he panted. "*Don't* climb down, they'll tear you to pieces!" Briefly, he wondered if he should tie her in place; but she might fall out and throttle herself, and there wasn't time.

Casting off all his gear but his weapons, he searched the approach to the thicket for Pirra's tracks. Found them— but she'd headed *south*. What was she *thinking*? That would take her to the edge of the cliffs.

The broom was too tall to see over, and he dared not shout in case he drew the Crows. He heard another frenzy of barks, much closer than before. He tried not to picture what they'd do to Pirra if they caught her.

Spiky branches blocked his way, but it would be no barrier to the dogs. No matter how fast he ran, they were going to reach her first.

Pirra's heart thudded in her throat as she crashed through the thicket. She could hear the dogs baying, but she couldn't tell where they were.

Suddenly the baying stopped. The silence was horrible.

They were following her scent.

Her scent.

That gave her an idea. She scrambled downhill, praying she would find the cave.

Spiny branches snagged her waterskin and the bag of olives, so she threw them off, keeping only her club. She dared not glance back, or stop to listen. The dogs could be anywhere.

At last through the branches, she glimpsed white rock. Skittering down, she crawled into the cave. Deep inside, the mudpool waited like something alive. Maybe it *was* alive, maybe some monster lurked beneath that murky green. But it was her only chance.

The mud was warm and sucked hungrily at her legs. She went under, slime filling eyes and ears and nose. Her foot struck rock and she boosted herself out, spitting mud and clawing it from her face. The stink was so bad she could hardly breathe: If this didn't throw them off the scent, nothing would.

Snatching her club and spattering mud, she fled, trying

not to retrace her steps. But if there'd been too many goat trails before, now there were none. She had to force her way through, and the broom fought back.

Suddenly she heard panting behind her and the clatter of claws. Panic seized her. The trick hadn't worked.

Her muddy sandals kept slipping, but there was no time to tear them off. Her breath sawed in her chest. She was spent, she couldn't go on.

She came upon a shallow gully choked with junipers, and climbed into it. Better to hide down here and fight with the earth at her back, than be caught on the run.

More clattering claws.

She braced herself. She heard panting breath, then a huge shaggy hound leaped the gully—and raced on.

Pirra dared not breathe. Had it worked?

And where was the other dog?

<hr/>

One moment, Hylas was crashing through the thicket. The next, the dog was slamming into his chest.

His axe went flying, but somehow he kept his footing and pushed the beast off. It was at him again in a heartbeat, sinking its teeth into his calf. With a cry he reached for his knife. It wasn't in his belt. He grabbed a rock and lashed out, catching the dog a glancing blow on the shoulder, which it ignored. He made to strike again, and it leaped at his throat. He seized its neck as its weight sent him crashing to the ground.

Gripping its scruff with both hands, he fought to keep

its jaws from his face. It snapped air a finger's breadth from his nose, spattering him with spit. Its meaty breath heated his cheek and its growls shuddered through him. He met its small yellow eyes and saw nothing but blood-hunger. His arms began to shake. He couldn't hold it off much longer.

He did the unthinkable: He shoved his fist into its jaws.

The dog was too startled to bite. With his free hand, Hylas found a rock and slammed it into its skull. The dog slumped on top of him and lay still.

Gasping for breath, Hylas yanked out his arm. It was covered in spit, but only scraped. The bite in his calf was worse, although it hadn't yet started to hurt. He was shaking all over.

Retrieving his axe, he lurched to his feet. The thicket was silent. Where was the other dog? Where was Pirra? As he stumbled through the broom, he imagined her standing at bay, with the great beast advancing upon her.

He was about to risk shouting to her when he lost his footing and fell.

A growl, horribly close. He scrabbled for his axe, couldn't find it. A red blur came hurtling toward him.

At the same moment, a snatcher sprang from nowhere, swinging a club, and the dog lay dead.

Hylas sat up and stared.

The snatcher was dripping green slime. "Are you all right?" panted Pirra.

22

"I thought you were a snatcher," gasped Hylas.

"What *is* a snatcher?" said Pirra.

"You're all covered in mud!"

"Where's the other dog?"

"I killed it." Dusting himself off, he got to his feet. Despite a few scratches and a bleeding calf, he looked unbelievably better than when she'd last seen him. He wasn't so thin, and instead of rags, he wore a rough hide kilt and a neatly plaited belt. Most striking of all, he was *clean*. His hair was no longer matted with filth, but shiny and the color of ripe barley. Suddenly, Pirra wished she wasn't caked in muck.

"Thanks for what you did," he said, stooping for his axe.

She pressed her lips together and tried to smile.

"I can't believe you found me," he said. "How'd you get out of the stronghold?"

"That was Hekabi. I—I found your signs."

"Why *are* you covered in mud?"

"Um—to throw them off the scent."

"That was clever."

She didn't reply. The dead dog lay between them. One of its claws was broken, which made it seem oddly vulnerable. Pirra loved dogs. She'd always wanted one. And now she'd done this.

I killed it, she thought. Her knees buckled and she sat down. Hylas said something, but she didn't hear. She was trying not to throw up.

"I said, do you have any gear?"

"Um . . . A waterskin and a bag of olives. Back there."

"I'll find them. You—"

"I killed it," she blurted out. "I never killed anything."

His jaw dropped. "What, *never*?"

They stared at each other, and the gap between them yawned. Hylas had hunted all his life: He had to, or he'd have starved. In the House of the Goddess, Pirra had simply clapped her hands, and slaves had brought whatever she wanted.

Hylas touched her shoulder. "It was either the dog or me," he said gently. "Besides, it's better off now. Maybe next time it'll come back as a sheephound, and have a good life in the mountains."

She gave a shaky smile.

"I'll show you what to do for its spirit," he said. Kneeling, he sprinkled dust on the dog's muzzle and put his hand on its flank. "No more hunger," he told it, "no more beatings. Be at peace." Then to Pirra, "Stay here, I'm going up to the ridge."

"Why?"

"The Crows, Pirra, we've got to be sure they've really gone; and I've got to fetch . . . Are you all right?"

"Fine," she lied.

As soon as he was out of sight, she threw up. Then she buried the sick, so that he wouldn't see.

A while later, Hylas returned with their gear. "They've gone," he panted. "They caught a deer, I saw them carrying it back to the Neck. They must've decided the dogs would find their own way."

"What's *that*?" cried Pirra, scrambling backward.

A weird yellow cat was peering at her from behind his legs.

Hylas grinned. "Her name's Havoc. She's a lion cub. Watch your gear, or she'll eat it. What've you got there, Havoc?"

The lion cub was scrabbling at the spot where Pirra had buried her sick. Pirra shooed her away, and the cub darted behind Hylas.

"She's just a bit wary," said Hylas, scratching the cub's ears. "She'll get used to you."

"I thought she was a cat," said Pirra.

"What's a cat?"

She stared at him. "Don't you have cats in Lykonia?"

"I don't think so."

"Oh. Well they're like—very small lions."

He burst out laughing. "You're making that up!"

She grinned. "No I'm not!" Suddenly, she felt better.

"Come on," said Hylas, grabbing her hand and hauling

her to her feet. "Camp's not far, and there's a nice warm spring. You can get yourself cleaned up."

Everything had happened extremely fast. The lion cub had been terrified that the dogs would kill the boy, and deeply impressed when *he* had killed *them*. But then he'd found the stinky human female, and now they were back at the den, and he'd gone off to hunt, leaving them together.

The lion cub sensed that the boy liked the female a lot, although he didn't want to show it; but the cub wasn't sure. Warily, she hid in the long grass and watched the female peeling off her stinky overpelt and climbing into the hot wet. She was in there for ages, making happy, spluttery little whimpers and sliding right under.

When she climbed out, her hide wasn't lion-colored, like the boy's, but pale—*and she had a long black mane.* The cub was astonished. Did human females have manes?

Now the female was slipping on her overpelt, which she'd also washed clean. She trailed the cub's ball of sticks temptingly past her hiding place. The cub couldn't resist. She pounced and swatted the ball, and in its amazing way it fled faster than she could run, even though it had no legs. The female caught it cleverly in her forepaws and tossed it high, and the cub leaped for it again.

They played this till the cub was tired. Then she rolled onto her back, and the female scratched her behind her foreleg *exactly* where she liked best.

"I think Havoc's getting used to me," said Pirra with her mouth full of deer meat.

"Told you she would," mumbled Hylas.

Havoc sat between them, glancing hopefully from Pirra to her wicker ball, and back. Pirra threw the ball to Hylas, who caught it one-handed and tossed it back to her over the lion cub's head. After a couple of turns, they let Havoc catch it, and she lay grasping it jealously between her fore-paws. Pirra smiled and scratched the cub's flank with her toes.

Hylas could tell that she was feeling better. She looked better too. She'd scrubbed off the mud and finger-combed her crinkly black hair, and the scar on her cheek was a smooth, pale crescent. Hylas thought it suited her—there was something of the Moon about Pirra—but when she caught him staring, she flushed and turned her head so that it didn't show.

He still couldn't believe that she'd managed to find him. On the way to camp, he'd told her about the snatchers and the cave-in, and she'd told him about the wisewoman curing Kreon, and that Zan, Bat, and Spit had gotten out alive. He sensed there was more, but he didn't ask. Right now, he just wanted to enjoy being with her and Havoc, away from the Crows.

He didn't want to think about anything else.

———

Dusk came on. Hylas cut more ferns and put them under the overhang for Pirra, then some for himself, beneath a bush a little way off. Pirra sat near the spring, feeding shreds of deer meat to Havoc.

"Hylas," she said in an altered voice. "I need to tell you something."

He put down the ferns in his arms. He knew from her tone that it wasn't good. "Can't it wait till morning?" he said.

"I don't think so." She hesitated. "The Crows. They know you're alive."

Hylas didn't reply.

"Did you hear what I said?"

Havoc padded over to him and rubbed her greasy muzzle against his knee. "How do they know?" he said quietly.

"Hekabi fell into a trance. She said: 'The Outsider lives.' Kreon heard."

Dread was a stone in his belly. "But they don't know I'm here, on Thalakrea."

"No."

"And they don't know what I look like."

"Some of them might—and certainly Telamon does."

Telamon. The name rose between them like a ghost.

"Telamon," said Hylas, "is far away in Lykonia."

"Yes, but—"

He jumped to his feet, startling Havoc. "That clump of fireweed over there. Can you pick some? I need to see to this dog bite, and those scratches on your legs could do with a salve."

In silence, Pirra handed him the fireweed, and in silence he made twine for tying on dressings. He didn't *want* to talk about the Crows, especially not Telamon. Telamon hadn't told him he was a Crow—*and yet*, without his help, Hylas would never have escaped with his life. Telamon had been his friend. He might be the Chieftain's son, but he used to like nothing better than roaming the mountains with Hylas and Issi. Once, he'd confessed that, at his father's stronghold, he never felt good enough.

"Father was a great warrior in his time, and I've always got the Ancestors staring down at me from the walls."

"I thought Ancestors were dead," Hylas had said.

"That's the point, Hylas, it means you can never get away from them. You can never be as strong or as fearless as them."

Hylas glanced around to find Pirra watching him.

"I'm sorry," she said. "I didn't mean to spoil things."

He sighed. "It's not you. It's the Crows."

He prowled about, picking rue for a salve. Pirra went on watching him. So did Havoc. The cub's ears were back: She knew he was upset. When he sat down and started mashing the rue between two stones, for once, she didn't push in to see what he was doing.

Pirra sat with her tunic tented over her knees. "I heard something else in Kreon's stronghold." She paused. "They're bringing the dagger here. To Thalakrea."

Fiercely, Hylas ground the rue to a gray-green pulp. "I don't want to hear about the dagger."

"Hylas. While they have it, they can't be beaten. No one is safe. You know that."

"All I want," he said stubbornly, "is to get back to Akea and find Issi."

She blinked. "I can't believe that's true. Where would you go? How would you get away from them?"

"I know the Mountains, I'd find a way."

"Oh, Hylas. Do you truly believe that?"

He threw her an agonized glance. Then he fetched his little bundle of deer fat and mixed it with rue to make the salve. He smeared half on the bite on his calf, and bandaged it with a giant mullein leaf tied on with twine.

"They're going to invade Keftiu," said Pirra.

"What's it to you? You ran away from Keftiu."

"It's still my country, I can't—"

"Here," he cut in, "rub the rest of this on your scratches."

"Hylas—"

"No. I can't talk about this now."

"But—"

"I said no!" He was glaring at her, but he couldn't keep the pleading out of his voice.

Havoc stood tensely, glancing from one to the other.

"We need more food," he muttered, "and we need to find a way off this island. Until we've done that, there's no *point* talking about the Crows. Agreed?"

Pirra met his eyes. Then she nodded. "Agreed," she said. "For now."

Pirra slept like a stone, and woke to find that Hylas and Havoc had gone to check his snares. She had another marvelous wash, and dabbed some mud on her cheek. Maybe the magic spring would get rid of her scar.

She was hungry—they'd finished the deer meat last night—but Hylas came back with nothing: His snares had been empty.

"Oh well," she said, "we've still got the olives."

"Mm," he said. "But we should save them till we really need them."

"I just remembered. When I was on the cliffs, I saw a white beach below the forest. It can't be far."

His face cleared. "Then let's go and catch some fish!"

Last night, Pirra had been too tired to notice the forest, but now she drank it in. She loved the scent of hot pines and the big glossy beetles bumping about among the thistles; the intense blue sky between the deep green branches, and the sunlight striping Hylas and Havoc with gold.

"It's beautiful," she exclaimed.

"What is?" muttered Hylas, casting about for signs of prey.

"This!" She flung up her arms.

He gave her a puzzled grin and shook his head. He'd grown up in a forest. He didn't know what she meant.

As they went farther, Havoc kept sneaking up on Pirra and swatting her ankles.

"Stop it," said Pirra, warning her off with a stick.

"She's just practicing hunting," said Hylas. "That's how full-grown lions trip up their prey."

"Well I'm not prey," retorted Pirra. "Havoc, *no*!" In the end, she had to distract the cub by dragging the wicker ball on some twine.

Suddenly they heard the voice of the Sea, and emerged from the trees into the glare of the strangest ravine they'd ever seen.

Great frozen waves of dazzling white stone swirled around them, as if the Sea had once attacked the land, and been stilled by the touch of an immortal finger. Ghostly white crickets sprang up at their feet as they picked their way between juniper and spurge pallid with dust. In pockets of bleached sand, they saw tall, stately white flowers.

"I don't know those flowers," said Hylas.

"I do," said Pirra with a flicker of unease. "They're Sea lilies. They're sacred, they only bloom in summer on the hottest shores. My mother uses them in spells of finding."

Hylas wasn't listening. "The Sea!" he shouted, racing up a huge crest of smooth white rock.

Pirra forgot the lilies and scrambled after him.

But when they reached the top, they found a sheer drop to the waves far below.

"We'll never get down there," said Hylas. "So no fish."

Hungrier than ever, they started back through the ravine.

All at once, Pirra spotted something behind a clump of junipers that she'd missed before. "Pomegranates!" she cried, running to see if any were ripe.

"What are pom—what are they?" called Hylas.

"You eat the seeds, you'll like them!"

"Well hurry up, I want to go and set some more snares." Pirra ignored him.

She'd picked three pomegranates and was reaching for a fourth when she sensed she was being watched.

High overhead, in the bushes on the edge of the ravine, something stared down at her. It was dark against the Sun: all she could make out was a pair of horns and two floppy ears. She had time to think *goat*; then a stone whistled through the air and the goat dropped with a thud at her feet.

"Is it dead?" shouted Hylas, tucking his slingshot in his belt as he ran toward her.

"Um—yes," she said. "That was a good shot. I didn't think you'd even seen it."

He grinned. "Main thing is, it didn't see me."

After they'd sent the goat's spirit on its way, Hylas split its leg bones and they gobbled the delicious, rich marrow.

Feeling much stronger, they carried the carcass back to camp.

Hylas insisted on using every scrap; he said it was disrespectful to the goat if you didn't. He set a haunch to bake in the mud along with some snails Pirra had collected, and after a squabble, she got the filthy job of scraping the hide clean, while he cut the meat, liver, and heart into thin slices and hung them to dry—out of reach of inquisitive paws.

They spent a peaceful afternoon curing the hide and stomach for a pouch and a waterskin, and making sausages by stuffing the intestines with clotted blood and chopped caper buds. (Pirra added the capers, which Hylas viewed with suspicion; she was glad there were some things she knew and he didn't.)

To make up for her cleaning the goatskin, he made her a knife. It had a lethal obsidian blade in a goathorn handle, wound with split pine root for a steady grip. Pirra loved it because it wasn't like anything from the House of the Goddess.

When the meat was cooked, they ate in ravenous silence.

Havoc had eaten till her belly was as big as a melon, and now she lay on her side, sleeping it off. A wilting Sea lily was tied around her neck. Before leaving the ravine, Hylas had made an offering of the goat's ears, and Pirra had smeared the juice of two flowers on their foreheads and garlanded the cub with a third, to include her in the blessing.

At last, Pirra heaved a sigh and wiped the grease from

her chin. "That was the best meal I've ever eaten. And so *hot*! On Keftiu my food's always cold. My room's too far from the cookhouse."

Hylas snorted a laugh. "You poor thing."

She chucked a snail shell at him, then lay on her side, chewing a fennel stalk. "So how come you know all about tracking and things?"

With a thorn, Hylas pried a snail from its shell and ate it. "An old Outsider taught me. I never knew his name. People called him the Man of the Woods, although he told me once he was from Messenia."

"What was he like?"

"He had one eye and one tooth, both dark brown, and he stank like a dung heap. But he knew everything about the Wild. He could tell when a storm was coming just by the way a raven flies. And he taught me tracking with a beetle and a pile of dust."

"A beetle?"

He nodded. "He'd smooth out a patch of dust, and I had to shut my eyes, and he'd put a beetle on the dust and make it crawl. I had to work out where it'd gone by its tracks. It was easy with dust, but then he did it again with grit, and that was harder. After that he used grass, then leaves. They were hardest of all. Went on for days. The beetle got really sick of it."

Pirra blinked. "You used the *same* beetle?"

He burst out laughing. "Course not! Sometimes you're just too easy to fool!"

She grinned and chucked another shell at him. "But you did use beetles?"

"Yes, but not the same one!"

Flipping onto his belly, he propped himself on his elbows. "I used to wonder if he was my father," he said. "I asked once, and he said no. I think he knew something, but then he died of fever, so I never found out." He glanced at her. "Who was your father?"

"I don't know," said Pirra. "When my mother decided to bear a child, she mated with three different priests, so that none of them could say I was theirs."

Hylas looked startled. "Did you know them?"

She shook her head. "They died in an earthshake when I was little. At least, that's what I was told, but I've always wondered if she got rid of them, so they couldn't make trouble."

Hylas whistled. "Didn't you want to find out about them? I've always wanted to know about my father."

"Why should I? It's bad enough having a mother." An image of Yassassara rose before her, and she pushed it away.

Hylas was watching her. "Will she come after you?" he said quietly.

She reached for another fennel stalk. "Oh yes, she'll send people to find me. She'll never give up." For a moment, she pictured her mother in the Hall of Whispers, breathing the mysterious scent of Sea lilies. Perhaps already the lilies of Thalakrea had sent their perfume on the wind, and told their Keftian sisters that Pirra was here—and they'd told Yassassara . . .

"I'm never going back," she said out loud. "If she locked me up again, I'd die."

She knew this didn't really fit with what she'd said about warning Keftiu of the Crows' invasion; and she could see Hylas thinking so too. But he didn't point it out, and she was grateful for that.

With a thorn, he pried another snail from its shell and held it out to her. "I still think you're lucky to have a mother."

"*Lucky?*" Pirra nearly choked on the snail. "I hate her and she hates me!"

"Yes, but . . . All I remember about mine is when she left me and Issi. Sometimes I think there's more, but it always slips away."

Pirra felt sorry for him. She thought how odd it was that while she knew and hated her mother, Hylas didn't know his, and yet he loved her.

"Do you think she's still alive?" she said.

"Maybe. Maybe someday we'll all be together, her and me and Issi." He frowned and scratched a circle in the dust.

Havoc woke up and padded over to sniff the snail shells. Hylas pushed her gently away. Then he said to Pirra, "When you escaped Keftiu, what were you planning to do?"

She spread her hands. "I hadn't really thought that far. I was just trying to get away. Why?"

He scratched another circle in the dust. "You could come

with me. To Lykonia. We could live in the mountains."

She flushed. "Thanks."

He shrugged.

Havoc spat out a snail shell and coughed. Hylas gathered the rest and put them out of reach in the fork of a tree.

It was getting dark, but Pirra didn't want to go to sleep yet, so she asked Hylas how far he could spit an olive stone.

His lip curled. "Farther than you."

"Oh yes? I don't think so!"

They delved into the bag of olives, and chewed and spat. Pirra had often played this game on Keftiu, and she was winning, until Hylas made her laugh and she gulped and nearly choked—which made her laugh even harder, so that she lost.

"You *cheated*!" she gasped.

"So what?" spluttered Hylas. "I won!"

They lay on their backs, chewing crunchy red pomegranate seeds, which Pirra had finally persuaded him to try.

"Where'd you learn to spit like that?" said Hylas.

"Userref taught me, he's really good at it."

Havoc climbed onto Hylas' chest, and he tugged her ears.

"Userref would love her," said Pirra. "One of his most powerful goddesses has the head of a lioness."

Hylas scratched the lion cub's scruff. "Hear that, Havoc?"

Havoc yawned so hard she fell off.

Idly, Pirra asked Hylas why the pit spiders had called him

Flea, and he told her it was the first name that came into his head. "It's what that stranger called me last summer, remember? Akastos?"

She shuddered. "The one who tied you up and left you for the"—she lowered her voice—"for the Angry Ones."

They fell silent. Pirra thought of the Crows worshipping the Angry Ones in their secret, terrible rites. She was about to tell Hylas—then decided against it. Not now. Not in the dark.

Night deepened around them. In subdued tones, they talked of what they would do tomorrow. Hylas wanted to climb the obsidian ridge and head west around the Mountain, in the hopes of reaching the Sea. He described a place high above the ridge, with strange hissing cracks where fire spirits lived. He said he thought Havoc could *see* them, and he had no desire to go near them again. "But I think we can avoid them if we keep lower down. There's bound to be a trail to the coast, and maybe a village where we can steal a boat."

"Or we could find a way to Hekabi's village," said Pirra. "They'll help us. And I've buried some gold behind one of the huts."

He took that in silence.

Pirra was uncomfortably aware that she hadn't mentioned the Crows, or the dagger.

She caught Hylas' eye, and he glanced quickly away, and she knew that he was thinking of them too.

24

"That Mount Lykas where you grew up," said Pirra in a low voice. "Is it anything like this?"

"No," said Hylas.

They'd been heading west over a black slope spiked with red grass, but had halted before what lay ahead. From the summit to the roots, a great shoulder of the Mountain had been scorched to cinders: a whole tree-covered spur blasted by poisonous breath.

"Could a forest fire have done it?" said Pirra.

"I don't see how. Those pines have all fallen downhill. Whatever it was, it came from above."

Uneasily, they craned their necks at the smoking summit.

"Look how it bulges," said Pirra. "As if something's trying to thrust its way out."

Or someone, thought Hylas.

Down in the forest, it had been easy to forget the Mountain. Up here, these blasted pines felt like a warning. *Know that I am all-powerful,* the Lady of Fire was telling them, *and that you only survive because I permit it.*

Havoc bounded onto the spur and sneezed, then

glanced back at him. She was right. They had no choice but to cross it.

A hot wind whirled ash in their eyes as they picked their way over the cinders. Charcoal branches were slippery underfoot, and the bitter smell reminded Hylas of the burned valley last summer, and of the Angry Ones, who haunt charred places.

In an undertone, he asked Pirra if she thought they haunted the Mountain too.

"I don't think even the Angry Ones would dare." She made to say something else, but just then, Havoc gave an excited little grunt and darted to a burned pine log.

"She's found something," said Hylas.

The lion cub was sniffing eagerly. She'd found a piece of scat. It was packed with deer hair and shards of bone, and when Hylas bent closer, he caught its acrid smell. "Lion," he said.

Pirra turned pale. "What, up here?"

"Look, there are the tracks."

He followed them, with Havoc sniffing each print. "They're widely spaced," he said, "that means it was going fast . . . Some of the paw prints are deeper than the others. It was wounded, dragging its right hind leg . . ." He lost the trail in a tangle of charred branches.

Pirra cast about her in alarm. "D'you think it's still here?"

He shook his head. "These tracks are old. Must've been made by Havoc's father or mother."

"What was a lion doing this high up?"

"Who knows? Maybe trying to escape."

Havoc had already set off across the blasted spur. Hylas noticed how starkly she stood out, a streak of gold against the charcoal slope. His own fair hair must show up like a beacon.

"Let's go," he said, scooping ash and rubbing it over his head. "Sooner we get under cover, the better."

It was a relief to reach the other side, even if there was no cover, and they rewarded themselves with some imperfectly dried goat meat and a few mouthfuls from their waterskins.

"Those tracks reminded me," said Pirra. She took something from her pouch and held it out to him. "I keep forgetting to give this to you."

Hylas stared at the lion claw in his palm.

"I thought you should have it for an amulet," said Pirra, "because you worship the Lady of the Wild Things, and because, well, lions are strong, and so are you. Anyway, you gave me that falcon feather, so it seems fair."

"Thanks," he muttered. First that lion on the day he was caught, then Havoc, then the lion scat, and now this. He had the alarming feeling that it made some kind of pattern.

"Put it on," urged Pirra.

He tied the thong around his neck.

She nodded. "It looks good."

It did make him feel stronger, but he didn't like the idea

of the gods pushing him about like a piece on a gaming board.

They found a goat trail and walked single file, trying not to glance up at the summit looming over them, or down to the broom thickets, dizzyingly far below. Then they crested another ridge and suddenly the wind blew fierce in their faces: they had reached the north coast of Thalakrea.

No settlements, not even a hut, and no way down to the Sea. Nothing but wind-battered cliffs and raging surf.

"No chance of a boat," said Pirra, narrowing her eyes against the dust.

"There might be, farther along," Hylas said stubbornly.

But they hadn't gone far when they caught a distant sound of hammering—and there below them lay the black plain and the Neck, and beyond it the snarling head of Thalakrea, with the red wound of the mines and the all-seeing eye of Kreon's stronghold.

The trail widened, and Pirra found a little hollow out of the wind. Flinging down her gear, she sat with her forearms on her knees. Havoc glanced uncertainly at Hylas.

He stood with the hot wind buffeting his face, and a wave of hopelessness broke over him. The only village was Hekabi's, dangerously close to the mines. Even if they reached it and bought passage on a ship, how would they avoid capture, when Kreon saw everything from his aerie?

"Hylas," Pirra said quietly.

He shot her a warning glance.

"We can't put it off any longer. We've got to decide what to do."

"You mean the dagger," he said between his teeth.

She nodded. "If we try to escape, we'll miss our only chance of stealing it. We have to choose."

Savagely, he hacked at the grit with his heel. "The dagger," he said curtly, "has nothing to do with me."

Her dark brows drew together. "Last summer, you were determined to stop them getting it. What's changed?"

"A year, that's what, and being down the pit. All I want is to find Issi."

"And if the gods won't let you?"

"What do they *want* from me?" he cried. "What do you *want*?" he shouted at the smoking Mountain—and it flung back his voice: *want, want, want* . . .

"You're frightening Havoc," Pirra said sternly.

Hylas turned his back on her. In his mind he saw the dagger of Koronos: its broad square shoulders and the beautiful deadly sweep of its blade. He wanted to seize it and make it flash in the Sun, to feel its power coursing through him . . . He wanted to fling it to the bottom of the Sea.

"It'll always be with us," said Pirra as if she'd heard his thoughts. "Whatever we do, wherever we go. No, don't walk away, *listen*. We don't know how long it'll be here on Thalakrea, but one thing's sure: It won't be forever. They'll take it back to Mycenae—and when they do, it'll be gone for good. This is our only chance."

"Why do you even care?" he retorted. "It's nothing to do with you!"

"Yes it is! Keftiu's my country. I can't walk away."

"Last night you said you'd die if they sent you back. Do you really think you can save Keftiu *without* getting caught?"

She flinched. "I can try." She touched the sealstone on her wrist, and the tiny amethyst falcon flashed in the Sun. "Hylas, I don't think it's by chance that you ended up here, or that I did, or that they're bringing the dagger to Thalakrea. It's not by chance that the Oracle mentioned you—"

"But I never *asked* to be in the Oracle!" he burst out. "It may not even *mean* me, I'm not the only Outsider! I won't *do* it! Since I lost Issi I've done nothing but get farther away from her! Well no more!"

"You're angry because you know it's the right thing to do."

"I don't *care* about right, I care about Issi!"

"And if you find her, how long do you think you can live on your Mount Lykas, with the Crows still in power?"

He glared at her. "Last night you asked about my mother. If I ever meet her again, what do I tell her, Pirra? 'The only thing you told me to do was look after my sister—and I *failed*'? I have to find Issi. Everything else— the Oracle, the Crows, the dagger—it's just in the way."

"And me?" Pirra said levelly. "And Havoc? Are we in the way?"

Hylas gave her a long look. Then he turned on his heel and left.

~~~

Some time later, he returned.

Pirra sat where he'd left her, in the hollow. Beside her sprawled Havoc, licking the ash off her paws. As he approached them, the lion cub bounded toward him with little *ng ng* greeting grunts. Pirra didn't turn her head.

"I'm sorry," said Hylas.

Pirra nodded. "So am I. Because I've made up my mind. Whatever you do, I'm going back. I have to find some way to steal the dagger, and send a warning to Keftiu. And yes, Hylas, I'm going to try to do both."

"That's madness. You told me what that stronghold's like."

She ground the butt of her axe in the dust. Her scar stood out pale on her cheek, and in her flinty resolve, Hylas saw traces of her mother, the High Priestess.

"What about you?" she said without looking up.

"I don't know." He walked to the edge of the trail and stared down the Mountainside. Distractedly, he took in the black slope falling away to the broom-choked gullies. He smelled dust and thyme and woodsmoke. He didn't know what to do.

"I can't let them invade Keftiu," said Pirra. "Even if all I can do is warn my people, I have to try."

He smelled woodsmoke . . .

He dropped to his knees.

"Hylas?"

Far below in the thicket, he caught the flicker of fire. Through the branches he made out men and dogs.

"Hylas?" repeated Pirra.

Hard to see at this distance, but he counted six or seven dogs and maybe seven Crow hunters. They looked as if they were setting up camp.

Then, through a gap, he saw a boy about his own age: tall and well-built, with long dark hair in warrior braids. He saw how he fiddled with the sealstone on his wrist in a way that was instantly, shockingly familiar. The blood roared in his ears. It was Telamon.

Havoc came to see what he was doing, sending pebbles bouncing down the slope. Telamon glanced up. Hylas grabbed Havoc by the scruff and hauled her out of sight.

"What is it?" said Pirra, coming toward them.

"Get down!" he whispered.

She ducked.

Too late.

Telamon had seen her.

25

Already the dogs were racing up the slope, the Crows spreading out to cut them off. Hylas jerked his head at the summit. "Only way's up."

Pirra nodded. "I saw a trail back there—"

"If we can get around the other side and down into the thickets . . ."

If it's not too steep, he thought, and *if* the dogs don't catch us first. He could tell from Pirra's face that she'd thought of that too.

Keeping low, they raced for the trail with Havoc streaking ahead: a horribly easy quarry for a pack of dogs.

To their astonishment, the trail turned out to be made of obsidian cobbles, and it snaked toward the summit; Pirra said the Islanders must have made it to take offerings to the Mountain. It was also treacherously smooth. Her sandals kept slipping, so she tore them off and ran barefoot.

Every moment, Hylas dreaded the clatter of claws and the whine of arrows, but all he heard was the hiss of wind and their own sawing breath. Then the Sun went dark and he ran into a wall of poisonous smoke. It bit his lungs and he fought the urge to cough. Through the murk he saw Pirra stagger and clap her hand to her mouth.

Havoc slammed against his legs, trying to keep him on the trail. Then the wind tore a rent in the smoke and Hylas saw why. Just off the edge lay the bubbling, yellow-crusted crack of a fire spirit's lair.

He grabbed Pirra's arm and pointed. "Stay on the trail," he gasped, "they're everywhere."

As the obsidian snake wound higher, the wind gusted more fiercely: now ripping aside the smoke, now swamping them in fumes. On either side, they heard the sputtering of the angry spirits. The Mountain was driving them toward the summit.

Hylas' gear bumped against his back, and Havoc's wicker ball broke loose and bounced into a fiery crack. A furious hiss, a jet of smoke—and the ball burst into flames.

Havoc didn't notice. She'd caught a scent. With an urgent grunt, she shot up the trail.

Hylas threw Pirra a startled glance. The lion cub hadn't seemed scared, she'd seemed *eager*.

Below them in the smoke, a man coughed.

They stared at each other in horror.

In the distance, a dog barked: three short, savage signals. Then another, farther down.

Hylas and Pirra fled up the trail. It grew steeper; soon they were using their hands. Craning his neck, Hylas saw that the summit was shockingly close, toxic vapor rolling off it in thick white waves.

The obsidian ended and he was running over unstable black scree. Through the haze, he saw Pirra stagger. Then the ground crumbled beneath her and she wasn't there.

She was clinging to the edge, her legs flailing for a foothold. Grabbing her wrist, he hauled her back from the brink.

"We're on a ridge," he panted.

It was as sharp as a knife, with barely space for them to stand abreast. On one side the Mountainside fell away to the thickets unreachably far below. On the other was the sheer drop that had nearly claimed Pirra. Because of the smoke, they couldn't see how far it went.

"What's *down* there?" breathed Pirra.

Hylas threw in a pebble: They heard it rattle and bounce, but no sound of it striking bottom. Then suddenly the smoke drew apart and they saw it. They had reached the summit of Thalakrea, and it was *hollow*: a vast, yawning cauldron rimmed with the burning lairs of fire spirits, its barren black sides sweeping down into the swirling fumes where dwelt the Lady of Fire. One wrong move, and She would swallow them whole.

From somewhere behind came the baying of dogs. Above, the rim of the crater rose steeply, studded with giant boulders flung from within by some shattering force. They had no choice but to climb even higher.

Suddenly Pirra's eyes widened and she yanked Hylas down.

Something whizzed past his head and stuck quivering in the ground.

It was an arrow fletched with crow feathers.

Pirra rearranged her grip on her club as she stood shoulder to shoulder with Hylas on the rim of the crater.

Apart from that arrow, the Crows hadn't shown themselves, but now two bristling dogs stalked toward them out of the smoke.

"Stay close," muttered Hylas. "You're smaller, they'll go for you first." His face was set, and with his rawhide kilt and the lion claw on his chest, he looked more like an Outsider than ever.

The dogs were shaggy red brutes with fangs like boars' tusks. As they came on, Pirra saw the blood-hunger in their eyes.

Without warning, one leaped at her. She swung her club. Missed. Hylas' axe caught the dog midair and it fell dead.

The other dog sprang at Pirra. She caught it a crack on the muzzle that flung it sideways, but with terrifying speed it attacked again. Hylas landed it a kick that sent it howling into the abyss and him lurching backward. He would have fallen in a fire spirit's lair if Pirra hadn't yanked him back.

Now two more dogs were advancing upon them, and

warriors were looming out of the smoke, some nocking arrows to bows, some gripping daggers in fists.

"Behind us," panted Hylas with a jerk of his head. "That boulder shaped like a lion, if we can reach it, we can make a stand . . ."

Dodging arrows, they edged backward up the slope. But as they neared the boulder, Pirra heard a growl so powerful it shook the ground beneath her feet.

"Oh no," breathed Hylas.

She glanced over her shoulder. That rock didn't just *look* like a lion—it *was* a lion.

In one appalling heartbeat she took in its massive head lowered with lethal intent, its huge claws raking the grit as it prepared to attack. Then she saw *Havoc* hiding behind its muscled haunches, and in a flash she knew that the tracks they'd found on the spur hadn't been those of the cub's parents, but of *another* lioness, *this* one, who was now bent on protecting the cub from all comers— including them.

Before them the Crows, behind them an angry lioness.

"Get down!" said Hylas, pulling her into a crouch.

The lioness snarled, baring massive yellow fangs.

Hylas unslung his waterskin and tossed it toward her, and with one huge forepaw she batted it into the crater. Pirra did the same with hers: anything to distract her.

The Crows were hanging back, but the dogs were racing toward them. Out of the corner of her eye, Pirra saw the lioness hunker down. She saw the jut of shoulder blades and haunches as the great beast tensed to spring.

"*Duck*," said Hylas.

Pirra felt a *whoosh* as the lioness sprang right over them and met the dogs head-on. There was a crack and a howl swiftly cut off, and a dog slithered limply over the edge.

The lioness lurched to her feet, but now Pirra saw how she staggered, her flanks heaving, spit trailing from her jaws. She was old and badly wounded.

She was also *between* the Crows and their quarry, so Hylas and Pirra seized their chance and fled. But while the men harried the lioness, two dogs scrambled past her, one hurtling toward Hylas, the other heading straight for Havoc.

Pirra saw Hylas fighting the dog with his axe in one hand and his knife in the other. She saw Havoc backed against a rock, snarling bravely at her attacker, who was three times her size. Pirra left Hylas and raced up the slope. As the dog leaped at Havoc, Pirra swung her club and killed it. For an instant the cub's eyes met Pirra's—then she turned tail and sped off into the smoke.

Hylas had killed his dog too, but as he turned to join Pirra, he stumbled and lost his footing. She caught his axe handle, checking his fall long enough for him to scramble back.

A few paces below them, the old lioness stood at bay before the Crows and the surviving dog. Arrows jutted from her flanks; she was failing fast. The dog leaped and sank its teeth into her throat. With a roar she raked it with her claws. It clung on, and in a blur of teeth and fur they disappeared into the crater.

Once again, Hylas and Pirra scrambled up the rim. But now the Mountain turned against them, gusting smoke in their faces and forcing them back.

As they staggered down the slope, a warrior loomed over Pirra and grabbed her by the hair. Another seized Hylas' arm and yanked it savagely behind him.

"Got him!" he shouted.

26

The warrior caught Pirra's wrists in a bone-crushing grip. She wriggled and kicked, but it was like fighting a boulder.

"Let her go!" cried Hylas. "She's the wisewoman's slave, she's needed to cure Kreon!" That earned him a blow to the face with the butt of a knife.

"We got them, my lord!" called his captor to someone farther down the trail.

Footsteps in the smoke, and both warriors straightened respectfully. Pirra saw a young man climbing toward them.

Hylas saw him too, and paled. He caught Pirra's eye. "Save yourself," he muttered, "you can't help me now."

The young man was darkly handsome, with high-boned features and a warrior's long braids. With a jolt, Pirra recognized Telamon, the boy she'd been meant to wed.

It's all over, she thought numbly. He'll take Hylas to Kreon and they'll feed him to the crows.

Telamon's gaze flickered over her, and although his expression didn't change, she knew that he'd recognized her. Then he turned to Hylas.

Hylas spat blood and glared defiantly back.

Nothing moved in Telamon's face, but Pirra saw his grip on his knife tighten.

"Do we kill them here," said Pirra's captor, "or take them back to the mines, so the others can watch?"

"This Mountain is sacred," said Pirra, "if you kill us, you'll be cursed forever!" She'd invented the curse; but it made them uneasy.

"Let her go," ordered Telamon. "She can make her own way back."

Pirra's captor released her with a suddenness that made her stagger. "And the Outsider?" he said.

Telamon's dark eyes flicked to Hylas. Abruptly, he sheathed his knife and turned away. Only Pirra saw how his face worked, as if warring impulses fought within him.

"It's not him," he said over his shoulder.

The warriors gaped. "Wh-at?" said one.

"My lord, are you sure?" said the other. "He's dressed in skins, I think he—"

"What you think doesn't matter," Telamon said coldly. "I knew the Outsider. This isn't him. It's just some runaway slave."

The men exchanged startled glances. "So then—do we take him back to the mines?"

"No. If we put him with the others, he'd spread rebellion."

"Then what?"

Telamon thought for a moment. "The furnaces. We'll give him to the smith. He won't last long up there."

"If I were to kill you now," said Telamon, "I'd receive nothing but praise."

"But you won't," said Hylas, with more conviction than he felt.

"You can't know that for sure," muttered Telamon.

"If you'd wanted me dead, you'd have done it already."

Telamon put his hands to his temples. "I want you far away from here," he said. "I want never to see you again. I hate this. Lying to my kin, and for what? To risk helping someone who was once my friend."

They were alone at the Crows' camp in the thicket; Telamon had gotten rid of his men by sending them in search of the missing dogs. Hylas sat with his arms tied behind his back. They were beginning to ache, and his cheekbone hurt.

He watched Telamon prowl around the campfire's dead gray ashes. His warrior braids swung, and the little clay discs at the ends made a faint clinking that was painfully familiar. He'd grown taller, but he was still the same boy who used to run off and join Hylas and Issi on Mount Lykas.

"If you're not going to kill me," said Hylas, "let me go."

Telamon snorted. "And tell them what? That fire spirits carried you away?"

"So what are you going to do?"

Telamon fiddled with the sealstone at his wrist. "I still can't believe it," he said. "You. Here. *Why?*"

"Not my choice. I got caught and sold as a slave."

Telamon shot him a searching look. "Is that true?"

"Course it's true, I've got the tattoo to prove it." He twisted around to display the mark on his forearm.

"But why *here*, on Thalakrea? And why now, when Koronos—when we're all here together?"

"I didn't know you were coming. Look. Telamon. I don't *care* about your wretched dagger. All I want is to get off this island and find Issi!"

Telamon studied him with an unreadable expression. "I want to believe you. But I believed you before, and you lied."

"So did you."

Telamon flinched. Then he walked to the dead fire and kicked it, raising a bitter cloud of ash.

For a heartbeat while his back was turned, Hylas thought about knocking him to the ground; but Telamon was stronger, and armed. Instead he said, "You don't seem surprised that I'm alive."

"That's because I'm not," retorted Telamon. "I've known for a while."

"How?"

He didn't reply. "I wept for you, Hylas," he said in a low voice. "I grieved for my dead friend. And all the time you were laughing at me."

"I wasn't laughing," said Hylas.

"No?"

"No."

Bleakly they stared at each other across the ruins of their friendship.

Men's voices came to them through the thicket.

Quickly, Telamon squatted beside Hylas and pretended to tighten his bonds. "When we reach the furnace ridge," he whispered, "you'll have to stay alive as best you can. They say the smith's a hard man with strange ways. He'll flog you, but if I stopped him they'd be suspicious, and I'm running enough risks as it is. Hold on for a few days, and I might be able to get you on a ship."

Hylas twisted around. "Are you telling me you'll help me *escape*?"

"Sh! Not so loud!"

"But *why*?"

"Why's it so hard to understand? You were my friend. Even after everything that's happened, I can't—I can't watch them kill you. If I get you off the island, I'll be rid of you, once and for all."

"But if you help me, you'll be betraying your own clan."

Telamon glared at him. "Do you think I don't know that?"

The men returned with three cowed-looking dogs at their heels. In the blink of an eye, Telamon became their haughty young leader and hauled Hylas to his feet. "Move," he snarled.

⚊⚊

The obsidian trail cut straight across the plain, so that by late afternoon they were already approaching the Neck.

Once, Hylas glimpsed Pirra following at a distance. He

hoped she'd have the sense to make for the village, and not try to rescue him. He'd seen no sign of Havoc. Had the lion cub made it down from the Mountain, or was she still up there, lost in the poisonous smoke?

Telamon picked up a horse at the Neck, then they started for the ridge. As they passed the mines, Hylas saw slaves toiling to clear the shafts. Soon it would be as if the cave-in had never happened. He thought of the snatchers deep underground. He could almost feel their anger through the rocks.

The track to the furnaces was steep, and edged with piles of burned slag. He trudged in a blur of exhaustion, surrounded by Telamon's men. As they crested the ridge, the din of hammers grew.

Telamon's horse shied. "Steady," he growled. He was trying to appear at ease, but Hylas could tell he was nervous. *Smiths are different*, Zan had said. *Even the Crows are wary of them.* Telamon was taking a risk, making the smith take on a new slave.

Grimy slaves tended the furnaces, like ants tending enormous grubs. Each was a squat clay column pitted with holes spouting evil-smelling brown smoke. The slaves had just cracked one open: Hylas saw liquid fire spattering into a stone trough. *Crush the greenstone, burn it till the copper bleeds out . . .*

From stone huts, fires glared and hammers rang. Hylas guessed that there, in some mysterious way, copper was being mated with tin to create bronze.

Then they were out on a windswept headland, hearing gulls and gulping salty air. The drop to the Sea was dizzying. No escape that way, thought Hylas.

Beneath a thorn tree, four slaves unloaded charcoal from an ox-wagon. Beyond, on the tip of the headland, a large stone hut stood alone. Hylas caught the sound of a single hammer. His belly tightened. That must be the smithy.

Telamon dismounted and ordered his men to untie Hylas. Then to the slaves, "Tell your master I wish to speak to him."

They tapped their lips and shook their heads.

"They're mute, my lord," said a warrior. "The smith only permits those who can't speak near his smithy."

Hylas had forgotten that. Uneasily, he wondered what it meant for him.

The warrior had had the same thought. "My lord, I'm not sure the smith will—"

"He'll do as I command," said Telamon. But he was sweating.

One of the slaves ran and beat a copper drum hanging from the tree.

The hammering stopped. A man emerged and walked toward them. He was powerfully built, with broad shoulders and muscled forearms flecked with burns. He wore a leather apron to shield him from the heat of the forge, and his dark beard was clipped short, his shoulder-length hair held back by a headband of sweat-stained rawhide. Hylas couldn't see the upper part of his face, which was hidden by a leather mask.

Telamon inclined his head.

The smith acknowledged him with the slightest of nods.

"Master smith," said Telamon with a careful blend of haughtiness and respect, "this slave's a runaway. I want you to keep him separate, so that he can't spread trouble."

Through the slits in his mask, the smith studied Hylas. Then he grunted at him to follow, and headed back to his smithy.

Hylas risked a glance at Telamon, but he'd already remounted and was riding off. Hylas wondered if he'd meant what he said about helping him.

"In here," growled the smith.

Rubbing the feeling back into his wrists, Hylas followed his new master inside.

He walked into a blast of heat and a strange sweet smell of raw metal that reminded him of fresh blood. A charcoal fire smoldered in a raised stone hearth. Beside it stood a massive stone block, and rawhide bellows with blackened clay snouts; stacks of bronze ingots shaped like oxhides, a cubit long; piles of axe heads, knives, spearheads, all with the pinkish luster of new bronze. On a workbench lay stone molds, hammers and chisels, a dish of dried anchovies and cheese, and a half-open pouch of leaves.

Hylas blinked. Something about those leaves had jogged his memory . . .

The smith took a horn cup and drank from a pail. "So," he said. "Why'd they really send you to me?"

That voice. Smooth. Powerful. He'd heard it before. And those leaves on the workbench were *buckthorn*. People chewed them to ward off ghosts—or the Angry Ones.

He mustered his courage. "Don't you recognize me?"

The smith set down the cup. Behind his mask, his eyes gleamed.

"It's me," said Hylas. "Flea. Last summer you took me captive. You weren't a smith then, you'd been shipwrecked, you called yourself Ak—"

Swift as a snake, the man called Akastos clapped a hand over his mouth. "The name's *Dameas*," he breathed. "Dameas the smith. Got that? Blink twice for yes, or you'll regret it."

Hylas blinked twice.

Akastos dragged Hylas to the forge and held his fist over the fire. "Swear that you'll never tell anyone my true name."

"I swear!" gasped Hylas.

"Say it. Tell your oath to the fire."

"I swear I'll never tell anyone your true name!"

Akastos plunged Hylas' fist into the water pail, then sat on a stool and forced him to his knees, bringing them face-to-face. Hylas knew better than to struggle; the grip on his shoulder could crush his bones like eggshell. He didn't know if he was frightened or relieved to be at Akastos' mercy again. This man had left him as bait for the Angry Ones; but at times he'd shown flashes of kindness.

Akastos pulled off his mask and fixed him with a penetrating stare. His hair was shorter, his sharp beard no longer crusted with salt; but his unsettling light-gray eyes were just as impossible to read.

"What are you doing here?" he barked.

Hylas gulped. "I'm a slave. I ran away."

"No tricks, boy, you're on a knife edge. Again. What are you doing here?"

"It's *true!*"

Akastos snorted. "Last summer you turned up on the Island of the Fin People. You said the Crows were after you, they were killing Outsiders, you didn't know why. You *said* you were a goatherd—and yet you knew about the dagger of Koronos. And now you just *happen* to cross my path again?"

"I was trying to get home. They caught me and sent me here."

"Why didn't they just kill you?"

"They don't know it's me—I mean, that I'm the Outsider."

"So you're asking me to believe that you've fetched up here on Thalakrea at the same time as the House of Koronos—*and they don't know?*"

Hylas nodded. "Don't give me away. They'll kill me."

Abruptly, Akastos released him and went to the forge. Firelight streaked his features with shadow and flame.

Hylas risked a glance at the door.

"I wouldn't," said Akastos, reading his thoughts. "You'd never get past the furnaces, and from the cliffs there's only one way down; it's quick, but you wouldn't survive."

Resuming his stool, he rested his powerful forearms on his knees. Then he spoke to Hylas in a low voice that made the rest of the smithy disappear. "What do you know about the dagger? Leave nothing out."

Hylas took a breath. "A dying man gave it to me in a tomb. He said he'd stolen it and to keep it hidden."

The smith went very still. "What was he like?"

"Young. Keftian. Rich, I think. Did you know him?"

Not an eyelash stirred, but Hylas sensed the rapid flow of thought. "So," said Akastos. "You had the dagger in your hands."

"Then Kratos got it back. We fought. He drowned. The Crows took it."

Akastos raised his eyebrows. "Kratos is dead? At last, some good news. But why are the Crows still after you?"

"There was an Oracle, it said *If an Outsider wields the blade, the House of Koronos burns.* They think I'm the one. But I don't *care* about any of that, I just want to find my sister."

Akastos took that in silence. "This has to be a trap," he said. "They must know you're here."

"They don't, I swear! At least—Telamon knows, but he—"

"Telamon?"

"The boy who brought me here, he's Thestor's son. We used to be friends—when I didn't know he was a Crow."

Akastos reached for a wineskin on a hook, half filled an earthenware beaker, and topped it up with water from the pail. Hylas watched thirstily as he drank.

"Thestor of Lykonia," said Akastos, wiping his mouth on his wrist. "That boy is his son?"

Hylas nodded. "He says he'll help me escape."

"And you trust him."

Hylas didn't reply.

Akastos turned the beaker in his long fingers. "So what am I going to do with you, Flea? I can think of one sure way of saving myself a lot of trouble."

"But you won't," Hylas said quickly. "You won't kill me."

"What makes you say that?"

It was a struggle to control his breathing. "You made me swear never to tell your name. If you were going to kill me, you wouldn't have bothered."

The lines at the sides of Akastos' mouth deepened, as if he would have smiled if he hadn't lost the habit.

Suddenly, Hylas remembered the mute slaves by the thorn tree. "P-please," he stammered, "don't cut out my tongue!"

That seemed to anger Akastos. "Why would you think I'd do that? Those slaves out there, they were born mute, I just took them out of the mines."

"Sorry," said Hylas. He eyed the beaker. "Can I have a drink?"

Again Akastos snorted. "Go ahead."

Hylas gulped three beakers of wine and water, then asked if he could have an anchovy.

Akastos shrugged.

"Aren't you even a bit glad to see me?" mumbled Hylas as he wolfed the lot.

"Why? You're bad luck, Flea, I told you that last summer."

"You also said that we're alike. We're both survivors."

"So? Does that make you think you know me?"

"No, but—"

"What do you think you know about me, Flea?"

Hylas swallowed the last of the cheese and decided it would be safest to hold nothing back. "You were a sailor. Maybe a warrior too, because you're so strong. You're cleverer than anyone I've ever met, and you've been on the run from the Crows for longer than I've been alive. Also you're on the run from"—he dropped his voice—"the Angry Ones. Which means you must have done something terrible, but I don't know what."

The fire crackled and spat. Hylas feared he'd gone too far.

Akastos scratched his beard and sighed. "Why did you have to cross my path again, Flea?"

"Wh-why?" said Hylas. "What are you going to do?"

Akastos rose to his feet and prowled the smithy. Then he barked a laugh. "What a sense of humor the gods have!"

"What do you mean?"

"Surely you can see that the best way for me to make use of you is to take you to Kreon?"

"But—you can't!"

"If I give him the Outsider, it'll gain his trust and get me inside his stronghold."

"But the Oracle! I could help you *defeat* them! That's what you want, isn't it? That's why you're here?"

"Oracles are tricky things, Flea, I never rely on them.

This one *could* mean the gods have a use for you; or you might just be some goatherd out of your depth. There's no way of knowing which."

"But—if you hide me from the Crows and I do turn out to be the one in the Oracle, you'll have a better chance of beating them!"

"True. But if I hide you, they'll also have a better chance of finding you, and making you tell them my real name."

"I swore I'd never do that!"

"Ah but Flea. Anyone can be broken if you know how."

Something in his voice told Hylas that Akastos knew how.

"I thought you liked me," Hylas said bleakly.

"That's got nothing to do with it," snapped Akastos. "The point is—" He broke off and stared at the doorway.

"What is it?" mouthed Hylas.

Akastos signed him to silence.

A sound outside: furtive. Listening.

Stealthily, Akastos approached the doorway, taking care not to cast a shadow that might alert whoever was out there. With the speed of a snake he sprang, dragging in a struggling bundle.

"Don't hurt her!" cried Hylas.

Akastos dropped the bundle and sucked a bitten hand.

Havoc shot behind Hylas and snarled.

28

"Don't hurt her!" repeated Hylas. He scooped Havoc into his arms and felt her shaking with fright, her heart hammering against his chest.

Akastos loomed over them with his knife in his hand. "What does this mean?" he said harshly.

"Please! She's only a cub!"

He was startled to see that Akastos' forehead was beaded with sweat. "A *lion*," muttered the smith. Then to Hylas, "Is this a trick? Making me think it's an omen?"

"No! I found her on the Mountain. Kreon killed her parents, she can't fend for herself!"

Akastos gave him a hard look. "Have you never heard of the Lion of Mycenae?"

Hylas shook his head.

"It's what people used to call the High Chieftain. I had a farm, not far from Mycenae. And now here's this cub. That's some kind of sign."

"But—it's not her fault!"

Slowly, Akastos sheathed his knife. "Get it out of here," he said thickly.

Hylas thought fast. "I could hide her behind the smithy. I could take her food—"

"Do it."

Hylas hesitated. He hardly dared remind Akastos of what he'd been saying before Havoc had appeared, but he had to know. "You won't—you won't give me to Kreon, will you?"

Akastos rubbed a hand over his face. "Just get that creature out of here."

~

The big dark-maned human glared at them as the boy staggered from the den with the lion cub in his forepaws.

She was too frightened to struggle. Her pads hurt and she was hungry. On the Mountain, the girl had killed a lizard for her, but on the plain they'd lost each other, and for a desperate time the cub had been alone.

At last she'd caught the boy's scent, but he was with the bad humans, so she'd stayed hidden. She'd followed him to this dreadful noisy place where humans attacked the earth as if it had done something wrong, and the earth growled back—although they didn't seem to hear. The lion cub hated it, but she had to stay close to the boy.

Now he carried her to some boulders behind the den. They smelled of dust and beetles. No lions. Fearfully, she padded to the edge. Far below, a vast glittery creature with a wrinkled gray pelt pawed at rocks with a low, unceasing roar. The cub flattened her ears and shot back to the boulders.

Speaking softly, the boy pushed her into a little hollow behind a bush. It smelled friendly. The cub felt a bit safer. The boy ran off and returned with some fish. While she was eating, he ran off again. Wearily, she heaved herself up to follow.

Something yanked her back. With an indignant yowl, she tried to pull free. The same thing happened. The cub was astonished. *Something was wound around her neck*. It was attached to the bush, that was why she couldn't get away. It wouldn't take long to gnaw through. But suddenly, she was too tired.

As her head drooped onto her paws, she thought of the dark-maned human. She wasn't sure what to feel about him. She sensed that he was always alert, like a hunting lion, and that his heart was a tangle of good and bad.

What frightened her most was that under his human scent, she'd caught a whiff of something else: the black, biting smell of the terrible spirits who haunted her very worst sleeps.

The molten bronze trembled like a pool of liquid Sun.

Hylas labored at the bellows. Akastos twisted a withe around the crucible and lifted it clear of the embers. Hylas dropped the bellows, and grabbed a stick with a flat piece of slate mounted on the end. Akastos poured a dazzling stream of fire into the mold, while Hylas held the slate's edge just above the lip of the crucible to keep back any specks of charcoal floating on the bronze. Blazing white flames splashed over the mold, and Hylas glimpsed the throbbing red form within. Akastos wiped his forehead. Another axe was born.

Hylas had been at the smithy for three days. Telamon hadn't been back, and there'd been no sign of Pirra. Hylas hoped she was all right, because there was nothing he could do to help.

Havoc had chewed through three tethers, but hadn't touched the fourth, which he'd smeared with scat. By day, the threat of buzzards and the din from the smithy kept her in her hiding place. At night she grew restless, and Hylas worried that she'd throttle herself, so he'd persuaded Akastos—who remained wary of her—to allow her in the smithy, *provided* she gave no trouble. Hylas kept her occupied with scraps of sacking and another wicker ball, which she loved just as much as the old one.

Akastos drove Hylas hard, making him tend the fire and burnish the newborn weapons; but he fed him well, and he taught him things. He said the most precious metal was silver, and the rarest was iron, which fell from the stars— but the most desired was gold. It came from rivers, and you found it by washing sand over sheepskins, so that the grains snagged in the wool and turned the fleece gold.

At other times, Akastos questioned Hylas closely. How long had he had the dagger? What could he remember of the cave-in, and Periphas? Then Hylas wondered if the smith was merely keeping him safe for some secret purpose of his own.

Hylas hoped he was wrong. Akastos was ruthless, but Hylas liked him and wanted his approval. If he'd had a father, he would have wanted him to resemble the smith.

"Wake up, Flea," growled Akastos. "Fire's dying down."

Hylas re-applied himself to the bellows. Their clay nozzle poked through a hole in a stone slab that shielded him from the embers, but he was still streaming sweat.

A hiss of steam as Akastos cooled the mold in the trough, then up-ended it and tapped the bottom with the butt of his hammer, to release the axe head. The new bronze was a beautiful, shiny dark-gold.

"Why *do* people make bronze?" said Hylas. "I mean, why not just use copper?"

Akastos' lip curled. "You're always asking questions, Flea. Bronze is harder than copper, and it takes a sharper edge."

"Is that why the Crows—"

"Yes." He lowered his voice. "The Crows made their dagger of bronze so that they could gain its endurance and strength." He studied the axe. "Bronze never grows old. It heals like flesh, and draws lightning from the sky. Which is why," he added drily, "it's a good idea not to raise your weapon in a storm."

He seemed to be in a forthcoming mood, so Hylas risked the question he'd been longing to ask. "How did you learn to be a smith?"

"On my father's farm," Akastos said curtly. With his hammer, he struck the axe. He went on striking, as if to obliterate his thoughts. Hylas knew not to ask any more.

Akastos made hammering look easy, but once, he'd let Hylas try. The hammer was so heavy he could barely lift it one-handed, and his blow had bounced off with a clang. "Harder, Flea, you won't hurt it! Bronze is a survivor, like you and me. The harder you hit it, the tougher it gets."

By now, the axe was battle-hard. Akastos turned to the crucible, where more bronze was heating, and they began again. And when they'd amassed a pile of axes, spearheads, arrowheads, and knives, that would be another day done.

Hylas had swiftly realized that by pretending to be a smith, Akastos had created the perfect disguise. The mute slaves kept others from the smithy and warned him when to don his mask; and as he ruled the ridge, he could order the ash from the forge and the slag from the furnaces hauled away each day, without anyone guessing that this was to avoid attracting the Angry Ones.

But *why* had he come to Thalakrea? And what terrible crime had he committed, that he was haunted by the spirits of vengeance?

Dusk fell and the furnaces went quiet—although at the smithy, Hylas and Akastos would take turns through the night to feed the fire and mutter the ancient spell against the Angry Ones.

It was Hylas' turn to stay awake. On a pallet by the wall, Akastos slept more restlessly than usual; he'd caught his thumb with his hammer, and the nail was turning black.

Hylas sat by the forge with Havoc at his feet. She seemed

subdued, and lay quietly shredding a scrap of sacking with her claws.

Hylas nodded with fatigue as he mumbled the charm. The smithy was full of shadows. He thought of the haunted gully last summer, where the Angry Ones had nearly driven him mad with terror. They were drawn to burned things. And the Crows daubed ash on their cheeks . . . Could it be that they *worshipped* them?

His head sank onto his chest. The spell blurred to a meaningless jumble.

From the rafters, something dropped to the floor and came lurching toward him—

He jerked awake.

On his pallet, Akastos stirred and muttered in his sleep.

Havoc stood tensely, her ears pricked.

"What is it?" whispered Hylas.

She turned her head, and her golden eyes threw back the firelight.

Despite the heat, he went cold. Something *had* thudded onto the roof.

Shakily, he took a burning brand and swept the smithy. Shadows fled the light. Nothing else. And yet his skin crawled and the hairs on the back of his neck stood up.

With pounding heart, he stepped outside. For once, Havoc didn't push past him, but stayed in the smithy.

The roof loomed against the stars. Hylas remembered that tomorrow was the dark of the Moon, when the Angry Ones would be at their most powerful.

Something black hitched itself off the thatch and flew away.

With a cry, Hylas recoiled—and backed into Akastos.

"It's not them," said the smith.

"Y-you're sure?"

"Oh, I'd know it, Flea."

Hylas breathed out. "How long till they find you?"

"Who knows?" He touched the thong at his wrist. "I bear the smith's sealstone; it'll help throw them off for a while."

"What happened to the real Dameas?"

Akastos hesitated. "Let's just say he gave it to me."

Back in the smithy, Hylas fed Havoc a rind of goat's cheese and sat hugging his knees to stop them trembling.

Akastos woke the fire in the forge and made it blaze. In the leaping light, Hylas saw the scars on his shoulders and chest. Not for the first time, he wondered if they were battle scars. He'd noticed that the smith's right arm was slightly more muscled than the left. Was that from wielding a hammer, or a sword?

"Why are the Angry Ones after you?" he said quietly. "Who did you kill?"

29

"Strange," said Akastos, watching the flames. "They hate fire because it gives light, and yet they're drawn to burned things. As bitter as guilt."

"I know about guilt," said Hylas.

"At your age? I doubt that."

Hylas told him how he'd decoyed the Crows away from Issi, then hadn't been able to find her.

"You were a boy against warriors," said Akastos. "It wasn't your fault."

"But she'll think I abandoned her." He picked a scab off his knee. "Sometimes I think that if I keep Havoc safe, the Lady of the Wild Things will look after Issi."

A shadow of pity crossed Akastos' face. "Be careful, Flea, you're growing too attached to that cub. If you become attached to things, you get hurt."

Hylas swallowed. "Do you still think Havoc's an omen?"

Akastos prodded the fire with a stick. "Well, people did call the High Chieftain of Mycenae a lion—I mean the real High Chieftain, before Koronos took over—and my farm was on the plains, just below the citadel. Then years later, a boy walks into my smithy: an Outsider with a lion claw around his neck and a lion cub at his heels. So yes, Flea, I think she's an omen—although I don't know what it means."

As if she knew they were talking about her, Havoc came and leaned against Hylas. He scratched her scruff, and she licked his knee, then lay down on his feet and went to sleep.

"I thought you didn't believe in omens," said Hylas.

"I said I don't rely on oracles. Oracles are riddles spoken by seers; omens are signs made by animals. Seers lie. Animals don't."

Hylas said, "Where I come from, farmers have bent backs and crooked legs. You don't look like a farmer to me."

Akastos shrugged. "The Mycenaean plains are the richest in Akea, the farming's easy. I had barley fields, olive groves. And vines . . . my wine was the darkest, the strongest . . . The Crows took it all."

"Did you have a family?"

He hesitated. "My son would be about your age if he'd lived." His face grew distant, remembering. "At first it was only Koronos and his blood kin, with a small band of warriors. They came from their ancestral chieftaincy, Lykonia, and they brought gifts. The High Chieftain wasn't fooled, but others were—till it was nearly too late. For a time, the struggle for power lay on a knife edge. It would be decided in the mountains around

Mycenae. They were home to a tribe of Outsiders—"

"Outsiders?" cried Hylas.

"They weren't outcasts, as they are where you come from, but proud people, incredibly skilled at woodlore. They knew the mountains like nobody else. You never heard of them?"

Hylas shook his head. "What happened then?"

"The High Chieftain went to their leader and sought his help against the Crows." His voice hardened. "The leader of the Outsiders wanted no part in it. He said it was no concern of his people. Soon after, the tide turned in favor of the Crows. The High Chieftain was killed. Mycenae fell to Koronos." He paused. "About that time, the Angry Ones came after me."

Hylas waited, not daring to breathe.

"I had a brother," said Akastos. "He was also my best friend. The Crows told him lies about me and we fought." He opened his hands and let something fall that only he could see. "I killed him. I killed my brother."

The fire crackled. The smithy felt airless and hot.

"The Angry Ones descended like a plague," Akastos told the flames. "Blighting my crops, my cattle. I had to leave the farm, or there'd have been nothing left." He drew a breath. "So. That's why I'm always moving on to the next hiding place, the next disguise. Because I killed my brother."

Hylas forced himself to look Akastos in the eye. "It was the Crows' fault, not yours. They made you do it."

"It was my fault, Flea."

"Maybe it was the will of the gods—"

"That's the coward's way out. *I* wielded the knife. *I* spilled his blood. Except 'spilled' sounds too clean, and there's nothing clean about killing a man. When you kill a man, Flea, you feel your knife pushing into his flesh. You hear his agony, you smell his terror as he realizes he's going to die. Then you see his eyes grow dull, and you feel the full horror of what you've done, but it's too late, you've taken his life, you can never give it back . . ." He passed his hand across his mouth, and Hylas saw how it shook.

"Sometimes they come to me in my dreams," Akastos whispered, "and they have my brother's face. I see him with the blood streaming from his eyes. Angry. Accusing me." He fell silent. "I'm doing you no favors by keeping you here, Flea."

"You're keeping me alive. But why are *you* here, on Thalakrea? I think the Crows worship the Angry Ones—so how can you bring yourself to stay here, when they might be so close?"

Akastos' light-gray eyes pierced his, and Hylas sensed his supple mind deciding what to reveal. "For fourteen years, I've been on the run. Two things I've sworn to do before I die. Nothing else matters. To destroy the dagger of Koronos—and appease my brother's ghost. For that I'll risk everything. Even getting caught by the Angry Ones."

A log shifted in the forge, and Hylas jumped. "How can you appease a ghost?"

"By feeding him the blood of vengeance: the lifeblood of a highborn Crow. Only then will his spirit be at peace. Only then will I be rid of the Angry Ones."

On the cliffs, the gulls were awake. Hylas heard the ox-carts rumbling up from the charcoal pits. Red light stole into the smithy and lit Akastos' haunted features.

Hylas thought of what he'd just learned. He said, "Why did you tell me all this?"

To his surprise, Akastos nodded approvingly. "That's good, you're thinking like a survivor."

"So—why?"

"I told you all this, Flea, because oddly enough, I'd rather not have to hand you over to Kreon to be gutted like a pig. But if you get in my way, I will. So now you know what I'm after. Don't get in the way." Before Hylas could reply, he'd gotten up and left the smithy.

Hylas ran to the doorway and watched him go. Akastos the wanderer had become Dameas the smith, heading off to see that the furnaces were properly loaded with green-stone and charcoal. He glanced back, and his meaning was clear: *What I've told you changes nothing. Now get to work.* Then he put on his mask and was gone.

As Hylas fed the fire, he wondered how Akastos had borne it. Most men haunted by the Angry Ones went mad within a year. Akastos had lasted fourteen.

Footsteps outside, and he turned to speak to the smith.

It wasn't him. It was a slave Hylas didn't know, a sweaty young man with the bulging eyes of a frightened hare.

"Message from the lord Telamon," he whispered. "*Midnight. Here.*"

"Here?" said Hylas. "I should wait here?"

"There'll be a boat below the cliffs. He knows a way down."

"Come back! Is that all?"

"That's all I know," muttered the slave as he scuttled off.

Hylas' mind reeled. But he had no time to take it in. Thirty paces away under the thorn tree, two people stood waiting.

One was a tall woman with a white streak in her hair and wild eager eyes fixed on him.

The other was Pirra.

30

"I'm so glad you found Havoc," said Pirra, kneeling on the floor of the smithy and rubbing foreheads with the cub.

"I didn't," said Hylas, "she found me."

They exchanged grins.

The lion cub stood with her forepaws on Pirra's thighs and gave her cheek a rasping lick. Hylas knelt and trailed a wicker ball—a new one—and Havoc pounced.

Hylas had darkened his hair with charcoal, which was wearing off in streaks. Pirra thought he looked stronger than she'd ever seen him. She was pleased that he still wore the lion claw on his chest, and relieved that there were no welts on his back.

"I was so worried the smith would have you flogged," she said.

He glanced at her. "I was worried you wouldn't get back to the village."

"I did, but Hekabi had been summoned by Kreon, and the guards on the ridge wouldn't let me past without her.

I had to wait. It was horrible, I had no idea what had happened to you."

Hylas ran his fingers through Havoc's fur. "It's really good to see you, Pirra."

"You too." She pushed her hair behind her ears, then remembered her scar, and turned her head so he couldn't see.

"Why do you do that?" he said quietly. "Your scar's part of who you are."

She flushed. "Well I wish it wasn't. I tried some of that magic mud, but it didn't work. I even got some powdered sulfur from Merops. That didn't work either." Shut *up*, Pirra. There was so little time, and she was babbling about her stupid scar.

Under the thorn tree, Hekabi was getting tired of waiting.

Pirra said, "She wants to talk to you."

Hylas was instantly on his guard. "About what?"

She hesitated. "I told her about the Oracle. She wants—"

"You told her who I am?"

"Listen to me, Hylas. She hates the Crows as much as we do. And she's—she's after the dagger."

Rising to his feet, he went to stand behind the forge; as if he needed to put something between them. "Don't you remember what I told you on the Mountain?" he said without meeting her eyes. "I don't care about the dagger anymore."

"I don't believe that."

"Well it's true."

Pirra stood and faced him. Between them the fire hissed and the air shimmered with heat. "Just listen to what she has to say."

"No. You listen to me." He scowled at the embers. "Telamon's going to help me escape."

Pirra caught her breath. "Telamon," she repeated. "Telamon the Crow. The grandson of Koronos."

He flinched. "If he'd wanted to betray me, he'd have done it by now."

"And if you're wrong?"

"I'm not."

"I see," she said with mounting anger. "And when is Telamon—your *friend*—going to help you escape?"

"Tonight. I'm meeting him here at midnight."

She felt as if he'd punched her in the chest. If she hadn't found her way to the smithy, he would have left her behind. "And—you believe him?"

"Pirra, this is my only chance. I've got to take it, I owe it to Issi. Can't you see?"

Hekabi left the thorn tree and started toward them.

"Come with me," Hylas said suddenly.

But it seemed to Pirra that she could see the dagger of Koronos between them: keeping them apart. "I can't," she said.

"*Why* not?"

"How can you ask? How can you turn your back on all this and run away!"

A flush stole across his cheekbones. "It's not running away."

"Yes it is," said Hekabi.

They turned and watched her enter the smithy. Her glance flicked to Havoc—who shot behind a stack of ingots—then back to Hylas.

He gave her a defiant stare. "What's it to you?"

"Everything," she said sternly. "If you *are* the one in the Oracle, we can't defeat them without you." Putting out her hand, she touched her finger to his brow. "You've been close to an immortal. I can feel it, crackling on your skin."

"No." He backed away.

"He has," said Pirra. "Last summer in a cave, we were in the presence of the Lady of the Sea. He touched the blue fire."

"Yes," murmured Hekabi, "the burning shadow of a god. I can always tell."

"*So?*" cried Hylas. "What of it?"

"It means you're the one," said the wisewoman. "It means you have a destiny. Your life is not your own."

"What's going on in here?" demanded a voice from the doorway.

Pirra turned to see a tall angry man with his hands on his hips. With a jolt, she recognized the shipwrecked stranger who'd once captured Hylas.

"Get out of my smithy!" he barked.

Before Pirra could say a word, Hylas had grabbed her wrist and dragged her behind the forge. "His name's *Dameas* now," he hissed. "You've never heard the name Akastos!"

She twisted out of his grip. "*What*? You mean he's the *smith*?"

"He hates the Crows, they took his farm. And he knows about the Oracle. We can trust him—I think."

"You *think*?" she whispered furiously.

There was no time to explain. Hylas' head was spinning. First the message from Telamon, then Pirra, and now Akastos, glaring at him.

"What's going on, Flea?" Akastos said angrily. "Letting *women* into my smithy? Don't you know that's the worst kind of bad luck?"

"And Dameas knows all about bad luck," put in Hekabi. "Don't you, Dameas? If that's your name."

He turned on her. "What's that supposed to mean?"

He towered over her, but she was undaunted. "Something's after you," she said. "I can smell it. Spirits of air and darkness."

Not a muscle moved in Akastos' face.

"I could give you a charm to keep them away—for a little while."

His beard jutted. "I don't take help from a woman who gives medicine to Kreon."

"And I don't take orders from a man who makes weapons for him. Give me the boy and I'll be on my way."

"Why would I give you the boy? He stays with me."

"You have no use for him. I do. Give him to me. I'll be grateful, I might leave you a salve for that hand of yours." She nodded at his thumb, which was purple and swollen.

"I don't need your help," he said calmly. Taking an awl, he jabbed it into his thumbnail, releasing a spurt of blood. "That's better," he said. "Now get out."

Suddenly, Pirra pushed past Hylas and went to stand between the seer and the smith. "What are you arguing about?" she cried. "We all want the same thing!"

"Who's this?" said Akastos.

"She's my friend," said Hylas, "she—"

Pirra silenced him with a look. "Hekabi wants to get the Crows off her island," she told them. "Dameas wants his farm back."

Akastos shot Hylas another angry glance.

"And I," Pirra went on, "want to stop them invading Keftiu. Only Hylas wants to run away," she added with such scorn that he felt the heat surging up his throat. "So why are we arguing? We need to steal the dagger. We have a better chance of succeeding if we act together, not apart."

"Who *are* you?" repeated Akastos.

Pirra didn't reply. Her color was high, her scar livid on her cheek. She was half his size, but something in her bearing made up for that.

"She's right," said Hekabi. "And I know how we can do it."

Akastos folded his arms across his chest. "And you want

me to believe that you came up here armed with a plan, even though you had no idea we'd even meet?"

Hekabi smiled thinly. "I'm a seer, remember?"

Akastos studied her. "And in return for your plan?"

"You give me the boy."

"No one's giving me to anyone!" shouted Hylas.

Akastos glanced from Hekabi to Pirra. Then he opened the pouch at his belt, drew out a buckthorn leaf, and chewed. "I don't trust you," he told Hekabi, "and we'll see about your plan. But get me into the stronghold, and I'll do the rest."

Pirra and Hekabi had gone ahead, and had already reached the steps to the stronghold. Hylas craned his neck at the crows wheeling about it like flakes of black ash.

He felt sick with dread. Kreon was within those walls, along with his deadly brother and sister, Pharax and Alekto—and the High Chieftain himself. *Koronos.* The very name cast a shadow on the heart.

"Keep up," muttered Akastos. "And don't even think about trying to escape. Those overseers will have you down the pit faster than you can crack a whip." He was wearing his mask, and to prevent the Crows recognizing his voice, he'd given out that he'd scorched his throat in an accident. "That's why you're coming," he'd told Hylas. "You'll speak for me."

"*Please* don't make me," said Hylas for the tenth time. "If I go in there, I'll never come out."

"Yes you will."

"Someone will recognize me."

"Only Telamon knows what you look like, and you say he won't betray you."

Hylas made to protest, but they were passing a troop of Crow warriors, and Akastos shot him a warning glance.

Hylas was trapped, and all the signs were bad. The smoke pouring from the Mountain had thickened and turned gray. Even the sunset looked wrong, the sky a sickly yellow streaked with poisonous green. You didn't need to be a seer to know that this was going to be a disaster.

"On the first night of the Moon's dark," Hekabi had told them, "Koronos will seek to invoke the Angry Ones, drawing them to Thalakrea to subdue the Lady. The rite will be in three parts. First the sacrifice—that'll be secret— then the feast. Lastly, the reading of the smoke. I've made Kreon believe that for the feast, the meat of sacrifice must be burned on a special fire: one kindled here in the forge, and brought by the master smith himself."

So. The plan. Akastos and his slave Hylas would take the fire to Koronos, while Hekabi and *her* slave Pirra would help with the smoke-reading. At a sign from Akastos, Hekabi would pretend to throw a fit, thus distracting the Crows. Then, *somehow*, Akastos would steal the dagger, and *somehow*, they would all escape before the Crows discovered it was gone.

Hylas thought this plan had more holes than a fishing net, but he couldn't get Akastos to see that. At the last moment, though, the smith seemed to have had second thoughts, because he was bringing two of his mute slaves, bearing a large covered basket. When Hylas asked what was in it, Akastos was evasive. "Let's just say that if the wisewoman lets us down, I'll create a distraction of my own."

The steps to the stronghold were steep, and Akastos went in front. He wore leather gauntlets, and he carried a pottery bowl with a bronze one inside, which held embers from the forge. Hylas could see the tension in his shoulders. Hekabi had given him a pouch with a charm to disguise him from the Angry Ones; but he didn't put much faith in it. He was dreading an encounter with the spirits who had pursued him for so long.

Glancing down, Hylas was alarmed to see that already the mines lay far below. They were crawling with slaves, like an ant's nest smashed open. Kreon had ordered all tunnels cleared, and even deeper ones dug. There had been tremors. Everyone knew the Mountain was angry. But Kreon believed the Lady of Fire could be placated by force.

In a low voice, Hylas asked Akastos if he thought the Crows' rite would succeed in invoking the Angry Ones.

"It might," Akastos said grimly. "But if the Crows think they can gain their favor, they're wrong. No one gains the favor of the Angry Ones."

Hylas climbed on with his head down, breathing in the stink of carrion and a sulfurous whiff from the Mountain. He couldn't see how he was going to get out of this alive. And he was worried about Havoc. He'd left her tethered behind the smithy; if he didn't return, she would starve. But if, by some amazing stroke of luck, he found his way back to the smithy and met Telamon as planned, how could he carry a struggling lion cub down the cliff?

A sound above him, and he was startled to see Pirra on the next step. She was holding out a leather cap. "Your hair," she said. "The charcoal's wearing off."

"Oh. Thanks."

Side by side, they mounted the steps in silence. Pirra looked pale and tired. Hylas wondered if she'd slept as badly as he.

"Are you really going through with this?" she said in a low voice. "Are you really going to run away?"

He flushed. "Doesn't look like I'll get the chance, does it?"

"I mean, if this works and we . . . If this works."

"Then yes," he said curtly. "I'm really going through with it."

Her brow furrowed. "I thought you were *better* than this."

That hurt. "You'd do the same thing if you had a sister," he muttered.

"No I wouldn't."

"Oh no? What about that slave of yours—Userref? You said he's like a brother to you. Well what would you do if he was in danger and you could save him? What would you do, Pirra?"

She didn't reply.

They climbed on in prickly silence. Suddenly Pirra turned and put her hand on his shoulder. "Good-bye,

Hylas," she said in a strangled voice. "I hope you find your sister."

"Pirra, don't be—"

But she'd gone, running up the steps to join Hekabi.

Hylas didn't go after her. He felt churned up and *angry*. He didn't know if he was angry with Pirra or himself.

For a second time, Pirra passed through the gates of Kreon's stronghold, between the great stone walls twenty cubits thick. For a second time, her breath echoed clammily in the passages.

She wished Hekabi hadn't insisted on going ahead of the others. She kept thinking there must be *something* she could say to bring Hylas around. It wasn't possible that she'd just said good-bye to him forever.

A shadowy figure stepped from a doorway and grabbed her arm.

"Leave her alone," snapped Hekabi, "she's with me."

"She'll catch up with you," retorted Telamon. Barking at the guards to go on without them, he pulled Pirra into a windowless side-chamber lit by a sputtering torch.

"What do you want?" she spat as she twisted out of his grip.

"What are you *doing* here?" he demanded.

"I'm Hekabi's slave, remember? And in case you're thinking of telling them who I am, I wouldn't. Then we'd have to wed."

"I'd rather wed a leper."

"Then we agree on something," she said crisply, although she spoke with more assurance than she felt. Telamon was prowling the chamber. He looked frighteningly strong. She thought of her obsidian knife, which she'd strapped to her thigh, under her tunic. But he'd be on her before she could untie it.

"*Why* did he come?" he burst out.

"Don't worry," she said scornfully. "He'll meet you at the smithy, just like you planned."

His jaw dropped. "He told you about that?"

"He's my friend. He tells me things." She paused to let that sink in. "What about you?" she said in a hard voice. "Why are you helping him?"

A Crow warrior appeared in the doorway. "The High Chieftain is asking for you, my lord."

"Get out!" shouted Telamon. But Pirra saw the sweat beading his forehead.

He's scared, she thought. Scared of his own kin.

Despite herself, she felt a flicker of sympathy. She'd been frightened of her mother for as long as she could remember.

Telamon planted himself before her, clenching and unclenching his fists. She saw the muscles in his arms and shoulders. She stared past him, refusing to be threatened.

"I need to know what's happening," he said. "Look at me, Pirra. *Look* at me! Why is he really here, in the stronghold? Why tonight?"

She met his eyes. "Why don't you ask him?"

"The smith won't let me near him. If I insisted, I'd make people suspicious."

"There's nothing I can do about that."

With a snarl he punched the wall near her head, making her flinch. He was breathing hard, grinding his fist into the stone.

"Telamon," she said as calmly as she could, "let me go. I need to get back to the wisewoman."

For a moment he stared down at her and she stared back, determined to stand her ground.

"You asked why I'm helping him," he said quietly. "We were like brothers. He's the only friend I've ever had."

Me too, Pirra thought bleakly.

"If I do nothing, I betray him," Telamon went on. "If I help him, I betray my kin. But if I can just get him off the island, I'll be free of him forever. I'll never have to face this again."

"Do you really believe that?" said Pirra.

He threw her an agonized look. "*Why* is this happening? I never asked for any of it!"

"So what?" said Pirra. "I didn't ask to be bargained off by my mother like a jar of olives—"

"You're a girl, that's what you're for."

Her sympathy for him vanished. "It doesn't matter *why* it's happening," she said coldly. "What counts is what you do about it. Don't let him down."

He bristled. "Why would I?"

"Because you're a Crow."

"How dare you call me that! We're a proud and ancient clan!"

"And do you worship who they do?" she said. "Do you, Telamon?"

He swallowed. "No."

"Really? At your uncle's funeral pyre, I saw you smear your face with ash."

"That was out of respect for the dead."

"Then why are you here now, when they're going to invoke the Angry Ones?"

"That's nothing to do with me, I'm taking no part in it!"

"But you're not trying to stop them."

"How could I?" In the torchlight he was very hand-some, with his strong jaw and his dark, glittering eyes; but Pirra thought there was a softness to his upper lip.

She said, "I think you became friends with Hylas because he's strong and you're weak. I think, Telamon, that you'll always be weak."

He glared at her with sudden hatred. "And I think it's time we sent you back to Keftiu."

"If you did that, we'd have to—"

"Oh there'll be no match, I'll make sure of it. You'll be returned to your mother for her to punish as she sees fit." He took her arm in a grip that was painfully strong. "Come with me. There's someone you should see."

Two warriors marched toward Hylas and he flattened himself against the wall. As they swept past, he caught the creak of rawhide and the stink of ash. His belly clenched. He was in the very stronghold of the Crows.

Akastos and the slaves were somewhere behind. In front, he could see Hekabi—but no Pirra. Had she gone on ahead?

The way she'd looked at him . . . *I thought you were* better *than this*.

Hekabi halted before a doorway shrouded in red.

"Where's Pirra?" he whispered.

"Sh!" she hissed.

Akastos and the slaves caught up with them, then the guards drew back the hanging and pushed them inside.

The chamber was dimly lit by smoky lamps at either end. In the gloom, Hylas made out a window hidden by a screen, and on the wall, the pelt of an enormous lion; he guessed it was what remained of Havoc's father. In the middle of the chamber stood a great bronze tripod piled with unlit charcoal. The air crackled with the aftermath of sacrifice. A black arc across the rush-strewn floor showed where a carcass had been dragged away.

A shadowy woman circled the tripod, dipping her fingers in a small crystal bowl and flicking oil on the charcoal. Hylas couldn't see her face, but from Pirra's description, he guessed this was Alekto. She wore a robe of strange shimmering stuff as fine as spiders' webs. Gold clinked at her wrists and ankles, and in her hair nested a diadem of gold spikes.

A warrior squatted by the tripod, spearing chunks of flesh from a heap on the floor and laying them on the charcoal. This must be Pharax. He wore a plain tunic with a studded swordbelt across the chest, but he wasn't using his sword to spear the meat, he was using the dagger of Koronos. Hylas knew it even in the dark. He felt its call. Beside him, he heard Akastos catch his breath.

A third man emerged from the murk. Kreon wore a mantle of red wool and a headband of hammered gold, but he seemed ill at ease, his face slick with sweat. "Is that the fire?" he snapped.

"Yes, my lord," replied Hekabi.

"This had better work." He jerked his head at Akastos, who emptied the embers onto the tripod. The oil-soaked charcoal caught, and in the leaping light, the shadows of the Crows reared to the rafters.

Alekto circled Akastos and Hylas, trailing a sweet smell with an acrid undertow of ash. "Why does the smith wear a mask?" she asked coldly. She was young, and so beautiful that Hylas could hardly look at her; but her great dark eyes were as empty of feeling as two holes cut in marble.

Akastos nudged him in the ribs.

"A-an accident at the forge," he stammered. "Scars too dreadful to be seen."

Alekto shuddered. "Get him out of my sight, I loathe ugly things."

"The smith stays," snarled Kreon.

"Can't he speak for himself?" said Pharax, rising to his feet.

"The f-fire scorched his throat," said Hylas. "I must speak for him."

Pharax took that in silence. He was leaner than his brother, and far more frightening. There was a peculiar fixity to his stare, and his free hand was half clenched, as if to grasp an unseen weapon.

"Why is the wisewoman here?" said Alekto with a frown.

"I need her to read the smoke," said Kreon. "I have to know this has worked. Or to put it another way, Alekto, she's here because I wish it."

His sister gave him a mocking bow. "So masterful," she murmured.

Kreon glowered at her, and Pharax barked a laugh. He'd been cleaning the dagger with rushes, and now he laid it in a narrow chest of dark wood that stood on a bench behind the tripod. His hand lingered on the lid, as if he wanted to claim the dagger for his own.

Telamon ran in, mumbling an apology.

"You're late," growled Kreon.

Telamon saw Hylas and glanced away. "I'm sorry, Uncle," he said again.

"He was with a slave girl," taunted Alekto. "A scrawny one with a scar. Nephew, what taste!"

Pirra, thought Hylas. He threw Telamon a furious look, but Telamon gave a faint shake of the head. What did *that* mean?

"And will our nephew join us in the feast?" said Pharax with an edge to his voice.

"I doubt it," said Alekto, enjoying Telamon's discomfort. "He's only a boy, he can't take strong meat."

Strong meat, thought Hylas. What had they sacrificed?

Then Alekto saw someone in the doorway, and the mockery died on her lips. Pharax and Kreon stiffened, and the flames in the tripod seemed to sink.

An old man entered the chamber, attended by four terrified slaves. He wore the purple tunic and white goatskin mantle of the High Chieftain, secured at the shoulder by a gold cloakpin the size of a clenched fist. Age had silvered his beard and scraped the hair from his skull, but instead of weakening him, it had turned him to granite. Fear flowed in his wake, and like the wolf who leads the pack, he regarded no one, but gazed stonily over their heads.

Pharax, Kreon, and Alekto put their hands to their breasts and bowed. "Koronos," they murmured. Telamon did the same.

The slaves set down more benches covered with black

sheepskins, put vessels on a three-legged table, then fled. Kreon approached his father, but Koronos drove him back with a cut of his hand, and took his seat on the central bench.

Hekabi cast Akastos an anguished look. The High Chieftain sat directly in front of the chest that held the dagger. There was no point feigning a fit now, it might as well be at the bottom of the Sea.

"What do we do?" whispered Hylas.

"We wait," breathed Akastos.

On the tripod, the meat of sacrifice was turning black, hazing the air with bitter smoke.

Alekto took a pitcher and poured water over her father's hands, then dried them with a cloth. She was trembling, and she made sure not to touch his flesh with her own.

Pharax grasped a tall vessel of polished obsidian and filled an earthenware cup so fine the firelight glowed through it. The liquid was red and thick: Hylas guessed it was blood and wine. With pounding heart, he watched Koronos drink. Hooded eyes like a lizard's. A slow pale tongue that slid out to lick a lipless mouth.

Kreon offered the High Chieftain a bronze platter of burned meat, and he ate one morsel. His fingernails were stained black and cut to points, and on his thumb he wore a ring of gray metal; Hylas guessed this was iron. "Now you, grandson," he said stonily.

The others waited.

Telamon licked his lips. He reached for a piece of meat and put it in his mouth.

Koronos nodded once, then ordered his sons and daughter to eat.

The Crows seated themselves and fell on the burned meat, snatching chunks and snapping it up with their sharp black talons. Hylas saw grease glinting in Kreon's beard, and a fleck of charred skin caught between Alekto's white teeth.

Again the High Chieftain drank, then flung the cup to the floor, shattering it to pieces. Hekabi had said that Koronos only used new vessels, and only ever once.

Hylas must have flinched at the noise, because Koronos saw him. Hylas bowed his head. He felt the lizard gaze sweep over him with the force of lightning. He swayed. This man had decreed the slaughter of all Outsiders. Because of him, Issi was missing, maybe dead . . .

A strong hand gripped his shoulder, and Akastos breathed in his ear: "Soon. I'll tell you what to say."

The Crows were daubing their cheeks with ash. The feast was over. It was time to read the smoke, to tell if the rite had worked.

With his sword, Pharax struck the bronze bowl that had held the embers, making it sing. Alekto began to chant, circling the tripod and crushing hemlock beneath her glistening feet.

Koronos rose and held his hands palms upward over the tripod.

Still chanting, Alekto took the obsidian vessel and poured a red stream over her father's hands and onto the charcoal, raising hissing clouds of smoke. The liquid that touched his fingertips was for the gods, that flowing between his fingers for the Ancestors, and that in his palms—which was most of it—was for the spirits whose true names not even Koronos dared utter aloud: the Angry Ones.

The vessel was empty, and Alekto withdrew. Koronos leaned forward, breathing the smoke. Hekabi moved closer, to read the signs.

In the silence, Hylas heard the crackle of embers and the whisper of breath. He clutched the lion claw on his chest. Beside him, Akastos gripped the pouch that held Hekabi's charm.

The lamps flickered and died. Now only the glimmer from the tripod held back the dark. The hairs on Hylas' arms rose. His flesh went cold.

Suddenly a fierce wind gusted through the window. The screen fell with a crash. Hylas sank to his knees. As the wind whirled around the chamber, he saw a deeper darkness: vast winged shadows that froze his heart with dread. He screwed his eyes shut, but he could still see them, their nightmare heads burned black by the fires of Chaos, their raw red mouths like gaping wounds . . .

Then they were gone, obliterating the stars as they sped toward the Mountain.

At last he opened his eyes.

The smoke had cleared. In the ember-glow, he saw Hekabi standing aghast. "It worked," she gasped. "They've come."

Telamon looked appalled. Kreon wiped the sweat off his

brow. Pharax beat his chest with his fist in triumph, and Koronos' stony grip tightened on his knees.

"Didn't you hear me?" Akastos whispered to Hylas. "Tell them what I just said! *Now!* It's our chance!"

But Hylas couldn't move, he was still frozen with dread.

With a snarl, Akastos pushed him aside. "Dameas the smith," he croaked in a hoarse whisper, "brings Koronos a gift to honor his triumph over the Lady of Fire." Then he withdrew into the shadows, and his slaves stepped forward. The Crows turned toward them, watching intently as they set down the covered basket before the tripod and pulled off the cloth.

Telamon gave a start, and the children of Koronos peered at the smith's gift. The High Chieftain didn't stir.

With a cry, Hylas sprang forward, but Hekabi held him back. "Hush!" she whispered in his ear. "Don't draw attention to yourself!"

The cage was so cramped that Havoc couldn't turn around. Her muzzle was bound with a strip of rawhide to keep her quiet, and she was shaking with terror.

Kreon glanced at Hekabi. "What do we do with it?"

Hylas saw the hard cruel faces bent on Havoc's cage. He felt Hekabi's fingers digging into his shoulders. "That's for you to decide, my lord," she said.

Kreon licked his lips.

Pharax went to the chest and lifted the lid. Firelight glinted redly on the dagger of Koronos. "It's a sacrifice," he said. "We kill it, of course."

33

"Go on, stick a knife in it," said Alekto, "that's your answer to everything."

"What's yours?" retorted Pharax.

Hylas couldn't stand it any longer. "The smith says it's got to stay alive!" he blurted out, ignoring Hekabi's startled glance.

"Why?" demanded Pharax. He'd raised the lid of the chest and was clearly keen to make use of the dagger.

"It—it belongs to Kreon," stammered Hylas. "It was found on his land."

Kreon's eyes glinted, and Pharax scowled. "So?"

Hylas thought fast. "So it must stay alive because—as it grows stronger, so shall the House of Koronos grow stronger. Like the Lion of Mycenae, only greater."

Kreon liked that. He cast his brother a triumphant look.

"Also it's female," Alekto added drily, "which means it's a better hunter than the male."

Koronos rose and signed to Pharax to shut the chest. "It lives," he declared.

In a daze, Hylas watched the High Chieftain leave

the chamber, followed by the others, Pharax bearing the chest in his arms, and the slaves hurrying behind with Havoc's cage. Hylas saw the lion cub trying in vain to turn her head and keep him in view. Then she was gone, and Akastos was dragging him out into the passage.

It was nearly midnight. Hylas quickened his pace. The furnace ridge was dark, except for the glare of watchfires, and the guards had let him through, as he was slave to the smith.

But where *was* the smith?

He'd been with them as they'd emerged from the stronghold. Then Hekabi had declared that she wasn't leaving without her slave, and had argued with the guards until Pirra was brought out, shaken but unhurt. After that, they'd made their way down the steps in the dark; then suddenly Hekabi and Pirra had headed off for the village, and Hylas was alone: Akastos was gone.

The wind roared over the headland and rattled the branches of the thorn tree. The door of the smithy stood ajar, casting a slab of yellow light across the ground. Hylas saw Havoc's paw prints in the dust, and her beloved wicker ball. His throat closed.

Akastos sat on his stool by the forge, calmly sharpening a blade on a whetstone. He was intent on his work, and didn't raise his head at Hylas' approach.

"*Why?*" cried Hylas.

Akastos sighed. "I'm sorry, Flea. I needed to distract them."

"But *Hekabi* was going to do that!"

"You think they'd have been fooled by some madwoman throwing a fit?" Holding up the blade, he scrutinized it with narrowed eyes. "It worked better than I'd hoped, thanks to you. You think fast, Flea, I'm impressed. What you told them saved that cub's life."

"And because of you, her life will be a miserable one in that terrible place!"

"Better than no life at all."

"Is that all you can say?" He wanted to rage and shout and fight: to do *something,* not just stand there and watch Akastos coolly passing the blade over the whetstone in long, sure strokes.

"I'm sorry," Akastos said again. "But I've been waiting too long to let pity get in my way."

"Don't you care about anything? Don't you even care that you couldn't steal your precious dagger?"

Akastos did not reply.

Hylas opened his mouth to berate him—then shut it. He saw the red gleam of firelight on the bronze knife in Akastos' hands. He took in its broad square shoulders and its strong straight spine sweeping down to a lethal point. He saw the three rivets on the hilt, and the quartered circle incised on the blade. A chariot wheel to crush the enemies of the House of Koronos.

"You did steal it," he said.

Akastos flicked him a glance.

"But—I *saw* it in the chest. I saw Pharax shut the lid and take it with him."

"You saw *a* dagger," said Akastos.

Everything fell into place.

"You made a copy," said Hylas. "You swapped them." His mind flew back to the moment when the slaves had uncovered Havoc's cage. Akastos had withdrawn into the shadows, and after that, Hylas hadn't seen him. Nor had the Crows. All eyes had been on Havoc. "But—they searched us going into the stronghold. How did you get the copy past the guards?"

Akastos snorted. "I know a thing or two about smuggling weapons. Unlike those idiots at the gates."

Outside, the wind moaned in the thorn tree. Hylas thought he heard hoofbeats in the distance.

Akastos had heard them too. Gripping the dagger, he moved noiselessly to the doorway and took up position behind it. He was no longer a smith, but a warrior trained to kill.

The hoofbeats came closer. It had to be Telamon.

Akastos too was listening intently.

Hylas went cold.

Two things I've swore to do before I die, Akastos had told him. *Destroy the dagger of Koronos—and appease my brother's ghost.*

How can you appease a ghost? Hylas had asked.

By feeding him the blood of vengeance.

The blood of vengeance.

The lifeblood of a highborn Crow.

"No," said Hylas. "I won't let you kill Telamon."

"He's the grandson of Koronos," said Akastos.

"He was my friend."

"He's a Crow."

Hylas planted himself in the doorway. "I won't let you kill him."

"Don't get in the way, Flea. I don't want to hurt you."

Hylas didn't move. He had no weapons, the Crows had taken them, while Akastos had the dagger and was a grown man twice his size.

"Out of my way, Flea," said the smith with an odd pleading note. "Don't make me do this!"

The hoofbeats came nearer.

Hylas turned to shout a warning, but Akastos lunged at him and clapped his hand over his mouth. Hylas bit hard. Akastos didn't let go. Hylas hooked his leg around Akastos' knee, trying to throw him off his feet. It didn't work, but Akastos lost his balance and staggered against the forge, dragging Hylas with him. Blindly, Hylas reached behind him, grabbed a burning brand from the fire and lashed out. Akastos hissed as it bit his calf, and for an instant his grip loosened and Hylas wriggled free.

"*Telamon!*" he shouted at the top of his lungs. "*Get out of here! Danger!*"

The hoofbeats skittered to a halt.

Clenching his teeth in pain, Akastos sprang at Hylas, who dodged behind the forge. They circled, now this way, now that.

"*Telamon go back!*" yelled Hylas. "*He's going to kill you!*"

Akastos lunged. Again Hylas dodged. It was a feint: Akastos nearly caught him.

"*Get out of here!*" shouted Hylas. "*He's not after me, he's after you!*"

The horse squealed, and he pictured Telamon yanking its head around. Then the hoofbeats went thundering down the slope and faded into the night.

Still Hylas and the smith faced each other across the smoldering fire. Akastos was breathing hard: The brand had scorched an angry wound down his calf. Grimacing with pain, he lurched against the wall and sank to the ground. "You *fool*," he gasped.

Hylas fetched the water pail and a jar of almond oil, set them within reach, then retreated. "I'm sorry I hurt you," he said. "But I couldn't let you kill him."

Akastos leaned back and shut his eyes. "*Sorry,*" he repeated. "What good to me is 'sorry'? Can I forge it into a weapon to kill Koronos? Can I make it into a chariot to ride against them?" He banged his head against the wall. "Fourteen years I've been on the run. Hiding. Plotting. Failing. Starting again." His forehead glistened with sweat. A vein stood out in his neck like rope. "This was the closest I've ever got. Everything would have ended tonight. I would have been *free*. If it hadn't been for you."

Hylas twisted his hands. "But you still have the dagger. We can destroy it right now, in the forge!"

Akastos opened his eyes and glared at him. "Do you think it's that easy?" he said as he struggled to his feet. "*Do you think it's that easy?*" he roared. "Then why didn't I do it the moment I got back here? *Why?* Because no forge made by mortal men will ever be hot enough to destroy it! Because the dagger of Koronos can only be destroyed by a *god*!"

34

Dawn was still far off, but the sky was aglow with a strange dark angry red. As Hylas ran down from the furnace ridge, the Mountain loomed into view. Smoke no longer seeped from its summit, but rose in giant plumes to touch the sky—and it was lit from beneath by the same furious red.

He thought of the Angry Ones doing battle with the Lady of Fire. Anger, all was anger.

Akastos had raged like a lion when he'd realized that he was too badly hurt to destroy the dagger. Then quite suddenly, he'd mastered himself. He'd trickled oil on his burn, and sent away the guards who'd come running at the uproar. He'd told Hylas to pour him a beaker of wine. Then, shockingly, he'd laughed.

"Well, well, Flea. It seems that you and the gods have done for me again."

Draining the beaker, he'd wiped his mouth on the back of his hand. Then he'd astonished Hylas by tossing him the dagger. "Take it. Find the wisewoman. She'll know how to destroy it."

It had fit Hylas' grip as if it was made for him, and as he'd rearranged his fingers on the hilt, he'd felt a jolt of cold power shoot through him. "There'll be guards on the way to the village," he'd said. "How will I get past them?"

Akastos had taken a lump of clay the size of a walnut, and stamped it with his sealstone. "The smith's mark, it'll give you safe passage. There. You hold your life in your hand. Mine too. Don't fail."

In the Moonless dark, Hylas made for the crossroads. On the cliffs, seabirds were flying up. Distractedly, he thought how odd this was; seabirds always roosted at night.

The dagger in its sheath bumped against his hip. Akastos had made him hide it under a scrap of sacking, but it still gave Hylas a heady sense of invincibility: as if he, not Akastos, had drunk that wine.

He hated it. The dagger had separated him from Pirra, and sliced through his plan for escape. It had severed his hopes of finding Issi.

He thought of his brave, fierce, reckless little sister, struggling for survival in the wilds of Messenia. "I'm sorry, Issi," he told her under his breath. "Turns out I can't come and find you. Not yet. Not till this is over." It flashed through his mind that if Issi knew what he was doing, maybe she would forgive him—because in his place, she would do the same thing.

On the hill, Kreon's stronghold was ablaze with torches. Had they discovered that the dagger was gone?

He drew it from its sheath, and in the starlight its edges gleamed faintly scarlet, as if stained with blood. Despite the heat of the night, he shivered. He wondered if the dagger knew that he was bent on ending its life.

But how *could* he, when it could only be destroyed by a god? Would even Hekabi know what to do?

Across the plain, the Mountain went on venting that angry smoke. Hylas thought of the fire spirits in their lairs: lairs that tunneled deep into its burning heart.

And suddenly he knew how to destroy the dagger.

Across the plain, the smoke rising from the Mountain was weirdly tinged with red.

"It looks angry," said Pirra.

"*She* is angry," corrected Hekabi. "The Crows have sent the spirits of air and darkness against Her. She will vanquish them. But She won't forgive."

The wisewoman was angry too. In bristling silence they'd picked their way down from the stronghold and started for the village. They had failed to steal the dagger, and by now Hylas would have fled the island, taking with him their chance of defeating the Crows.

But halfway along the trail, Hekabi had halted. "It isn't over. I can feel it. We've got to go back."

So once again, they were nearing the crossroads. In the starlight, Pirra saw the silent ponds where she'd first encountered Hylas, it felt like months ago.

She had railed at him for putting his sister before everything, and he'd said, *If Userref was in danger and you could save him, what would you do?*

Well, now she knew.

"There's someone you should see," Telamon had snarled as he'd dragged her off to another chamber in the stronghold. Then he'd left her to face the man who waited inside.

At first she didn't recognize him. He was richly dressed as an emissary of Keftiu: a fine green cloak and a braided blue kilt cinched with a belt of gilded calfskin. On his chest, along with the familiar eye amulet, hung a wax tablet mounted in lapis lazuli and bore the seal of High Priestess Yassassara.

Being Userref, the first thing he did was scold. "Pirra, *look* at you! Dressed like a peasant, hair far too short—and your *feet*, they're filthy!"

"I've missed you," she said simply. But when he stepped toward her, she put up her hands. "It's no use, Userref. I can't go back."

"You must," he said gently.

"This isn't about being free anymore, it's more than that now." She dared not mention the dagger in case they were overheard, but in an undertone she told him about the Crows invading Keftiu.

To her astonishment, he already knew. "The High Priestess has known for months. Part of my mission is to learn more."

"She *knows?*"

"Pirra, when will you learn? The High Priestess knows everything."

She struggled to take that in. "I still can't go with you."

"You *must*," said Userref in an altered voice.

Then he told her. Yassassara was clever. *Bring back my daughter, or you forfeit your life.*

Pirra stood facing this gentle young man who'd cared for her since she was a baby. "I can't," she said again.

"Pirra. For me."

"But—you can run away too! Now's your chance! Go to Egypt, find your family, you've always longed to! You can be *free*!"

In the torchlight, his handsome face became stern. "How can I ignore the will of the gods? They made me a slave, they sent me to Keftiu. I have to return, no matter what."

She didn't know what to do. Right now, the others were trying to steal the dagger; she should be helping them.

"Come with me," urged Userref.

Things had happened quickly after that. With a cry she'd fled the chamber, stumbling through a maze of torchlit passages, trying in vain to find the others. Then, somehow, she'd fetched up at the gates—and found Hekabi clamoring for her release.

Seagulls wheeled above the crossroads, calling in the dark, and Hekabi hissed at her to hurry.

What would you do, Pirra? Hylas had asked.

Well, now she knew. She was just as ruthless as her mother. She had condemned Userref to death.

And in the end, it had been for nothing, because the plan had failed. The Crows still had the dagger. And Hylas was gone.

Without warning, Hekabi grabbed her arm and yanked her behind a thornbush. "Someone's coming!" she breathed.

A figure was approaching the crossroads. Pirra watched it whip off its cap and wipe its brow. She saw the starlight gleam in its fair hair.

She stepped out from behind the thorns. "You didn't leave," she said.

Pirra looked very pale, and she was staring at him as if he was a ghost. "I thought you'd left," she said. "I thought—"

"No time to explain," he cut in. Then to the wise-woman: "We've got to take it to the Mountain, yes?"

She didn't reply. She was transfixed by what he held in his fist. "Is that . . ."

"Yes," he said impatiently.

"The *dagger*," gasped Pirra. "How did—"

"Let's just say Akastos is a better thief than we thought. Hekabi, the Mountain. That's what we've got to do, isn't it? Find the lair of a fire spirit and throw it in; then the Lady will destroy it."

Hekabi clutched his wrist. "And it must be you who does it."

"Of course," said Pirra. "*An Outsider wields the blade and the House of Koronos burns . . .*"

"And then at last," said Hekabi, "Thalakrea will be free."

Hylas glanced at the dagger in his fist. He didn't like the way things were coming together. He was being pushed around by forces beyond his power to understand.

In the starlight, he made out great flocks of crows cawing in alarm around Kreon's stronghold. He had the uneasy feeling that somehow, they were part of it too. But how? What was he missing?

"We've got to hurry," said Hekabi. "There's no telling when they'll find out it's gone."

Pirra snapped her fingers. "Horses! They keep them at the Neck, if we could steal some . . ."

Hylas didn't move. He was watching the gulls and the crows cutting across the stars.

"Hylas?" said Pirra. "What is it?"

He thought of the wild creatures who'd been acting so oddly: the mice fleeing the deep levels, the birds who should have been roosting but weren't, the frogs who'd disappeared from the ponds. In his dream, Issi had tried to warn him. *Where are the frogs, Hylas? Where are the frogs?*

He thought of the blood spurting from Akastos' swollen thumb, and of that blasted spur on the Mountainside, which bulged as if something vast was trying to force its way out . . .

Then he knew. Kreon had dug too deep, and the Lady of Fire was angrier than anyone imagined.

He turned to Pirra. "It's going to blow up."

"What is?" she replied.

"Thalakrea."

35

"It's not true," Hekabi said fiercely. "The Mountain's been angry before—but She would never destroy Her own people!" Her arms were tightly crossed, as if to keep out the dreadful suspicion that Hylas might be right.

Pirra felt wrenchingly sorry for her, because she knew that he was. "The red river swallows Thalakrea," she said.

He shot her a glance.

"I just remembered. Hekabi said it when she was in a trance."

"I say lots of things in a trance," spat Hekabi, "that doesn't make them true! We *know* the Lady of Fire, we've worshipped Her for thousands of years!"

"The Crows haven't," cut in Hylas. Swiftly, he told her about the restlessness he'd observed in the wild creatures at the mines. When she brushed that aside, he described the bulge in the Mountainside.

At that, the spirit seemed to go out of her. She was shaking her head, but Pirra could see that the truth was sinking in.

"Hekabi," said Pirra. "Your people need you more than ever."

Hekabi stared at her in a daze of shock.

"Go to your village," Hylas told her. "Warn them, warn the slaves at the mines. Tell them to get off the island!" Then to Pirra, "You too, you go with her."

"No! I'm going with you, you can't do this on your own."

"Yes I can, there's no sense in your staying."

"Hylas, if we can find just one of those fiery cracks and throw in the dagger, we can be back at the village before the last boat leaves!"

"Like I said, there's no sense in your staying—"

"And like *I* said, yes there is, because *you* don't know the way to the village."

He chewed his lip. "Come on, we're wasting time."

⚍

The Mountain was spewing columns of smoke that towered above the plain. Lightning split the darkness. The horse squealed, nearly bucking them off.

Hylas clung to handfuls of mane and dug in his heels. He smelled the beast's terror, and felt Pirra clinging to his waist. He strained for the sound of hoofbeats behind them. So far, nothing.

Thanks to Akastos' seal and a story about making an offering to the Mountain, Pirra had talked the guards at the Neck into letting her through, and while she distracted them, Hylas had sneaked into the horse pen and stolen a mount. Now its hooves struck sparks off the obsidian trail as it flew across the plain, and the Mountain loomed closer with astonishing speed.

They reached the edge of the thickets and slid off to let the horse catch its breath. Pirra had persuaded the guards to give her a waterskin, and they both took a pull; but when she poured some into Hylas' hands for the horse, it shied, too frightened to drink.

"Not much farther," he told it, stroking its neck.

Lightning flashed and thunder rumbled. Hylas and Pirra exchanged glances. The Lady of Fire had woken the Earthshaker, and now She was calling on the Sky Father too: Commanding both Her immortal brothers to help fight the Angry Ones, and rid Her of these upstart mortals who'd been gnawing at Her innards.

From where they stood, the Mountain's flanks were dark with broom. Pirra pointed to a shadowy outcrop just above the thickets. "I remember those rocks; weren't there fire spirits just beyond?"

"That's good," said Hylas, "they're closer than I thought."

The horse sidestepped and rolled its eyes, but he managed to scramble back on. As he pulled Pirra up behind him, the earth shook and the obsidian trail heaved like a snake. The horse reared—flung them off—and galloped into the murk.

Hylas got to his feet, and saw Pirra rubbing her elbow. "You all right?"

She nodded. "You still got the dagger?"

He gripped the hilt.

The earth's growls died away. The smoke venting from

the summit thinned, and a weird calm descended. The Mountain was holding Her breath.

The obsidian trail cut a swathe through the thicket, which made climbing much easier, and they emerged above the broom sooner than they'd expected. Hylas cast about him in the eerie red glimmer. No crusted yellow rocks, no hissing cracks. This part of the Mountain had utterly changed.

"Where have they gone?" said Pirra.

He shook his head. The fire spirits had fled. In Pirra's eyes, he saw his own dread. What if they couldn't find any?

She jerked her head at the summit. "There were lots farther up."

He didn't reply. What was that pattering? Something was falling from the sky: softly, like gray snow. But it was *hot*.

Pirra coughed. Her dark hair was speckled with gray. Hylas picked a flake off her shoulder. "It's ash," he said.

She motioned him to silence.

Through the pattering of the ash, he heard it too. Many hooves clattering on obsidian. The Crows.

Together they raced higher, but soon reached a dead end. A landslide had buried the trail. Above them, steep slopes of black rock gleamed in the weird red light.

"We'll have to climb," muttered Hylas.

He'd scarcely started when Pirra yanked him sideways. A heartbeat later, a giant slab of rock broke off and slid over where he'd been standing.

They watched it crash into the thickets and disintegrate in clouds of dust.

Pirra broke a chunk from the slope and crumbled it in her fingers with startling ease. "It's not stone," she said in disbelief. "It's sand. How can we climb sand?"

Hylas craned his neck. If that slope came down on them, they'd be buried alive—or sent hurtling to the plain. But the hoofbeats were gaining on them. "We'll have to try," he said.

To spread the load, they separated. Hylas took a step up. His foot sank and slid, sending sand hissing down the slope. He waited till it had settled, then tried again. This time, he managed to climb a little higher. He went on sinking and sliding, climbing with nightmar-ish slowness. He saw a boulder jutting from the sand, and hauled himself onto it. He saw Pirra do the same. From there, he worked sideways to a patch that looked firmer . . . And still the ash fell, speckling the slopes with deathly gray.

At last he reached a ridge of solid rock. He hauled him-self over and lay gasping. Pirra had reached it too, she was on her knees not far off. They were back on the obsidian trail.

But where were the fire spirits?

"They *can't* be much farther," panted Pirra.

Hylas lurched to his feet and started up the trail.

They hadn't gone far when it came to an abrupt end. They had reached the summit. Only here it wasn't a knife edge, it was ten paces wide, and jagged with huge black boulders like broken teeth. Peering between them, Hylas glimpsed the far side of the crater, and the bulging spur. It had swelled to a huge canker, and was spewing smoke. When it burst, it would destroy Thalakrea.

"Where are the fire spirits?" cried Pirra.

Hylas tried to reply but his mouth had gone dry.

Between the giant teeth, he could see down into the crater, and it was no longer a cauldron of cold gray stone, but a blinding red glare. He felt its heat, he saw how it heaved and rocked, spattering the sides with liquid flame.

The hollow heart of the Mountain had become a lake of fire.

Pirra came to stand at his shoulder, and he heard the hiss of her breath. "Throw it in," she said. "Forget about the fire spirits, the Lady will destroy it!"

She was right. But first he had to reach the crater's edge, and to do that he had to find a way between the giant teeth.

They were clustered too tight, he couldn't get through.

"Maybe I can do it from here," he said, drawing the dagger from its sheath. If he threw with all his strength, it might clear the boulders.

Behind him, Pirra cried out.

He glanced over his shoulder, but she wasn't there anymore.

"Don't move!" shouted a voice.

Telamon stood five paces away, legs braced, arrow nocked to his bow. "One move," he said, "and you're dead."

36

"Where's Pirra!" shouted Hylas.

An arrow struck the ground by his foot, forcing him sideways. "I kept my word to you!" Telamon yelled. "I had a boat waiting!"

"And I would have gone, but I had to warn you, he was going to kill you!"

Another arrow thudded into the dust. Again he leaped sideways.

"You're making that up," snarled Telamon. "You just needed time to destroy the dagger! Throw it over here!"

In the red glare they faced each other, while the Mountain shook and the ash hissed down like poisonous snow.

Telamon was clever: Hylas saw how he'd been driving him with his arrows away from the rocks. Now he was too far from the crater; if he tried to cast the dagger from here, it would clatter harmlessly to the ground.

"I will do it," said Telamon, taking aim at his heart.

Hylas rearranged his grip on the hilt. A few paces to his

left, a clump of boulders offered cover and maybe a way through to the crater's edge.

"No," he said.

Telamon's arrow trembled. "Hylas. Throw me the dagger." His features were set, but his voice shook. "It belongs to *us*! It's got nothing to do with you!"

"Or Issi? Or Scram? Or all the Outsiders the Crows have slaughtered? They're evil, Telamon. This ends here!"

Telamon's face worked. "They're my *kin*!" His arrow sang as Hylas leaped for the boulders, and he heard it strike the rock a hand's breadth behind him.

"*Coward!*" roared Telamon. "Come out and fight!"

Hylas scrambled between the rocks. Spotted a gap. Too narrow, he couldn't squeeze through . . .

"Hylas, above you!" screamed Pirra from somewhere he couldn't see.

Glancing up, he saw Telamon crouching on a boulder and reaching into his quiver for another arrow. Hylas turned sideways and forced himself through the gap, shot out the other side, and landed on his knees.

A thud behind him. Telamon had jumped down. Ahead of them, more rocks were wreathed in smoke. As Hylas lurched to his feet, the fumes blew hot in his face, engulfing him in the choking breath of the Mountain. He heard Telamon coughing. Then the smoke sucked back and he saw it, just beyond the rocks: the throbbing red glare of the abyss. He drew back his arm . . .

"*No!*" screamed Telamon.

. . . Hylas threw the dagger as hard as he could.

Time stopped as it flashed over the rocks—struck the last one—and clanged to rest on the edge.

Hylas stared in disbelief.

Telamon's jaw dropped.

The dagger of Koronos refused to be destroyed.

The rocks sloped steeply down to where it lay on a boulder that jutted over the crater like a broken fang. Hylas started toward it, pebbles rattling past him to the burning lake far below.

A hand grabbed his shoulder and hauled him back. He hit the ground with a thud and Telamon was on him, crushing the breath from his chest. Hylas tried to squirm free, but Telamon was too strong. Grabbing Hylas' hair in one hand, he drew his knife with the other. Hylas gripped his wrist with both hands and fought to keep the point from his throat. It came steadily closer. With a supreme effort, he boosted himself sideways with his legs, bucking off Telamon and knocking the knife from his hand. It clattered across the stones and Telamon lunged for it—but Hylas seized his long locks and dragged him out of reach.

Still holding Telamon by the hair, Hylas bashed his head against the ground, but Telamon dug both thumbs into his throat, cutting off his air. Hylas clawed at his hands. Telamon kneed him in the belly, then flipped him over and knelt on his upper arms. Hylas felt the grip tighten on his throat. Black dots darting before his eyes, hot ash raining into his mouth, everything going black . . .

Telamon howled in pain and rolled off his chest.

⸺

Pirra saw Hylas taking great heaving gulps of air. She saw Telamon clutching his thigh in disbelief as she scrambled away.

She staggered, nearly dropping his knife. She was still dizzy from the blow he'd struck her earlier, but if she could distract him for long enough, Hylas might be able to get to the dagger.

"Call yourself a warrior?" she sneered. "Squealing like a girl at a pinprick like that?"

Still on his knees, Telamon swayed. Blood trickled between the fingers clamped to his thigh. Squinting in pain, he looked from her to Hylas, who was making his way down toward the dagger.

"Coward!" taunted Pirra, waving Telamon's knife in his face.

Suddenly he stiffened. Pirra glanced behind her. The insults died in her throat.

Out of the whirling smoke came a man, a warrior in black rawhide armor. Swift as a lynx, Pharax raced down the rocks, flung Hylas aside with one thrust of his hand, and snatched the dagger from the brink.

Hylas lost his balance and slid off the boulder.

Pirra rushed to help him, but Telamon grabbed her and yanked her back.

In triumph Pharax held up the dagger of Koronos, its blade flashing scarlet in the glare. At his feet, Hylas clung desperately to the edge.

"Kill him, Pharax!" shouted Telamon. "He's the Outsider in the prophecy!"

Pirra struggled and kicked, but Telamon was too strong. In horror, she watched Hylas fight to haul himself back onto the boulder. She saw Pharax towering over him. She heard his cold voice ringing out above the thunder of the Mountain:

"If an Outsider wields the dagger, the House of Koronos burns . . . But if *Pharax* wields the dagger—it's the Outsider who burns."

With his heel, he stamped on Hylas' hands.

"*No!*" screamed Pirra.

But Hylas was gone.

37

He was falling through scorching red smoke: bouncing off rock-faces, clawing at stones that snapped off in his hands. Then the Mountain punched him in the back and he wasn't falling anymore.

The air was black and bitter with ash. His eyes stung and every breath hurt. He felt battered and scraped—but he could move.

Coughing, he rolled onto his knees. Beneath his palms the earth was restless and hot. At any moment it might open up and swallow him. Lightning speared boiling clouds of ash. Fireballs hissed through the air, striking the ground around him.

Craning his neck at the crater wall, he saw the edge, dizzyingly high above. Behind him, not twenty paces away, lay the heaving red chaos of the burning lake. Its heat blasted him. He heard it thickly bubbling, spurting jets of liquid fire that netted the darkness with dazzling scarlet, before spattering back into the crater.

If it spattered him, he was dead.

Through the murk, he made out a small hillock of

cinders at the foot of the crater wall. He stumbled toward it. It wasn't very tall, but when he'd scrambled to the top, the stink was slightly less biting.

To his surprise, he still had his lion claw around his neck, and this heartened him a little. At his belt, he found the rag that Akastos had given him to hide the dagger. He tied it over his mouth and nose—and breathed a bit easier.

The crater wall sloped outward like a giant cauldron, but as he groped for handholds, it crumbled in his fingers. He tried again and again. The truth sank in. He wasn't going to be able to climb out.

Is this how it ends? he thought hazily. The Crows keep the dagger, and it was all for nothing?

Then across the burning lake, he made out the cankerous bulge. It had grown so huge that it thrust like a hunchback above the crater's edge. It came to Hylas that the dagger didn't *matter* anymore, because when that burst, everyone on Thalakrea would be killed.

Strangely, he felt no fear, only a weird kind of peace. Now that the worst was happening, there was no more dread.

Then he thought of Zan and Bat and Periphas, and all the other slaves. Hekabi and the Islanders. Akastos and Havoc and Pirra. Anger flared within him. They didn't deserve to die.

Lurching to his feet, he stood swaying on his hillock of cinders. "Why punish us all?" he croaked. "*We're* not Crows! We didn't *do* anything!"

The Mountain growled, spattering the rocks around him with liquid fire.

"What do I care?" he shouted. "I'm going to die anyway!"

The Mountain roared—and Hylas roared back. "I did *everything* I could! I gave the deep levels back to the snatchers! I saved Havoc—one of *your* creatures! I did my best to destroy the dagger—but *you* stopped me, *you* did! What more do you *want*?"

Lightning flared, the Mountain shook, and Hylas thought it was the end.

Then, abruptly, the roars sank to a rumble. The lightning died. The cankerous bulge stopped venting smoke.

Hylas sank to his knees. "What do you *want*?" he panted.

The liquid fire ceased to bubble and spurt, but now its glowing heart began to heave. The air quivered with the presence of an immortal.

And from the blazing lake rose the Lady of Fire.

———

She walked in a crackling glare of light, and Her burning shadow seethed behind Her. Her floating hair trailed filaments of flame, and Her face was more terrible than a thousand Suns.

Hylas knelt on the hillock with his arms across his eyes. "Please," he gasped. "Let the people get away!"

She turned toward him and he felt the full blast of Her gaze. *And in return?* Her voice rushed through him like a forest fire.

He clutched the lion claw. "T-take me," he stammered.
Fiery laughter engulfed him. *I already have!*

"Let the others get away. Just give them time!"

Though his eyes were shut, he felt Her stoop over him, dripping fire. He didn't dare look, but in his head, he saw Her bright hair blazing in the black air. He tasted Her bitter breath as she reached down to him. He cried out in pain as She touched his temple with one searing finger.

The fire gives . . . whispered the Lady. *And the fire takes . . .*

With a jolt, his wits returned. His head throbbed where the Shining One had touched him—but She was gone. Again, thunder crashed and lightning speared the clouds. The cankerous bulge vented smoke, and liquid fire spurted from the lake.

Something shifted painfully in his chest, and everything changed. He could hear the snatchers far away, burrowing under the earth, and every particle of ash pattering onto the Mountainside. On the lake, he glimpsed figures as insubstantial as flame. He heard their high thin voices and saw their fierce, inhuman faces.

This must be death, he thought, and those are the fire spirits coming to get me.

And yet—his bruises still hurt, and he could still taste the gritty bitterness of ash, so he must be alive.

As he squinted at the burning lake, a small, bright ball of flame that didn't feel frightening detached itself from the fire spirits and bounded toward him.

In her sleep, the lion cub wasn't caught by the bad humans in the horrible cramped tangle of branches.

In her sleep, she was sleek and strong, hurtling as fast as a full-grown lioness: up the Mountain and down into its fiery belly. In her sleep, she was racing to help the boy.

He was stuck, and he couldn't climb out. It was just like the time when she'd been stuck down the hole—only now it was *her* turn to help *him*.

Fast as a flame, she left the fire spirits on the burning lake and bounded toward him. She felt amazingly sure of herself: She knew exactly where to place each paw, when to grip with her claws, and when to push off and go leaping through the air.

For the first time ever, she could really *climb*.

The ball of fire bounded toward him, and Hylas shielded his face with his hands as it quivered and resolved into Havoc.

Except—it wasn't really Havoc, she kept blurring and scattering sparks. He sensed that what stood gazing up at him with those great golden eyes wasn't Havoc as he knew her, but her spirit.

There was no time to wonder what was happening. The spirit-Havoc flicked one fiery ear and scampered past him, leaping—with un-Havoc-like grace—for a boulder that he hadn't noticed before, which jutted from the crater wall not far above his head. Her paw prints left a glowing trail over the cinders, and when she glanced back at him, her meaning was clear.

Follow.

The boulder looked big enough for him to crouch on—*if* he could reach it. But he was dizzy with exhaustion, and his limbs were made of stone.

And yet—Havoc's bright spirit wouldn't let him give up. With an impatient glance at him, she climbed deftly higher, lashing her glowing tail for balance as she found another boulder: another small island of solid rock in the crumbly wall, which Hylas would never have spotted without her.

When she reached it, she peered down at him, her ears expectantly pricked. *Now it's your turn. Follow me. I'll lead you to the top.*

Hylas heaved to his feet and began to climb.

38

With every step, Pirra sank ankle-deep into fine black ash, then slid two paces farther, down a choking tunnel of darkness.

She told herself that Hylas might still be alive. She hadn't actually *seen* him killed; and if the dagger could get stuck on a boulder, then so could he. He was a mountain boy, he could climb anything.

"Keep up, Telamon!" barked Pharax from somewhere in front.

"It's the girl, she's slowing us down," called Telamon behind her. "Can't we just leave her?"

"No," Pharax replied coldly. "If she's the daughter of the High Priestess, the Keftians will pay to get her back."

"Oh they'll pay all right," muttered Telamon. Since the fight at the crater, there was a new grimness in him. As if, thought Pirra, the Mountain had scorched away the boy he had been.

They hadn't bothered to search her, so she still had the obsidian knife strapped to her thigh—but she knew that trying to reach it would be fatal. To Pharax, she was nothing but flesh and bone to be used as he saw fit. If she made trouble, he'd slit her throat.

He and Telamon had come alone to the Mountain—she guessed they hadn't told their men the dagger had been stolen—and now he strode with it in his fist, scorning danger. The Mountain was merely another obstacle to his will.

At last dawn came, but it was unlike any she'd ever seen. It didn't begin in the east, where the Sun woke up, but lit the whole sky with an angry red glow.

It was the end of the world.

~

The day had been born in a welter of anger, but it hadn't lived long. The ash spewing from the Mountain had spread in a vast pall across the Sun, and for a long time now, Hylas had been riding through a ghostly gray twilight.

He galloped with his head against the horse's straining neck. Although he was exhausted, his mind felt sharper, now that he was out of the crater's toxic fumes.

He missed the company of the spirit-Havoc. She had led him up the crater wall, then down the Mountainside to the thickets, where she'd vanished in a shower of sparks. Shortly afterward, he'd heard a desperate whinnying and found the horse he and Pirra had stolen, struggling with its reins snagged on a root.

At last he reached the Neck and skittered to a halt. All was eerily silent: The guards had fled. Jumping off and winding the reins around his wrist, he searched the camp. He found a waterskin and drank greedily, splashing some in a trough for the horse.

He tripped over a guard sprawled in the dust with a knife-hilt jutting from his belly: Killed in some desperate struggle to escape. Hylas yanked out the knife, wiped the blade on the dead man's tunic, and jammed it in his belt. No time to spare for the man's angry spirit. Not even a ghost could follow him in this.

As he galloped for the crossroads, he passed signs of flight, but no people. He wondered if they'd all gone, and he was the last one left on Thalakrea. Then through the murk he made out figures swarming down from Kreon's stronghold, and more fleeing the mines. Where was Havoc? And Pirra? Had Pharax killed her on the Mountain, or taken her with him?

Suddenly the earth roared and a great crack zigzagged across his path. With a squeal the horse flung him off and thundered into the gloom.

Painfully, Hylas got to his feet. A trail led north, that must go to the village; if he took it, he might find passage on a boat. To the south, another led past the mines and down to the shore. If Pirra was still alive, Pharax would have taken her there.

Hylas leaped the crack and headed south.

Chaos on the shore. The fury of the Earthshaker had ripped a great chunk from the western cliffs and flung it into the Sea. The furnace ridge no longer existed; Hylas hoped Akastos had escaped in time.

The Sea was sludgy with ash, the beach crammed with fallen boulders and panicking people desperate to get on a ship. Hylas saw three ships packed with Crow warriors heading into the bay, and many smaller fishing boats bobbing near the shore. In one he spotted Hekabi; he guessed the villagers had come to rescue as many as they could. Far out to Sea, he glimpsed a splendid ship with bellying black sails. Koronos and his kin were saving their skins and leaving the rabble to take their chances. Hylas prayed they'd taken Havoc.

Farther along the shore, someone was shouting. "Flea! Flea! Over here!"

A small battered-looking ship packed with escaped slaves was rolling in the shallows, and Periphas was beckoning. "Flea! Hurry!"

"I can't!" shouted Hylas. "I've got to find Pirra!"

"Who's Pirra? We can't wait!"

Hylas raced off along the beach, dodging carts, donkeys, people. No Pirra. Then the wind tore a rent in the ash and a ship loomed over him. Astonished, he took in its beaked prow and huge painted eye. What was a *Keftian* ship doing here?

On the deck, he made out a young man with a shaven head and black-rimmed eyes, shouting at the oarsmen. Hylas recognized Userref, Pirra's Egyptian slave, but as he opened his mouth to call to him, someone blundered against him and he fell over a crate.

The crate yowled. It was Havoc: upside-down, half-dead with fright, but alive. The Crows had brought her this far, then abandoned her.

"I'm here," Hylas told her, righting the cage and pushing his fingers through the bars, while the frantic lion cub mewed and tried desperately to lick his hand. "It's me, you'll be all right now, I'll get you out."

But as he drew his knife to cut her free, he hesitated. If he freed her, she'd be off like an arrow, he'd never catch her again. He would have to leave her to wander alone until Thalakrea blew up.

In consternation, Hylas glanced at the Keftian ship, then back to Havoc. His heart twisted. She would never understand. She would think he was dooming her to captivity; which he was—but at least she'd be alive.

"Userref!" he yelled, staggering into the surf with Havoc's cage in his arms.

The Egyptian saw him and his jaw dropped. "Who are you?"

"Doesn't matter!" gasped Hylas. "Take this!" His arms shook as he held up the cage. "Her name's Havoc! Pirra said you worship lions! You've got to save her!"

"You know Pirra? Where is she?"

"Take her! *Please!*"

He felt the cage lifted out of his hands as the Egyptian swung it aboard. Then the oars creaked and the ship was pulling away, and Hylas stood with the gray water swirling about his waist and the ash raining down like thick tears, watching Havoc struggling wildly in her cage. Her yowls pierced his heart. *Why are you abandoning me?*

"Hylas!" shouted someone behind him.

And there was Pirra. Bizarrely, she still had the water-skin slung across her back, and she was filthy and grinning from ear to ear. "I can't believe you got out!"

"What about you?" he panted. "How'd you get away from Pharax?"

"There was a landslide, I—"

"*Pirra!*" shouted Userref, signaling to the oarsmen to stop rowing. Pirra saw Userref and the Keftian ship. Her face worked.

Userref yelled something in Keftian and threw her a line.

It struck the waves near her. She shook her head. "No! I can't go back to Keftiu!"

Hylas stood blinking seawater from his eyes. There were no more boats, and at any moment, Thalakrea might blow up. "You've got to," he told her.

She turned on him. "We'll find another boat—"

"What boat?" he shouted. "They've all gone!"

"I told you, I'm never going back!"

"This is your only chance!" Grabbing the line, he splashed toward her and slung it around her waist.

"What are you *doing*?" Desperately she clawed at his hands but he ignored her, securing a knot she wouldn't be able to untie. "Pull her in!" he yelled to Userref.

"You can't *do* this!" screamed Pirra. But Userref was hauling her in and lifting her struggling on board, while barking orders to a seaman to cast another line to Hylas.

"You too!" cried the Egyptian.

Hylas waded for the line—but the Keftian oarsmen were pulling hard and the ship was moving too fast, dragging the rope out of reach.

A massive crash behind him, and another vast chunk of cliff toppled into the Sea. The impact sent a huge wave racing toward him. He was rolling over and over in gray sludge, he couldn't tell up from down. When he surfaced, spitting sludge, the Keftian ship was already far out in the bay.

Hylas floundered ashore. No one left except a panicking donkey and a litter of discarded possessions. Not long now, he thought numbly.

Then through the pattering ash, he glimpsed a small scruffy ship rocking in the shallows. He saw the escaped slaves thronging the deck, and Periphas leaning over the side. "Swim, Flea! We can't wait any longer!"

With the last of his strength, Hylas flailed toward them; then many hands were reaching down and hauling him aboard.

As the oarsmen brought the ship about and headed into the bay, Hylas pushed through the crowd to reach the prow.

The Keftian ship had set sail and was speeding away from him across the ashen Sea. Pirra stood in the stern, her hair wild, her face ablaze with fury.

"I *told* you I couldn't go back!" she screamed. "I hate you, Hylas! I'll hate you forever!"

Thalakrea was far away, but the Sea was still rough and the ash was still falling. It had turned the whole world gray: the waves, the sails, the silent, fearful people.

Like a ship of ghosts, thought Telamon.

He watched the gray oarsmen rowing the gray Sea. The gray deck was sticky with a scarlet tracery of blood: They'd sacrificed a ram to beg safe passage of the Sky Father and the Earthshaker.

Telamon was sick with fatigue and his thigh throbbed where Pirra had stabbed him, but as he looked at his hands gripping the side of the ship, he felt fiercely proud. These hands had dug himself and Pharax out of the landslide. The Mountain had tried to kill them, but he'd fought back. He'd called on the Angry Ones to help him—and they had.

They had saved him, as they had saved his kin. And although the dagger was missing, the fact that the House of Koronos had escaped unharmed told Telamon that the dagger had not been destroyed on Thalakrea. And he sensed that the others believed this too.

A few paces from where he stood, a canopy covered the stern. Beneath it, Kreon sat brooding over the loss of his mines, while Pharax sharpened his sword and Alekto combed the ash from her hair. Koronos gazed out to Sea, as inscrutable as ever. For the first time, Telamon felt they were truly his kin.

The High Chieftain turned his head and met his eyes, and Telamon bowed. Then he moved away. It wasn't yet time to tell his grandfather what he'd learned in those last moments at Thalakrea. He must keep his knowledge to himself till he knew how to use it.

Hylas was alive. Telamon had spotted him on the shore as their ship was leaving.

Anger, fear, outrage seethed inside him. But he felt no pang for the friendship that had been. That was good. It was all over now.

Suddenly a fierce wind gusted out of nowhere, rocking the ship and blasting him backward—and from the east came a deafening roar. People were shouting and pointing, clutching amulets and falling to their knees. In awe Telamon watched a black cloud rising from the horizon.

"That's Thalakrea," said Pharax, come to stand beside him.

"It's the end of the world," said an oarsman.

"If it is, then it is," Pharax said grimly.

Telamon cast him an admiring glance. Here was a man who would meet the end of the world as he met everything: with a sword in his hand.

Yes, thought Telamon. That's the way to be.

He realized now that the Angry Ones had saved him for a reason. *He*—not Kreon, not Pharax, not even Koronos—would be the savior of his House. He would crush Keftiu and seize the whole of Akea in his grasp. He would raise his clan to undreamed-of heights.

And no Outsider—no filthy barefoot goatherd—would get in his way.

⸻

Pirra heard the blast as she crouched on deck, trying to calm Havoc in her cage.

Gulls flew up from the cliffs and oarsmen shouted in terror. Userref gripped his eye amulet and chanted prayers to his gods. Havoc—who'd been seasick the whole way—flattened her ears and tried to make herself very small.

Pirra watched the ashcloud slowly darkening the Sun and turning the air chill. Even here, with Keftiu within sight, the Sea was scummed with ash. No one near Thalakrea could have survived that blast.

Userref finished his prayers and came to kneel beside her.

"Is it the end of the world?" she said.

"I don't know. But my father was a scribe, and he knew many Words of Truth. I remember one: *I am the Lord of the Horizon. I will darken the sky and separate myself from mankind. I will show you calamity over all the earth . . .*"

Pirra clutched her sealstone and thought of Hylas in

that scruffy little ship overburdened with escaped slaves. Had he reached safety before the Lady of Fire blasted Thalakrea to the sky?

"That boy on the shore," said Userref. "Was he the one you met last summer? The one named Hy-las?"

Pirra stiffened. "Don't ever speak his name again. I hate him."

"No you don't."

"Yes I do." She'd shouted it till she was hoarse, so it must be true. I could have been on that ship with him, she thought. If it wasn't for Hylas, I'd still be free.

The deck creaked and rocked, and Pirra watched Keftiu drawing inexorably closer. She had begged Userref to set her down on the coast somewhere far from the House of the Goddess; at least that would have given her a chance. "Don't take me back to Yassassara, she'll never let me out. I'll never see the sky again!"

But Userref—gentle, kind Userref—had been relentless. Pirra knew that it wasn't to save his own skin, but because, in his obedient Egyptian way, he was convinced that his gods wanted him to do the will of the High Priestess.

Pirra watched him pushing scraps of fish through the bars for Havoc, who'd recovered enough to snuffle them up.

"I'm sorry I can't release you, little daughter of the Sun," he told the lion cub respectfully, "but when we get ashore, I'll build you a fine large cage. You shall have many playthings, and meat every day. You shall be honored as a sacred creature of Sekhmet."

Without turning his head, he said to Pirra, "You know, that boy was only trying to save you."

"I could have saved myself," she said hotly. "I could have found another boat. He did."

"An overcrowded vessel, too low in the water. He might not survive. Do you really wish for that?"

Pirra glared at him. Turning aside, she unstrapped the obsidian knife and held it up. "See this? He made it for me." She flung it across the waves. "There. That's what I think of Hylas."

Userref frowned. "That was unwise. Now you have no knife."

Pirra rose to her feet and walked away.

But I do have a knife, she told Userref silently.

What he didn't know was that after the landslide, when she'd dug herself out, she'd found something lying beside Pharax's half-buried hand.

Userref didn't know what she kept hidden in the empty waterskin slung over her shoulder.

Slipping her hand inside, she touched the cold smooth bronze of the dagger of Koronos.

———

Hylas watched the cloud spreading across the sky like a giant hand reaching south—toward Keftiu.

He kept seeing Pirra standing on deck with the wind whipping her hair about her face. The way she'd glared at him . . . *I hate you! I'll hate you forever!*

Even here, so far from Thalakrea, the ash was still

falling. Earlier, Periphas had sacrificed a seabird to the Earthshaker, and it seemed to have worked, because now, in the distance, a blur of land appeared on the horizon. The freed slaves gave a ragged cheer.

Periphas picked his way along the crowded deck toward him. Like everyone, he was grimy and haggard with exhaustion; but there was a glint of good humor in his brown eyes.

"Any idea where we are?" said Hylas.

Periphas shook his head. "That's for the gods to know and us to find out."

Hylas hesitated. "A long time ago, you told me you were from Messenia."

"And so I am. Why?"

"My sister—she may be in Messenia. She's ten. Did you ever hear of someone like her?"

Periphas' face became grave. "I'm sorry, Flea. I wish I could tell you I knew of a girl with yellow hair and a ruthless expression, like her big brother. But I can't. All I know is that the Crows didn't get them all."

Hylas sucked in his lips and nodded. So he was back where he'd started. The Crows had the dagger and Issi was missing. The only thing that had changed was that he'd doomed Havoc and Pirra to captivity.

Periphas clapped him on the shoulder. "Cheer up, Flea, you're not dead yet."

Hylas scowled. "Why did you come back for me?"

"We owed it to you. You warned the wisewoman, who warned us. It's thanks to you we're alive." He paused.

"I don't just mean the people on this ship, Flea, I mean everyone. The Islanders, the other miners, your fellow pit spiders. They're all alive because of you."

Hylas hadn't seen it like that. But now he thought of Zan and Bat and Spit—whom Periphas had seen being picked up by an Islander's boat—and of all the others.

The ship lurched, then righted itself. Periphas shouted at the helmsman to watch where he was going, and several people laughed.

It seemed astonishing that they could laugh at such a time, when a vast cloud of ash was darkening the Sun. Hylas asked Periphas if he thought the world was going to end.

Periphas scratched his beard and squinted at the sky. "I don't know." He glanced at Hylas. "But until it does, someone's found a sack of olives we didn't know we had. So when you've finished being miserable, come and get your share."

Hylas watched him work his way back along the deck.

The land drew steadily closer, and he leaned over the side, gazing down at the scummy gray Sea.

Suddenly, a flock of seabirds flew over the ship. They were wheeling and crying, and in the ashen twilight, their wings flashed brilliant white. Unexpectedly, Hylas' heart lifted.

Periphas was right. He *had* saved them: Hekabi and Zan and Bat and Spit; the Islanders, the miners; Akastos too, if he'd managed to get away. Maybe that was why the gods had sent him to Thalakrea.

In his head, he spoke defiantly to Pirra. I know you're angry with me, Pirra. But you've got to be alive to be angry. I *saved* you. I saved Havoc too. And I'd do it again.

For a long time he watched the white birds wheeling and crying overhead.

Then he went to join Periphas and claim his share of the olives.

Author's Note

The Burning Shadow takes place three and a half thousand years ago in the Bronze Age, in the land we call ancient Greece. This was long before the time of marble temples and classical sculpture with which you may be familiar. It was even before the Greeks ranged their gods and goddesses into an orderly pantheon of Zeus, Hera, Hades, and all the others.

We don't know much about Bronze Age Greece, because its people left so few written records, but we do know something about their astonishing cultures, which today we call the Mycenaeans and the Minoans. Theirs is the world of Gods and Warriors. It's believed that this was a world of scattered chieftaincies, separated by mountain ranges and forests, and that it was probably wetter and greener than today, with far more wild animals both on land and in the Sea.

To create the world of Hylas and Pirra, I've studied the archaeology of the Greek Bronze Age. To get an idea of how people thought and what they believed, I've drawn on the beliefs of more recent peoples who still live in traditional ways, just as I did when I wrote about the Stone Age in *Chronicles of Ancient Darkness*. And although people in Hylas' time lived mostly by farming or fishing, rather than by hunting and gathering, I've no doubt that much of the knowledge and beliefs of the Stone Age hunter-gatherers lived on into the Bronze Age, particularly among the poorer people, such as Hylas himself.

Here's a quick word about place-names. Akea (or Achaea, as it's usually spelled) is the ancient name for mainland Greece, and Lykonia is my name for present-day Lakonia. I've kept the name Mycenae unaltered, as it's so well-known. I've adopted the name "Keftian" for the great Cretan civilization we call Minoan. (We don't know what they called themselves; depending on which book you read, their name may have been Keftians, or that may just have been a name given them by the ancient Egyptians.) As for Egypt, although that name derives from the Greeks, I've kept it because, like Mycenae, it felt artificial to change it.

Concerning the map of the World of Gods and Warriors, it shows the world as Hylas and Pirra experience it. Thus it includes some islands that I've made up, and omits others which form no part of the story. What Pirra calls the Obsidian Isles are what we now call the Cyclades: the islands east of Mainland Greece. I made up the island of Thalakrea, based on my research trips to several volcanic islands—Milos and Sifnos in the Cyclades, and the Aeolian Islands of Vulcano and Stromboli—while Kreon's stronghold was based on a visit to the spectacular hilltop ruins of Aghios Andreas on Sifnos.

To get a feel for Thalakrea's mines, I visited the largest Bronze Age copper mines in western Europe, at the Great Orme in north Wales. Crawling through those claustrophobic tunnels really helped me imagine what it was like for Hylas. Then on Sifnos in the Mediterranean, I hiked out to the isolated ruins of the Bronze Age mines at Aghios Softis. I didn't enter those tunnels—they're unstable and I was on my own, miles from anywhere—but again, being there brought home to me how awful it must have been to be a slave, working by lamplight in such cramped spaces.

Although Thalakrea is invented, its volcanic features were inspired by the real ones I experienced on my travels. Milos gave me the astonishing white ravine that Hylas and Pirra find; the vividly colored rocks and caves; the smelly hot springs; and, most memorably for me, the obsidian ridge, with its great drifts of obsidian shards and hammerstones left behind by stoneworkers many thousands of years ago. (The lonely wild pear tree is real, too. Many times I sat in its shade, watching falcons patrolling the ridge.)

Vulcano gave me Thalakrea's black plain; the broom thickets, the smelly green mudpool, and the Mountain's great smoking crater—not to mention Thalakrea's headachy smell. On several solo climbs of the (dormant) volcano, I had unforgettable encounters with its many fumaroles: the hissing, sulfur-crusted cracks that become the fire spirits' lairs in the story. I was often driven back by their choking smoke, and although I never spotted a fire spirit, it was easy to imagine how such a place would affect a Bronze Age boy like Hylas.

I'll admit that I haven't spent time *inside* the crater of an erupting volcano; for that part of the story, I've relied on the accounts of accident victims who survived to tell the tale. But to observe an eruption at first hand, I climbed Stromboli (off the coast of Sicily), which is in a state of almost constant activity. We reached the summit at nightfall, and watched fierce spurts of lava shooting from the crater. That was followed by an equally memorable nighttime descent down the black ashen slopes, which inspired Pirra's descent in the story.

I want to thank the many people—too numerous to name—who gave me advice and assistance while I was exploring Milos and Sifnos, Vulcano and Stromboli. I'm also extremely grateful to Todd Whitelaw, Professor of Aegean Archaeology at the Institute of Archaeology, University College London, for his help. He gave so generously of his time in answering my questions on the prehistoric Aegean, as well as providing detailed and invaluable guidance on which sites to visit on Milos and Sifnos and the significance of what I might see. He also let me handle many Mycenaean and Minoan artefacts (with gloves on, of course!) in the Institute's collection. To hold in your hand a small Bronze Age earthenware bull which might once have been someone's precious offering, and to see the painter's brushstrokes and even their fingerprints, is to feel very close to those long-ago people.

Finally, and as always, I want to thank my wonderful and indefatigable agent, Peter Cox, for his commitment and support, and my hugely talented editor at Puffin Books, Elv Moody, for her endless enthusiasm and unfailing support for the story of Hylas and Pirra.

Michelle Paver, 2013

THE QUEST CONTINUES IN

THE
EYE OF THE
FALCON

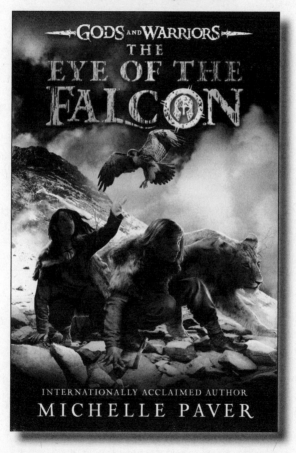

TURN THE PAGE FOR A SNEAK PEEK!

1

"What *happened* here?" said Hylas. "Where are all the people?"

"There's one over there," said Periphas, "but he's not going to tell us." He pointed at a ship that the Sea had flung halfway up a hill. Snagged in its rigging was the skeleton of a man. Shreds of rotten tunic flapped in the wind, and one bony arm swung in a grisly wave.

"Looks like the gods punished Keftiu worst of all," said Glaukos.

"Smells like it too," said Medon. The others muttered and gripped their amulets.

Hylas was stunned. Over the winter he'd seen many horrors, but nothing like this. The Sea had smashed huts, boats, trees, animals, people. The shore was eerily silent, and wherever he turned, he saw mounds of rotting wreckage. Dirty gray surf clawed at his boots, and he breathed the throat-catching stink of death. How could Pirra and Havoc have survived this?

With his knife, Periphas turned over the skull of an ox. "This happened months ago. Everything's covered in ash."

"But someone must've survived," said Hylas. "Why didn't they come back and rebuild?"

No one answered.

"This *can't* be Keftiu," said Hylas. "It's a huge rich island with thousands of people, Pirra told me!"

"I'm sorry, lad," said Periphas. "You won't find your friends now. We'll see if there's anything worth taking, then we're off."

While the others spread out to forage, Hylas spotted a hut farther down the shore and picked his way toward it, desperate to find someone alive.

The icy wind tugged at his sheepskins, and he startled a vulture, which flew off, raising a haze of ash. He hardly noticed. All through the winter the Great Cloud had hidden the Sun, plunging the world into perpetual twilight and shrouding it in ash. He'd grown used to the gloom, and the black grit that got into hair, clothes, food. But *this* . . .

He thought of his friends as he'd last seen them, seven moons ago on Thalakrea. The Mountain had been spewing fire and there'd been chaos on the shore, people fleeing in whatever boats they could find. Somehow, he'd gotten Havoc and Pirra on a ship: Havoc scrabbling in her cage and yowling at him, *Why are you abandoning me,* and Pirra white with fury—for the ship was Keftian. "I *told* you I couldn't go back!" she'd screamed. "I'll never forgive you, Hylas! I'll hate you forever!"

He'd done it to *save* her. But he'd sent her to this.

The hut was mud-brick and thatch, and someone had crudely repaired it after the Sea's attack. They'd also marked the wall with a stark white handprint. Hylas didn't know what that meant, but it felt like a warning. He halted some distance away.

The wind flung more ash in his face. As he brushed it off, he felt an ache in his temple, and from the corner of his eye, he glimpsed two ragged children. They vanished inside, but he saw that they were girls, one about ten, the other younger. Both had bizarrely shaven heads, except for one long lock hanging from the temple, and angry boils on their necks the size of pigeons' eggs.

"I'm not going to hurt you!" he called.

No answer, but he knew they were listening. And he caught a sense of anger, and hopeless searching.

To reassure them, he turned his back.

Again they appeared at the corner of his vision.

"Are you looking for your parents?" he said without moving his head. "I'm looking for someone too. My friends. Is anyone else alive?"

Still no answer. The anger and loss came at him in waves.

Belatedly, he remembered that he was a foreigner here, so they wouldn't understand him. "I'm Akean," he explained. "I can't speak Keftian!"

Once again when he looked, they vanished inside. After a moment's hesitation, he followed.

The hut was empty.

Yes, empty—and no way out except for this door. The back of his neck began to prickle, and his hand went to the lion-claw amulet at his throat.

Dim gray light filtered through the thatch, and the air was thick with the stench of death. Then on a cot against the opposite wall, he saw the bodies of two girls.

His heart hammered against his ribs.

One girl looked about ten, the other younger. Both had shaven heads with a single lock of hair at the temple, and terrible boils on their necks. A dark haze seemed to boil and swarm around them, like ash—only this was alive.

With a cry Hylas staggered from the hut.

Farther up the shore, the others were already splashing through the shallows to the ship, and Periphas was hastily untying its line from a boulder. "Where've you been!" he yelled at Hylas. "We're clearing out, we found bodies!"

"So did I!" gasped Hylas.

"Did you touch them?" barked Periphas.

"No, I—no." He didn't dare mention the children. His mind shied away from what they might be.

No one sees ghosts, he told himself. And yet I saw them. They were there.

"We found three fresh corpses in a shelter," muttered Periphas. "Black in the face, and all over with boils."

"What *is* it?" said Hylas.

"Plague," snapped Periphas.

The men within earshot blanched.

Hylas' mind reeled. "M-maybe it's only on this part of the coast," he stammered. "If we go farther—"

"I'm not risking it," said Periphas.

"Then inland! There are mountains, we can—"

"Let me tell you about the Plague," Periphas cut in. "It comes with the unburied dead. That's what happened here. First you get a fever. That's the Plague making its nests in your flesh. Soon those nests swell into great agonizing boils. They hurt so much you can't stop screaming, but the Plague doesn't care, it's breeding inside you. Now the boils are bursting, and the pain's so bad you're going mad." He chucked the line toward the ship. "It only ends one way."

The others had stopped what they were doing and were gaping at their leader.

Hylas glanced from Periphas to the ruined shore and the hazy mountains beyond. "I-I have to stay," he said.

"Then you're already mad," retorted Periphas. "I thought you were desperate to reach Messenia and find your sister!"

"I am, but . . . The gods didn't send us to Messenia. They sent us here. To Keftiu."

"Look around you, Hylas! Your friends won't have survived this!"

"But if they did—"

"A girl and a lion cub? There's no one here but the dead! If you stay, you'll become one of them!"

Hylas licked his lips. "Pirra and Havoc are my friends. I sent them here. I can't abandon them."

"What about us? Aren't we your friends?"

Hylas glanced at the others on the ship. They were tough men—escaped slaves like him—and used to unimaginable hardship. At nearly fourteen, he was the youngest by far, and yet they'd treated him with rough kindness. For seven moons they'd been trying to get back to Akea, but the Sea was full of huge floating islands of pumice, and they kept losing their way. Once, they'd run aground; it had taken two moons to repair the ship. And now they'd fetched up here, on Keftiu.

Hylas looked at Periphas, with his broken nose and his brown eyes that had seen too many bad things. Periphas had saved his life by hauling him aboard as the ship left Thalakrea. He'd been a warrior once, and over the winter he'd taught Hylas a bit about fighting. In a way, they'd become friends.

But Pirra was different—and so was Havoc.

"They need me, Periphas," said Hylas. "It's *my fault* that they're here. If there's a chance they're still alive . . ."

Periphas gave him a strange, angry look. Then he scratched his beard with one grimy hand. "It's your choice," he growled. "A pity. I liked you."

After that, things happened fast. Hylas already carried his axe, knife, slingshot, and strike-fire, but now Periphas gave him a waterskin, a sack of provisions, and a coil of rope. "That always comes in handy," he said with a scowl.

Soon afterward, Hylas was watching the ship heading

out over the gray Sea. He watched till it was gone, and he was left alone with the vultures and the icy wind: a stranger in a haunted land ravaged by Plague.

What have I done? he wondered.

Then he hoisted his gear on his back and headed off to find his friends.

2

Hylas could see snow on the mountains, and here on the coast the wind was freezing, but the cold didn't bother the lumpy little creature squatting in front of him. It was about knee height and made of dirty wax, with hair of moldy straw and fierce red pebble eyes.

Periphas had warned him about these as he was leaving. "They're Plague traps, they draw it away from the living. People call them pus-eaters. Make sure you don't touch."

As Hylas edged past the pus-eater, he felt an ache in his temple, and rubbed the scar from the burn he'd received on Thalakrea. The ache faded, but from the corner of his eye, he glimpsed dark specks crawling all over the pus-eater. He'd seen the same black swarm on the ghostly children. Was it Plague? Periphas hadn't said anything about being able to *see* it, so how could this be?

And how was it possible that he was seeing ghosts?

There was no one to ask. He hadn't met anyone all day, either living or dead. To his right, the gray Sea sucked at the shore, and to his left, low gray hills barred the way inland. Halfway up, a dark band of wreckage was a grim reminder of the Sea's attack.

Periphas had told him that if he followed the coast west for a day or so, then headed inland, he would reach the House of the Goddess, where Pirra's mother ruled. "Although who knows what you'll find. There used to be villages and ship-sheds all along this coast. Where we're standing used to be a town."

"What's a town?" Hylas had asked.

"Like a village, but bigger. Thousands of people."

"Thousands?"

"Keftiu is vast, Hylas, it takes two days to sail from one end to the other. Even if your friends are still alive, how will you find them?"

That had only been this morning, but already Periphas seemed long gone. Hylas felt lonely, vulnerable, and *cold*. He wished he had something warmer than a sheepskin jerkin whose sleeves were too short, and leggings with holes in the knees.

Up ahead, he saw smoke rising from behind a spur. Drawing his knife, he crept forward and peered around a boulder.

He blinked in disbelief.

Below him at the head of a bay clustered several makeshift huts with people bustling about in between, oblivious to the desolation. Some stirred huge steaming cauldrons; others bent over stone vats cut into the hillside, or unloaded dripping baskets from boats in the shallows. Even more bizarre, women stood at drying racks, hanging up sodden armfuls of astonishing colored wool. Scarlet, yellow, blue, purple: The brilliant clots of color seemed to throb in the grayness all around.

The wind gusted in Hylas' face, and he inhaled an eye-watering stench of urine and rotting fish. In astonishment, he realized that these people must be dye-workers. But why would anyone bother to dye wool in a Plague?

He was debating whether to go down and seek shelter or avoid them altogether, when a stone struck the boulder near his head. He spun around—guessed it was a trick—flung himself sideways. Too late. A noose yanked tight around his neck, his knife was kicked from his hand, and spears pinned him front and back.

"I *told* you, I'm not a thief!" shouted Hylas.

His captors yelled at him in Keftian, brandishing fishing spears and big double axes of tarnished bronze. There were ten of them: squat beardless men in ragged sheepskin tunics baring muscular limbs stained a weird, blotchy purple. Their faces were purple too, and they stank of urine and rotting fish. Hylas had never seen anything like them.

One man hooked Hylas' axe from his belt, then they hauled and pushed him down to the huts, keeping him at a distance with their spears, for fear of Plague.

Still yelling in their strange bird-like speech, they halted at the largest hut, and an old woman appeared in the doorway: Hylas guessed she was the headwoman of the village.

She was enormously fat, and swathed in layers of filthy gray rags. She had a spongy purple face crowned with a few greasy threads of hair. One eye socket was empty, the other eye was a cloudy gray. It skittered about alarmingly, then fastened on Hylas and gave him a hard stare.

One of the men pointed to the tattoo on Hylas' forearm: the black zigzag that marked him as a slave of the Crows. Over the winter, he'd tattooed a line underneath, to turn it into a longbow. That didn't seem to fool the old woman.

"What's a Crow spy doing here?" she rasped in Akean.

"I'm not a Crow," panted Hylas, "and I'm not a spy, I—"

"We drown Crow spies. We feed them to the sea snails."

"I *hate* the Crows! I'm just trying to find my friend! Her name's Pirra, she's the daughter of High Priestess Yassassara."

The woman snorted. "As if she'd be friends with the likes of you." Barking a command in Keftian, she jerked her head, and the men began to drag Hylas toward the Sea.

"I can prove it!" he shouted. "Pirra grew up in the House of the Goddess, she told me it's huge and—they do rites with men jumping over charging bulls—"

"Everyone knows that," sneered the woman.

They were hauling him over stinking mounds of crushed sea snails, past conical baskets baited with rotting fish. Was that how he was going to end up? As bait?

"Pirra hated the House of the Goddess," he shouted over his shoulder, "she called it her stone prison! Then her mother tried to strike a bargain with the Crows, she was going to seal it by giving Pirra in marriage—but Pirra burned her own face to spoil the match! She—she's got a scar like a crescent moon on her cheek—"

"Everyone knows that too," called the woman.

"You can't *do* this!" he yelled. "I'm a stranger here, it's against the law of the gods to kill a stranger!"

"The gods have abandoned Keftiu," snarled the woman. "Around here, *I* make the law!"

Now they were dragging him into the freezing shallows and kicking him to his knees. Icy waves stung his face. The tines of a pitchfork enclosed his neck, forcing him toward the water . . .

Something Pirra had said came back to him. "She had a tunic of Keftian purple!" he blurted out. "She said they make the purple from mashed-up sea snails, thousands of them, and it costs more than gold!"

The woman barked a command, and the pressure on his neck lifted. Panting, he lurched to his feet.

"Quite a few people know that too," the woman called drily. "You'll have to do better if you want to live."

"She—um—once she told me there were only two robes like it in all Keftiu," he gasped, "but nobody's ever seen the other because it's Yassassara's, they made it in secret, she only wears it for secret rites."

Silence. The gray Sea lapped hungrily at his thighs.

"I dyed that wool myself," said the woman. "By moonlight. In secret. Now, how'd you know that?"

"Like I said, Pirra told me!"

Another command—and Hylas was hauled back to the shore. The noose was removed, the spears withdrawn. Someone chucked him his axe and his knife.

The old woman hawked and spat a gobbet of purple snot on the stones. Then she turned and lumbered back into her hut. "Yassassara's dead," she said over her shoulder.

Hylas flinched. "What about Pirra?"

"You better come inside."

3

The lion cub heard ravens calling from the ridge and quickened her pace. Ravens meant carcasses, and she was hungry.

The Bright Soft Cold lay deep on the mountain, and by the time she'd struggled onto the ridge, the ravens had left only bones. The cub crunched them up, but the hunger didn't go away.

The cub was always hungry. Long ago, men had brought her to this horrible land of shadows and ghosts. She remembered fleeing in terror as the Great Gray Beast came roaring in and savaged the shore. Afterward, there had been piles of carcasses—dogs, sheep, goats, fish, humans—and swarms of vultures. The lion cub had fought for her share, until men had chased her away with their great shiny claws.

She'd fled to the mountain, because she *knew* mountains, but this was nothing like the fiery Mountain where she'd lived with her pride. *There were no lions,* only frozen trees and Bright Soft Cold; hungry creatures, ragged men, and ghosts.

It was a land of shadows. When the cub sat on her

haunches and gazed at the Up, she couldn't see the Great Lion whose mane shone golden in the Light and silver in the Dark. And there was no real Light, only this gray not-Light, in between the Darks.

The cub had grown used to the not-Light, as it helped her hide from men; but as the Darks and the not-Lights passed, the cold bit harder. Her breath turned to smoke, and she couldn't find any wet to drink, so she ate the Bright Soft Cold. She learned to crawl into caves when the white wind howled, and her pelt grew thick and matted with filth. It kept her warm, but she was too hungry and frightened to lick herself clean.

Then, alarmingly, her teeth started falling out. She was horrified, until new ones thrust painfully through. They were larger and stronger than the old ones: She could rip open a frozen carcass with one bite. And she got bigger. Now when she stood on her hind legs to scratch a tree, her forepaws reached much higher than before.

Here on the mountain, there weren't as many dead things as on the shore, so as well as scavenging, the cub tried to hunt. Mostly she did it wrong, charging too soon, or getting confused about which prey to chase; but *finally* she felled a squirrel with a lucky swipe. It was her first kill. If only there'd been someone with her, to see.

That was the worst of it, the loneliness. Sometimes the cub sat and mewed her misery to the Up. She longed for warmth and muzzle-rubs—and to sleep without fear, because other ears and noses were keeping watch.

THE
✦GODS AND WARRIORS✦
SERIES

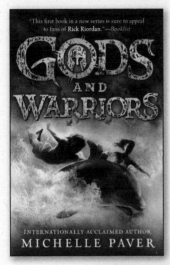

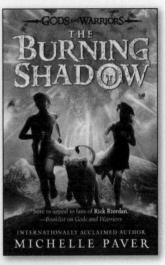